Penny Wanawake – big, black and sexy – exploded onto the detection scene in *Penny Black*. This is her second adventure.

When Max Maunciple, a novelist feared for his vitriolic pen, dies from an apparent surfeit of gin, only Penny suspects that his death may not be from natural causes. Aided by a handsome American policeman holidaying in England, she sets out to discover the truth.

The novel is full of splendid characters and elegantly set in Canterbury where historical and Chaucerian references abound. There is a memorable visit to a health farm and another to Boulogne. The action is fast. The dialogue sparkles. The story maintains its pace right to the very last page.

Zest and fun adorn a classic whodunnit plot. The disciplines of the detective novel are observed, the murderer's identity coming as a real surprise when the red herrings have been disposed of.

Very contemporary, full of zip and fizz, Penn's latest case as a sleuth comes as a fine successor to the first. It is a spectacular crime novel and a gripping piece of story-telling.

by the same author

PENNY BLACK

SUSAN MOODY
PENNY DREADFUL

MACMILLAN

ISBN 0 333 36532 1

First published 1984 by
MACMILLAN LONDON LIMITED
4 Little Essex Street London WC2R 3LF
and Basingstoke
Associated companies in Auckland, Delhi, Dublin, Gaborone,
Hamburg, Harare, Hong Kong, Johannesburg, Kuala Lumpur,
Lagos, Manzini, Melbourne, Mexico City, Nairobi, New York,
Singapore and Tokyo

Typeset in Great Britain by
WILMASET
Birkenhead, Merseyside
Printed and bound in Great Britain by
ANCHOR BRENDON LIMITED
Tiptree, Essex

For F. C. Horwood

Seven o'clock on a summer morning. And unless you counted the seagull, she was entirely alone. A wet stain on the pavement suggested a dog had recently passed by. Otherwise, that was it. In the guidebook, it said Deal was a former Cinque Port. It also said it had a population of approximately 30,000. Approximately all of them must still have been abed. OK. So it was early. But this was summer, after all. There should have been retired bo'suns peering through telescopes. Kids with spades. Fishermen hauling in nets with a shanty on their lips. What there was, was zilch.

She squinted through her camera lens at a street full of Georgian cottages. Penny Wanawake, Girl Photographer. Chelsea's answer to Julia Margaret Cameron. Fighting fit and ready to go. Except that there was nobody to go with. Not until she found Max Maunciple. She wished that she hadn't left his address behind in London. She wished she knew in which of the chintzy cottages he was staying. She wished she hadn't agreed to get him safely back to the school in Canterbury where he taught. Trouble was, she was all heart.

The seagull stared at her nastily from a chimneypot. She stared right back. Don't give me that seagull shit, or I'll bust you right in the beak. The air was salty. Light as pale and sharp as lemon juice lay over the empty street. A cloud appeared. It moved slowly across the sky like a nonchalant meringue. Her shadow lay on the pavement under her feet, long and thin and black. Just like she was. You could hardly tell where she left off and it began. She shook her corn-row braids. So did the shadow. Who knows what evil lurks in the hearts of men?

She bent again over her camera. She checked the shutter-speed setting. She adjusted the centre column of her tripod. Recording, not thinking.

'Man. That is what I call an ass,' someone said behind her.

She straightened up. 'Thank God,' she said. 'I was beginning to think the rest of mankind had been wiped out by killer tomatoes.'

'You been watching too many late-night movies.' A dude with a suntan stood smiling at her. The smile was terrific. So was the body that went with it. She reckoned he was just about six foot. Maybe an inch shorter than she was. He looked like he worked out a lot. And made out pretty good, too.

'Hi. I'm Penny Wanawake,' she said.

'Sorry to sneak up on you like that,' he said, 'but I hated to ruin your – uh – exposure. I'm Charles Yeoman. Most people call me Chips.'

'Bet that's because you come with everything.'

'Everything I got.' He deliberately widened eyes as blue as mussel-shells. 'Given half a chance.' One of his front teeth was slightly crooked. He shifted the hold-all he was carrying from one hand to the other, then put it on the ground. A St Christopher medal glinted round his throat. He wore a white open-necked shirt. And a pink linen suit.

'You gay or something?' Penny said.

'Are you kidding?' Yeoman pulled his chin in and stared down at himself. 'It must be this suit.' He wore white leather moccasins with tiny coloured beads on the tie-ups. His hair was short, the colour of a canteloupe.

'You look like a strawberry popsicle in it,' Penny said. 'Good enough to eat.'

'Honey, you want to leave that sort of thing to the experts,' Yeoman said. He rubbed his finger behind his ear. 'Guess this suit is kinda loud, at that. I got it two-thirds off in a sale in some fancy London store.'

'I don't suppose they could give it away.' Penny stepped away and looked him up and down. He was a big man. Maybe a couple of years older than she was. Which would make him about twenty-eight.

'Think they'll like it back home in Detroit?' he asked.

'They'll go crazy.' Penny said. There was a lot of hard muscle under the suit. Yeoman looked the macho type. He also looked as though he liked women, which lots of macho types don't.

'Say, will people here really think I'm bent?' Yeoman said. But not as if he gave a damn.

'Not when you tell them what you paid for it,' said Penny. 'To understand all is to forgive all.' She began packing up her camera equipment. 'Detroit, huh? I could tell straight off you didn't belong here.' She'd always been quick like that.

'In Michigan I just melt into the landscape.' Yeoman stared hungrily at her white tracksuit. 'Among other things. Tell me, Miss Wanawake, what are you doing in this former Cinque Port, population approximately 30,000?'

'You been reading my book.'

'Can't be too many coloured gals living in a place this size.'

'I have to pick someone up,' Penny said. 'The cousin of what used to be a friend. Until he landed me with this job.' She waved her hand at the street. 'The guy's staying someplace round here for the night.'

'Bugger's Alley,' Yeoman said. 'That's what they call it locally. Least, so they told me in the pub last night.'

'Probably figured you were cruising.'

'Look, I'll take the damned suit off if it bothers you.'

'Don't worry on my account,' Penny said. 'I have a pair of sunglasses in the car.' She put a hand on his arm. Close to, she could see that there were small black flecks in the blue of his eyes. She smiled at him. He smiled back. It really was a terrific smile.

She set off up a side street towards the beach. Yeoman walked beside her, swinging his bag. The slight rise of the roadway hid the sea ahead, but she knew it was there, all right. She could hear it crunching and slobbering as it gnawed away at the shingle. Ready to sock it to any smart-ass who showed up with a crown and an armchair, looking for a spot of direct confrontation. She looked at her Nautilus watch. She glanced fretfully at the quiet bedroom windows on either side of the street, their curtains still drawn tight.

'What are these guys waiting for?' she said. 'Judgment Day?'

'Way I heard it, a prince could wake them with a kiss. Any old time,' said Yeoman.

'Pity I didn't bring one with me.'

They passed colour-washed houses. Pernod-yellow, tuna-pink, nappy-green. *Très* chic. *Très* chichi. They passed gleaming brass doorhandles. They passed a ceramic plaque with handpainted flowers. Round the rim, it said Don 'n' Dunc live here.

'Jesus,' said Penny.

Once this had been the fisherman's quarter. The place where smugglers snuck brandy and baccy past the Excisemen. Now, the cottages provided weekend retreats for really super guys in the media. And their friends. One of the friends being Maunciple. If only she knew which.

They emerged on to the front. A cold wind slapped at them. The sea dazzled them. There was a wraparound sky, full of creamy light. Stones shifted and scratched at the water's edge, each one shiny with wet. It made you want to do something creative. Like write a poem. Or at least read one.

Yeoman took a deep breath and pounded at his chest. 'Man,' he said. 'That air's like wine.'

Penny frowned at him. 'It pays to improve your word power,' she said. She unlocked the door of her Porsche Targa, a recent gift from her father, and slung her camera stuff into the back. She ran up and down on the spot. She windmilled her arms. 'Want to come jogging with me?'

'Jogging?'

'You know. Like running. Moving forward at a fast but steady pace.'

'When I'm with a lady like you, I always prefer to define my terms,' Yeoman said.

'Ain't no ladies like me.'

'You might have been using a euphemism,' Yeoman said. He gazed with interest at Penny's breasts, which were jouncing around quite a bit inside her loose top.

10

'Language is never in a state of fixation,' Penny said, 'so keep on your toes. Next time I use the word jogging, it could mean something entirely different.' She ran backwards a few yards. 'Sit in the car, if you want to get out of the wind.'

'You trust me, then?'

'With my car? Sure I do. Don't know about anything else.'

She set off down the empty promenade towards the dunes at the edge of town. The coastline curved away from her to the right, cradling a semicircle of tossing water. A bracing wind blew down her neck and billowed the top of her tracksuit. Along the horizon, masts stuck up like dead toothpicks, marking the line of the Goodwin Sands. She'd been here before, as a child. The wind had been pretty damned bracing then, too. It was what she remembered most clearly about the place. Gulls screamed along a thin line of oil which floated parallel to the shore. The beach was unbeautiful. Seaweedy, stony, littered with plastic bags and frayed nylon rope. Wooden-boarded steel groins jutted out from the promenade at regular intervals, dividing the beach into equal portions like a giant ruler. They were covered in spray-painted slogans: SKINS RULE. MODS ARE SODS. FUCK THE IRA. Oh, I do like to be beside the seaside.

The houses thinned out as she left the town behind. They had a nautical flavour to them now. There were telescopes at upper windows. Widows' walks along the roofs. One had a ship's figurehead in the front garden, a fierce lady with streaming hair and enormous boobs. Her nipples were painted scarlet. Sand appeared in feathery skeins along the sea wall as Penny neared the dunes. To one side there was a golf course. To the other, the sea. On the dunes, the ground was soft and yielding, held together by determined clumps of grass. Where the tide had receded far into the sun-glittering distance, there were signs of humanity at last. Bait-catchers, dark against the light, their reflections seeping blackly into the wet sand as they bent and probed for the unwary lugworm. Sea lavender brushed her ankles. Sea holly crackled under her feet. A rusty tin lay half-buried in sand. She trod on a used condom. Dammit. High overhead, a lark did its best to compensate for

11

man's vileness.

Penny though uncharitable thoughts about Peter Corax, the Literary Gent who inhabited the top floor of her house in Chelsea. OK. So it wasn't Peter's fault that she had left his cousin's Deal address behind in London. But it was his fault that she was here now, chin-deep in other people's débris, waiting for Maunciple to surface from what was undoubtedly disreputable sleep.

She did a spot of aerobic breathing. In through the nose. Out through the mouth. Could you get cancer from breathing in too much salt? Her lungs felt barnacle-encrusted. She did a few squats, thinking about Max Maunciple, schoolmaster, historian, writer of ingenious crime fiction. And, by all accounts, a Grade-A jerk. If she hadn't let it slip that she was visiting friends in South-East Kent, she wouldn't now be trying to locate one of the truly great slobs of the twentieth century. Or maybe of all time. But she had.

'The Lensbury-Smiths?' Peter had said. 'My *dear*. I don't know her, but I knew him *very* well at Cambridge. Before I got sent down. They only live a few miles from Deal. How marvellously convenient it will be. Poor Max can't drive at the moment. He's spending Friday night with friends in Deal, and you'll be able to pick him up and take him back to Canterbury.'

Poor Max, it appeared, had fallen, while in his cups, off the edge of his bedroom carpet and had fractured a toe.

'Suppose I don't want to.'

'How grudging you sound.'

'If I sound grudging, it's because I feel grudging. Can't your cousin take a bus?'

'A *bus*? My dear, I don't think Max would *recognise* a bus,' Peter said, wrinkling his nose in a way that had been quite delightful when he was a Rising Young Novelist, but now just looked as if he were trying not to sneeze.

'A bus ride is an experience no novelist worthy of the name should pass up,' Penny said. 'Or there are taxis. He'd recognise one of those, wouldn't he?'

Peter had spread his hands. 'But they're so fiendishly

12

expensive. We poor scribblers 'can't afford such luxuries.' He moved as quickly as fat allowed to stand between Penny and the almost-empty bottle of Sainsbury's whisky on his bedside table. He knew Penny had seen him carrying it upstairs the previous evening. It had been full then. 'Besides, you'd be able to join in the junketings at his school if you took him over to Canterbury.'

'I'm not the junketing kind.'

'Oh, but these are rather special. World famous, I do assure you.'

'Why haven't I heard of them, then?'

'Perhaps you don't keep your ear to the cultural ground, Penelope.'

'I've got better places to keep my ears, thank you.'

'The point is, Abbott's lays on a series of intellectual entertainments at the end of each summer term, partly to show the parents that they're getting their money's worth for the stiff fees they pay, partly to keep the examination candidates out of mischief once they've finished taking their papers. Probably pinched the idea from the King's School, which does the same sort of thing only better, but the standard is still pretty high, and the programmes varied. There's drama. Orchestral music. Choral music. Pottery. Parents come from all over the world to attend. Not to mention Old Boys.'

'Oh God.'

'Besides, I've told Max so much about you. I know he'd love to meet you.'

'Would I love to meet him?'

'Think of driving him back to Abbott's as a charitable act,' Peter had said. 'The Lensbury-Smiths only live a few miles from Deal, so it's not out of your way. And at least Max doesn't smoke. I know how you hate that.'

'Peter, you are so blisteringly persuasive,' Penny said.

In the end, she'd agreed, as Peter had known she would. All she had to do now was to track Mr Maunciple down and convey him safely to Canterbury. Then she could wash her hands of him. Using carbolic soap. She turned and began to run back towards the town. The trouble was, she wouldn't actually recognise Max Maunciple if he poked her in the eye with a pogo-stick. Short of walking round the old part of Deal ringing a handbell and calling his name, she didn't see how she was to winkle him out of whatever cosy little den of vice he was in. On the other hand, he must be known locally, if he had friends here. He was a well-known author, after all. He appeared on TV talk shows to promote his latest books. He was reputed to be urbane and witty. Someone would probably be able to point him out. Once he'd got out of bed.

The sea was on her left now. Across the Channel, a low dark outline above the horizon confirmed the nearness of France. In the distance, a pier stuck out from the land, and a long way beyond it, a headland. White chalk with a green cap of grass. Very English. Very inspiring. This blessed plot. Cry God for Harry, England and St George. Though all that patriotic crap about the Falklands had been enough to make one apply for Estonian citizenship.

She knew that Max Maunciple had begun writing blood-and-thunder pulp fiction to supplement his income as a schoolmaster. Penny dreadfuls, with tough-talking villains and blood-spattered pages. A popular historical text about English shrines had made his name. A no-holds-barred memoir brought him to the attention of a wider public. They adored his air of disgusted malice. As he became sought-after, his fiction changed. Peter had told her once that all his cousin's crime novels were fact lightly gilded with fiction. No one was safe. He knew people in high places and used their secrets for his plots. Only the names were changed to protect him from being sued. Not that anyone would have dared. Prescriptions for tranquilisers doubled all over the English-speaking world, prior to the launching of a new Max Maunciple. A couple of famous marriages had broken up, following *Tennis Balls, My Liege*. A Hollywood name had gone into premature retirement, after the publication of *Star Scattered on the Grass*. A senior civil servant had resigned when *My Nancy Tickled My Fancy* came out. Max Maunciple sounded like a really sweet human being. And she was the one

14

privileged to drive him the eighteen miles between Deal and Canterbury. Some people had all the luck.

When she got back to the car, puffing and sweaty, Yeoman was hunkered down on the beach, sheltering under the lee of the promenade wall. He held a frying-pan over a Camping Gaz burner. There was bacon in it. And sausages. A red enamel teapot sat nearby, wrapped in a towel.

'Where'd all this stuff come from?' Penny said. She pulled her sweaty headband away from her forehead and snapped it back. It felt very odd. She did it again.

Yeoman jerked his head at his hold-all. 'Iron rations,' he said. 'I never travel without them. This is nearly ready. How about you?'

'Let me have a quick dip, to cool off.'

'I'd skip it if I were you,' Yeoman said.

Penny unzipped her top.

'I really would,' Yeoman said.

Penny shucked off the top half of her tracksuit.

'I mean, it's cold,' Yeoman said.

Penny removed the rest of her clothes.

'Man,' said Yeoman.

Slick with sweat and shiny as a seal, Penny ran naked down to where the ripples broke gently onto the shingle. She looked back. Yeoman was rubbing a finger slowly behind his ear. A man in a terry robe was watching her from a window. A paperboy wobbled by on a bike, his eyes glazed as though he were having a wet-dream. Oh well.

She plunged into the sea. The shock almost killed her. She plunged right back out again. Jee-sus. She sucked air into her chest. She ran back up the sloping beach and into the towel Yeoman was holding out for her. 'Why didn't you warn me?' she said.

'I did.'

'That is as cold as I ever want to be.'

'I nearly lost three toes from frostbite yesterday.' Yeoman handed her a polystyrene cup of hot tea. 'Drink that and you'll feel human again.'

'I'm not that ambitious. Just so I don't feel dead.'

15

'You look very much alive to me,' Yeoman said. He didn't turn his back as she shrugged into her tracksuit. She didn't mind. He gave her a paper plate with fried things on it.

'What are you back home? A short-order cook?' Penny ate a sausage as though her life depended on it. The way she felt, it probably did.

'I have been,' Yeoman said. 'On my way through college.'

'And when you graduated?'

'Police academy. I didn't figure there was much work for a guy who'd majored in nineteenth-century English Literature. Besides, I was feeling idealistic at the time. Saw myself as a one-man crime prevention agency.'

'So you're a cop?'

'Right. Detective squad and all.'

'Are you really?'

'Sure. Wanna see my credentials?'

'Not now. We've only just met.' Penny gulped at the hot tea. The rim of the mug tasted of salt. 'Where are you headed?'

'Canterbury.'

'No kidding.'

'None. Why?'

'How are you getting there?'

'Bus.'

'I'll take you,' Penny said, 'if you like. I'm driving over there this morning. Soon as I've located someone called Max Maunciple.'

'What?' Yeoman put down his plate and stared at her. 'Did you say Maunciple?'

'Yes.'

'You're not going to believe this.'

'Try me.'

'He's an author, right? I read this fantastic book about shrines and pilgrimages that he wrote. He really made all that bloodshed and faith come alive for me. I wanted to visit all the places he wrote about and it seemed like a good peg to hang a vacation on, so here I am.'

'History doesn't record too many miracles taking place in

16

Deal, as I recall.'

Yeoman looked momentarily confused. Then he said, 'I met this guy on a train. Said I really should take Deal in, if I could. Something to do with Henry Eighth.'

'And now you're on your way to Canterbury, since *The Pilgrimage of a Passionate Man* states that it was the foremost shrine of the fourteenth century, right? As well as being the cradle of Anglican Christianity.'

'Hey, how'd you know that was the book I read?'

'I have this electronic mind-scanner planted deep in my brain,' Penny said. 'Also, I occasionally read myself. If you take me up on that lift to Canterbury, you'll get to meet the passionate man himself. Once we find him.'

'I don't believe it,' Yeoman said. His face was one incredulous smile. 'The guy that wrote *The Pilgrimage of a Passionate Man*? That's great. That is really great.' He gazed at her with the kind of mingled disbelief and greed that a gourmet might display on hearing that the Troisgros brothers were offering him a meal on the house. 'Fancy you knowing this Maunciple guy.'

'I don't. Not yet. But unless my luck's in, I soon will.' Penny folded a piece of bread and wiped her plate with it. This wasn't the place for party manners. She needed stoking up. From a wooden post, a bird with a black head watched her, its beak hanging open.

'That's some coincidence, when you think about it,' Yeoman said.

'Yeah.'

'Terrific title, isn't it?'

'Real catchy,' Penny said. 'Except he stole it.'

'Who from?'

'Doing literature and all, I'm surprised you don't know. Walter Raleigh, is who.'

'The guy with the cloak who invented lung cancer? Is that right?'

'You learn something every day, don't you?' Penny reached for her mug of tea. It fell over. The contents drained away into the shingle. 'Shit.' she said.

17

The bird with the black head did so. It rose on tiptoe, stretched its neck about in a way a Burmese temple-dancer might have envied, and backed off into the air.

Above them, the promenade was busier now. Old ladies tottered along, heads bent against the wind, thin hair escaping from headscarves. A military gentleman galloped past in plimsolls and a pair of long shorts. Windows were being flung open in the houses which fronted on to the sea. A man with three Yorkshire terriers on different coloured leads sauntered by. He wore a red yachting cap, a white V-necked sweater with the sleeves pulled up above the elbows, and yellow espadrilles. At the sight of Yeoman, he stopped. He stood close to the edge of the sea-wall, gazing out towards the horizon, eye attractively crinkled. He ran the middle finger of his right hand across his brow. Terribly Christopher Columbus.

He dropped his eyes with a sudden start to where Penny and Yeoman stood below him. 'Hell-*o*,' he said. 'Didn't we meet in the pub last night?'

'He talking to me?' said Yeoman.

'Or your suit,' Penny said.

'Beat it, buster.' Yeoman clenched a fist.

'Wait a minute.' Penny put a hand on his arm. She smiled up at the man. He looked like the sort who numbered assholes like Max Maunciple among his acquaintance. Lots of them. 'Do you by any chance know a person called Maunciple?' she said.

'My dear,' cried the man. 'Who doesn't?'

'I believe he's staying overnight in Deal,' Penny said, ignoring several alternative replies. 'I'm not sure of the address, though.'

'Know Max?' The man tugged savagely at the yorkies, two of whom were trying to mount the third. He clasped his index fingers together in front of his nose, causing the dogs to yelp painfully. 'Why, Max and I are like *that*.'

'I can well believe it,' Penny said.

'He's staying with a dear friend of mine, actually,' said the man. 'Only two minutes from here. I'd be delighted to show

18

you.' He leered at Yeoman.

'How awfully kind of you,' Penny said. 'Isn't it, Chips?'

'In a pig's ear,' Yeoman said.

'Dear me. Did some of us get out of our sleeping-bags the wrong side this morning?' said the man. Penny hated the way his skin didn't move when he said it.

'Let's go,' she said. The sooner she found Max Maunciple, the sooner she could deposit him in Canterbury. Deposit. It made him sound like a turd. But that was undoubtedly what he was.

'. . . real turd. I mean the genuine, gold-plated article,'
Penny said. She lay on the bed in her hotel room. She had the
phone in one hand and a glass of Jack Daniel's in the other.
She wasn't about to quarrel with their claim that it was the
world's smoothest whisky. High clouds drifted across the sky
outside. A Gothic belltower loomed through the windows, its
stonework as intricate as a cable-knit sweater. 'He's one of
those creeps who refuses to face up to the fact that whether he
likes it or not, half the human race is female.'

'Does that include those Czech women sprinters at Hel-
sinki?'

'The thing I love most about you, Barnaby, is your ready
sympathy.'

'I've been meaning to talk to you about that. I've got so
much more to offer than mere sympathy.'

'I'm telling you, the only time this Maunciple jerk even
acknowledged my existence – and I'm doing him the favour,
driving him and his broken toe over to Canterbury – was when
we met a haulage truck in the middle of a narrow country
lane.'

'What did he say?' Barnaby Midas, friend, lover and
business colleague, sounded sincerely interested.

'He called me his dear girl. I don't take that kind of talk
from anyone.'

'What was he doing when he wasn't insulting you?'

'Sitting in the passenger seat, chatting up Charles Yeoman
in the back. All the way to Canterbury. Ended up inviting him
to spread his sleeping-bag on the floor of his elegant lodgings.

20

They're apparently right on something called the Great Court and have been untouched since Tudor times when they were erected. Or something. Not to be missed, according to Maunciple. And do you know what else? This'll really turn you on.'

'You turn me on.'

'Yeoman mentioned that he came from Michigan, and this creep launches into a long spiel about some kid he'd met last year while he was on a sabbatical in the States. Apparently she took an overdose on account of him, and guess what: Maunciple actually laughed while he was telling us. Jesus. He ought to be put down.'

'How did friend Yeoman take it?'

'He looked so embarrassed, I thought he'd self-destruct.'

Penny sipped at her drink. It had two icecubes in it. Really extravagant. A couple of years ago she'd trekked alone round Africa for nine months, sleeping rough, eating what she could buy from the local population, helping out in refugee camps. It had all been a lot easier, in retrospect, than prising icecubes out of the management of this nice family-run hotel. That appeared to be its only disadvantage. Besides, it would be churlish to complain about a hotel full of four-poster beds and deep window embrasures and oak staircases. The building had once been the guesthouse of a former Augustinian abbey, and was built into the precinct walls. The abbey now housed the Abbot's School, an establishment of modest academic repute that, until the 1970s, had provided the sons of the professional classes with the kind of classical education needed to get them into university. After that, according to Peter Corax, the rot had set in. Faced with the need for urgent reform, Abbott's had admitted girls, though only into the Sixth Form. Those who had expected a disaster second only to the Dissolution of the Monasteries had been disappointed. In fact entrants to Oxbridge, that apparent barometer of academic success, had almost doubled. So much for prejudice.

'Who's Yeoman, anyway?' Barnaby asked.

'That's all you've got to say when I tell you about a guy who drives a girl to suicide and then treats it as a joke?'

21

'Who's Yeoman?'

'A vacationing detective from Michigan I happened to bump into in Deal this morning. Comes from Detroit.'

'Do I hear a girlish quiver in your voice?'

'Certainly not.'

'What was he doing in your car?'

'What's with you, Barnaby? I was giving him a lift to Canterbury, that is all. No need to get neanderthal about it.'

'What's he like? Six foot tall with dark-blue eyes and an all-over tan?'

Penny had trained herself never to blush. Otherwise, she might have done so now. Not that anyone would have noticed. She got her height from her mother, Lady Helena Hurley, whose pedigree stretched traceably back over six hundred years of English history. She got her colour from her father, Dr Benjamin Wanawake, Permanent Ambassador to the UN for the African Republic of Senangaland. It made blushing redundant.

'I know nothing at all about his tan,' she said. Very coldly. Barnaby might be her long-time lover. That didn't give him any rights over her. Any more than she had rights over him. The trouble with living with someone was that after a while they got to know you too well. And the kind of men you were likely to fancy. 'As a matter of fact, he's five foot nothing and totally bald.'

'And this is a policeman?' Barnaby made noises indicative of derision. 'I've heard of New York's Finest. What's this guy with – Detroit's Tiniest?'

'Barnaby.'

'The Only Pygmy Police Force In the World.'

'Barnaby.'

'Yes.'

'You're being ridiculous.'

'Yes.'

They both knew he wasn't.

'To change the subject,' Penny said. 'How is Miss Ivory?'

'Miss Ivory is all of a flutter, wondering whether to take her hotwater-bottle with her tomorrow,' Barnaby said. 'She's

22

cornered the market in Rennies, in case her digestive system acts up. She's rung the Racegoers' Association three times today to make sure there's been no change in the arrangements, and the Met Office twice to check on the forecast for East Anglia. She told me she fears there may be a sudden unseasonal snowfall.'

'In July?'

'That's what I said. She was able to give me chapter and verse on at least three occasions when it had snowed in July. I'll tell you what else she's done.'

'Go on.'

'She's just placed a mother's-help with an Iranian family near Andover. A rich Iranian family.'

'Terrific.'

'Quite. The secretary of the local golf-club will almost certainly call upon Mr Almouni shortly. Guess who that'll be.'

'Is it wise? Suppose he starts asking you for application papers and enrolment forms.'

'I've already established that he doesn't play golf.'

'What does he do?'

'Spends enormous sums in Bond Street. And I'm talking money. He collects Oriental art. He has some Persian illustrated manuscripts that would make you drool.'

'Not me, they wouldn't. Nanny Simpson never let me drool.'

'Mr Almouni has recently married and, subsequently, we hope, impregnated a young and lovely wife. Hence the need for a mother's-help. In his spare time, he loads this wife down with expensive jewels.'

'Wish someone would load me down with expensive jewels.'

'Come back to Chelsea tonight and I'll see what I can do.'

'Not tonight, sweetheart. There's an open-air concert I'd like to go to. In some cloisters. Or somewhere ancient like that.' Penny drew in another mouthful of bourbon. She had a feeling she sounded evasive. She certainly felt it.

'Concert? What're they playing that you're so anxious not to miss?'

Penny stared at the icecubes in her glass. They'd almost

23

melted. She looked round the room. Just below her open window, someone said loudly, *'Ich habe mein Fotoapparat verloren.'* A strong smell of French cigarettes blew in as the trees outside tossed in a sudden breeze. 'I'll tell you if you promise not to give me any shit.'

'I promise,' Barnaby said. He started to laugh.

'Madrigals.'

Barnaby stopped laughing. There was silence on the other end of the phone. She could just see him, lying back on their bed in the big white bedroom in Chelsea. He would be staring at the Georgia O'Keefe she'd bought from Sotheby-Parke Bernet last time she was over in the States. His red hair would be flaming against the pillow. She could hear him saying nothing. She could have hit him.

'Dowland,' she said. 'Tallis. Ayre. Like that.'

'Since when did you know Tallis from a teapot?'

'I was raised on that kind of music,' said Penny, snippy as hell.

'And I was raised on strained carrots. That didn't stop me puking them up on my bib as soon as I realised what a load of crap they were.'

'Sometimes you can be awfully coarse.'

'Madrigals,' Barnaby said. 'I suppose the Archbishop himself takes the bass line.'

'Possibly.'

'Want to know what I think?'

'No.'

'I think that dwarf detective from Detroit is just crazy over madrigals. I'll bet he wouldn't miss something so terrifically English as madrigals in the cloisters for anything.'

Since this was a fairly accurate paraphrase of what Yeoman had actually said, Penny remained silent. Barnaby didn't.

'I'll also bet he's picking you up in the hotel lounge or lobby or some damn place and taking you out for dinner before the concert. All six foot of him.'

This was also true. 'Am I listening to the authentic sound of naked jealousy?' Penny asked. 'You sound like something out of a Mills & Boon novel.'

24

'I feel like it, sometimes.'

'Honey, with you I feel like it all the time.'

Outside, a deep bell began to clang. Birds wheeled into the sky from the ledges and alcoves of the belltower, their wings bright in the lowering sun. Shadows lengthened across lead roofs, heightening the details of carving and decoration that full daylight had smoothed out. Penny wondered if one could do for the Abbey what Monet had done for Rheims. With a camera instead of a paintbrush. The Abbey, much less famous than the Cathedral, had been founded by a twelfth-century splinter-group objecting to mainstream religious orthodoxy and some of the buildings were magnificent, particularly the polygonal chapterhouse and the splendid gatehouse, built after the licence to crenellate had been granted in 1382. Through the open window, a fine tilth of many touristic tongues overlaid the sound of footsteps passing and repassing in the Great Court. Someone was burning something in the hotel kitchens. It wasn't joss-sticks.

'What are you doing?' Barnaby asked.

'Drinking sour mash bourbon and missing you.'

'Good.'

'You'd love it here,' Penny said. 'The place is wall-to-wall with likely lads who're all bee-stung lips and cricket flannels and golden down on their arms.'

'I've just been through a homo phase,' Barnaby said, 'but I'll bear what you say in mind for next time.'

'You'll see Miss Ivory off safely tomorrow, won't you?'

'Of course.'

'And did Peter catch his train? He hasn't shown up here yet.'

'I took him to Victoria myself. He cast covetous eyes at a stripling pushing a broom around the station concourse, but I got him into a first-class compartment and waited until the train was pulling away. He ought to be there by now.' There was a pause, then Barnaby added, 'Just in time to go to the concert with you guys.'

Penny ignored the remark. 'And you. What're you doing?'

'I'm off to Andover tomorrow, with my golf-clubs on my

25

knee, Barnaby said.'

'Don't overdo it, will you? No hairy socks and brogues with fringed tongues. There's trouble brewing in Angola again, and we're going to need the money. Even if it doesn't erupt into full-scale civil war, the way it did last time, there'll still be people suffering. Children suffering.'

'I know,' Barnaby said. 'I do know. Look, I'll see you when I get back.'

'Hey, Barnaby.'

'Yes.'

'Is you is, or is you ain't my baby?'

'One guess.'

They hung up. Penny smiled to herself. Barnaby Midas, antique dealer and jewel thief, was a very satisfactory companion. In every way. They had met in Paris when Penny, studying for a year at the Sorbonne, had returned to her Left Bank apartment to find him examining the contents of her jewel case. They had been lovers ever since. Which in no way restricted their freedom of choice. Most of the time, their choice was each other. In the Paris days, Barnaby had been little more than a common cat-burglar, despite his education at Eton and Oxford. Now he specialised in sophisticated breaking-and-entering, combined with a high-class line in con tricks. His brainchild, R. H. Enterprises, had proved a most fruitful source of cash, fronted, as it was, by the innocent Miss Ivory and her domestic agency. He hadn't done a golf-club secretary before, but Penny had no doubt that he would be as convincing in the role as he was in any other. He'd been robbing the rich for the past ten years. Since he met Penny, he'd also been giving to the poor. He'd only been caught once. It was the time in Parkhurst that had honed his natural dramatic flair into the useful tool of his trade that it had now become. Penny hoped the young and lovely Iranian wife enjoyed her jewels while she still had them.

She leaned out of her window. Petunias and tobacco plants bloomed in the tiny courtyard below, separated from the Great Court of the Abbey by a length of iron railings set into ancient stone. An arched gateway led directly into the grassed

26

quadrangle of the Court itself, which was dominated by the bulk of a huge church. The abbey grounds had originally been contained behind a massive precinct wall, much of which remained, making of the school an enclosed world. It was hard to believe that twentieth-century England bustled and thrummed beyond the gatehouse. It made Penny feel very privileged. She watched a large number of boys walk rapidly here and there. They had their hands in their pockets. Many of them wore boaters. They looked incredibly suave. As well they might, being pupils at what must be one of the loveliest schools in the world.

As well as the boys, there were tourists. Two Japanese stood on the grass below some flying buttresses and snapped each other standing beside a notice which said DO NOT WALK ON THE GRASS. Perhaps they thought it was a quotation from the Bible. A busload of Hitler's master-race was clustered round a Führer in a green felt hat. The hat had a feather in it and was too small. A booth discreetly sold souvenirs. A litter bin leaked empty Coke tins. It seemed that nothing much had changed since Chaucer's day.

Max Maunciple strolled past below her, limping slightly. He was carrying something bottle-shaped wrapped in blue tissue paper. Seen from above, he was no more than a horseshoe of grey curls, a freckled scalp, a shapeless linen jacket. Vulnerable. Until she saw his shoes. A man who had the nerve to wear shoes like that obviously feared nothing and nobody. You wouldn't have bought a used Bible from him. You wouldn't have sold a used Bible to him. He stopped directly below her and stood watching a man who appeared to be in charge of a group of French teenagers. Nearly all the boys wore army fatigues six sizes too big, and bowler hats made of red-white-and-blue plastic. All the girls had hairy underarms.

Their leader was of medium height, with thick dark hair cut *en brosse*. He had a moustache that looked as though it had been chasing sheep. His shirt was open at the neck and tucked into very tight blue jeans. He clearly dressed to the right. Penny certainly liked his style. For a man standing against a shop whose window featured several gross of souvenir

27

teaspoons and a cardboard model of the Abbey, he had a great deal of what could have been insouciance but was more probably panache. It was a word she intended to look up in the French dictionary as soon as she could, just to make sure.

A raucous voice launched itself onto the evening air from somewhere beyond Penny's vision. 'Hey, you. Maunciple. I want a word.'

It sounded like trouble. With Maunciple on the receiving end. Penny was all for that. They bay window of her room gave her a panoramic view of the Great Court. If anything was going on, she had a front-row seat. She waited. A large man with a very red face appeared, walking fast towards Maunciple, waving one arm. It wasn't a friendly wave.

'Yes. You,' he said. The tie of a not very old school flapped at his throat. Some of his belly lay below the waistband of his trousers. Quite a lot more bulged over a belt of black alligator skin. Or possibly plastic. Though he didn't look like a man who wore plastic belts. More like the sort of man who took them off and hit people with them. Penny rather hoped that was what he had in mind for Maunciple.

'I'm sorry?' Maunciple was saying. Although he had his back to her now, she knew his sandy eyebrows would be raised fastidiously, indicating distaste in a piss-taking kind of way.

'Look here, Maunciple. I've had just about as much of you as I can take,' the big man was saying. Or bellowing. A man in search of garters and looking for Maunciple's guts to do the job. 'My boy tells me he's done very badly in his A-Levels. And I'm telling you now, I hold you directly responsible. I've had you, Maunciple, up to here.' He slashed a thick finger across his Adam's apple.

'Have we met?' Maunciple said.

'I should bloody well say so,' shouted the man. 'I'm Ken Sumnour. Don't you come the old soldier with me, Maunciple. Have we bloody met.'

'Sumnour? Sumnour?' Maunciple was doing a line in vague perplexity it was impossible not to admire. When Ken Sumnour lunged towards him, he added quickly, 'Ah yes. You must be James Sumnour's father.'

28

'I'm Jeremy Sumnour's father, too,' said the man. Seen from closer at hand, the redness of his face turned out to be some kind of skin disease. His eyebrows seemed to leap forward of their own volition, black and lustrous, so much so that Maunciple started back.

'Uh – yes,' he said. Not very urbane. Definitely not witty. It was a real pleasure to watch him.

'I told you before, Maunciple, you're no better than a bloody murderer,' Sumnour went on. 'I warn you. It had better not happen a second time.'

Maunciple had recovered. He smoothed down the paper round his bottle. 'My dear Mr Sumnour,' he drawled, 'I really cannot take the blame for every boy who fails to do himself justice in the examinations. The importance of A-Level is drummed into everyone even before he enters the Sixth. There is a point at which the boy must stand alone. If he has the requisite information inside his head, he will pass. If he has failed to absorb the knowledge we have been thrusting at him for two years or more, he will not pass. It is as simple as that.'

'That's exactly what it's as simple as,' Sumnour said roughly. 'My boy feels he didn't have the requisite knowledge, as you put it, inside his head. And why not? Because you, Mr Max bloody Maunciple, refused to give him the extra coaching he asked for. Coaching for which I would have coughed up without a murmur.' He thrust his chin aggressively in Maunciple's direction. The blemishes on his face stood out. 'People like you shouldn't bloody well be allowed.'

During this exchange, another man had been hurrying towards them from the far end of the Great Court. He now joined them. Penny knew him at once though she had never seen him before in the flesh. This was Marius Knight, who taught chemistry at the school, and was a Housemaster. He was also Max Maunciple's closest friend. Possibly his only friend. As dozens of photographs on the walls of Peter Corax's rooms could testify, he was also a close friend of Peter's. The three of them, Peter and Max and Marius, had been up at Cambridge together years ago. Young, handsome, blurring now at the edges, they lolled in punts, lay awkwardly on

29

college lawns, hugged cricket bats or girls, Max and Peter with flat slicked-back hair, Marius curly and intense between them.

'Mr Sumnour. Please,' he said, tugging at Sumnour's sleeve. He had a beautiful voice, deep and resonant. A preacher's voice. A rabblerouser's voice. 'I'm sure you will find that James has done better than he expects when the results come out. I can assure you, from long experience of such matters, that boys tend to feel gloomy about their prospects once they have completed their papers. It's the opposite of hubris, if you like. A desperate attempt to coax the gods into giving them better marks than perhaps they feel they deserve.' He gave a gentle laugh in which neither Maunciple nor Sumnour joined. He drew Sumnour with him towards the vast gatehouse which led to the grosser world outside. Maunciple stood looking after them.

A youngish man with a thin ascetic face loped past in a pair of Fila running shorts. Penny could see the F quite clearly. A lock of very serious hair bobbed up and down on his forehead as he ran. He had the finely-crafted but superfluous look of a silver swizzle-stick. The muscle-definition of his legs was fantastic.

When he saw Maunciple ahead of him, he speeded up. He spoke, not breaking his stride. Maunciple looked away. The clock on the belltower struck the quarter. The birds flew up. Probably did that every time. Penny thought she'd better hurry if she was to be ready when Charles Yeoman dropped by to pick her up for dinner. He'd been invited to leave his sleeping-bag in Maunciple's rooms, and had then gone in search of an off-licence, saying he'd better take the old gazebo something in return for the use of his floor. Penny hoped it would be something lethal.

As she showered, she wondered. What Maunciple had done to Sumnour's son. Why Maunciple had been staring at the Frenchman like an egg-bearing cuckoo sighting a temporarily unoccupied nest. Where the Frenchman was now. She sighed. He was probably on his way back to France with his flock. Canterbury was always full of French day-trippers and school-kids, over to buy *le Marks et Sparks* sweaters and *le junk anglais*, and possibly to soak up a bit of cultch in the process. She put on a white dress of heavy knitted cotton which swirled around her long legs when she turned. It was very snug over the hips. She rather thought it would set Yeoman's eyes twinkling when he saw it.

She picked up its matching white jacket and the keys to her room. She went down to the hotel lounge. The room smelled strongly of expensive perfume. The ceiling was covered with authentic Chaucerian beams. There were pilgrim-type chintz-covered sofas. Shiny bits of brass. A television set the size of a small council flat. Flowers. It was very cosy. A woman sat on one of the sofas, staring at nothing. She wore a long-skirted dress of some silky material dramatically emblazoned with big scarlet flowers. There were dark red stones in her ears. Penny didn't need Barnaby around to know that they were rubies. The woman was Spanish-looking, her black hair pulled into a heavy knot on her neck. Like everyone else in the country that summer, she was deeply tanned. Her eyes were dark, surrounded by skin that was darker than the rest of her face. She was middle-fortyish and as sexy as hell.

Penny rarely gave the English a chance to keep themselves to themselves. She crossed the room with her hand out and her best watermelon smile. 'Hi,' she said. 'I'm Penny Wanawake.'

'Oh.' The woman was startled. 'I'm – uh – I'm Margaret Curteis-Squire.' Her fingers flashed as she twisted them together in her lap. She had big square hands. On each, was a big square ruby.

'I bet you're going to the school concert this evening,' Penny said.

If the woman was impressed by Penny's powers of deduction, she didn't show it. She picked up the programme lying beside her on the sofa-cushions and leafed idly through it. 'Yes,' she said. 'My son is playing the flute.'

'If he's at Abbott's, you must come every year, don't you?' Penny asked. 'It's the first time I've been.'

'As a matter of fact, it's my first time too,' the woman said. 'I've always – uh – been prevented from coming before. But as

31

this is Adam's last term. . . .' The sentence trailed away. She pressed a tendril of hair back into place. The movement made Penny realise that she was the source of the perfume in the air. The insides of her wrists were very white. Her eyes were sad. Penny wanted to know why. She sat down in a chair covered in huge tulips and improbable foliage.

Footsteps pounded in the creaking passage outside. The door burst open. A David Gower clone stood there, all tanned muscles and golden curls cascading down the back of his neck. A real *Sonnenkind*. Penny swallowed.

'Mother,' said the clone. He held out his arms. 'So sorry I'm late. They kept us down at the river.'

Penny wondered where Peter had got to. He really shouldn't miss this. Perhaps he'd been distracted by the sight of so much other healthy young flesh about the place. One of the things she and he had in common was a susceptibility to youthful male beauty. In Penny's case this usually took the form of nothing more than admiration. In Peter's, it usually didn't. She could sympathise.

'Darling,' said Mrs Curteis-Squire. She no longer looked sad. She turned to Penny. 'This is my son. Adam.' She turned back. 'Miss – uh – Wanawake is coming tonight to hear you play,' she said fondly. She made it sound as though Penny had scaled mountains and crossed deserts for the privilege.

'It wasn't my main reas – ' began Penny scrupulously.

'And sing too, I hope,' Adam said. He grinned at Penny in a way she felt was a little lusty for a lad of his years. Which didn't stop her from grinning back. 'I'm alternating between my flautist's cap and my tenor's one tonight,' he said. He flickered honeyed eyelashes at her. She hoped his mother hadn't noticed. Where had she read about some kid who was as fresshe as is the monthe of May? Forget May. This one was just plain fresshe.

'Sounds like fun,' she said.

'Oh, I think it could be,' said Adam. He licked his bottom lip. No doubt about it. He was definitely giving her the eye. She wanted to tell him to behave himself. She wanted to say that she was old enough to be his mother. She didn't think he'd believe her if she did.

More footsteps sounded on the old planked floor outside the door. Charles Yeoman came in. He had a plaid rug over his arm. He had changed into a pair of dark trousers and a yellow button-down shirt that matched his hair. He looked just fine. Penny moved so that her skirt swirled. His eyes twinkled. She'd known they would.

'This is Charles Yeoman,' she said. 'He's over here from the States.'

Adam introduced himself and his mother. 'You've chosen a good year to come to England. Our summers aren't usually this fine,' he said.

'Are you on holiday, Mr Yeoman?' asked Margaret Curteis-Squire. She sounded as if she really needed to know.

'That's right.'

'Are you planning to spend the whole time in Canter-bury. . . .' Again she let the sentence trail away, like fishing-line floating above a pike.

'No.' Yeoman turned on his smile. Penny distinctly saw Margaret blink. 'I'm aiming to visit most of the other major English shrines while I'm here.'

'How very interesting,' said Margaret. 'You know, there's a rather good book on the subject, if you're—'

'Mother, I don't want to hurry you, but we'd better go if we're going to find somewhere to eat before the concert,' Adam said. He looked at the rug Yeoman was carrying. 'And I'll have to go back to Ashmole and get something for you to sit on. Ashmole is one of the school Houses,' he added kindly, for Yeoman's benefit. Yeoman didn't look as if he'd benefitted an awful lot.

'I'll wait for you outside,' his mother said quickly. 'It's a warm evening.'

'Can't you come with me?' Adam said. 'Mr Knight's always saying how much he'd like to meet you.'

'Yes. Well,' said Margaret. 'No. I think I'll wait.'

'Clever of you,' Penny said to Yeoman, 'to think of bringing a rug.'

'Maunciple insisted. Said the dews get pretty heavy after nightfall.'

33

Margaret's face changed. She no longer looked sexy. Obdurate was the nearest approximation to what she looked. 'Maunciple,' she said. She could have been chipping ice with her teeth.

'He's the one who writes thrillers,' said Adam. 'A real bastard.' He spoke with the bravado of a boy in the last few days of his school career. 'He used to be head of History here. Now he does special coaching for A-Levels.'

'I've heard of him,' Margaret said. She gazed into the middle of the room, where some lilac hung decoratively out of a copper bowl on a table. The way she gazed, it seemed quite surprising that it went on hanging, instead of falling into a heap of withered petals. Penny hoped she'd be wearing protective clothing if Margaret ever turned that gaze on her.

'He can't be all bad,' Yeoman said. 'He's offered me the use of his floor for the duration of my time here in Canterbury.'

'If you've got any sense, you'll refuse. You can't trust him,' Adam said. There was a flush under the tan on his cheekbones. He pulled in the corner of his mouth. 'He's got a perverted mind.'

Bells chimed somewhere in the sky above the hotel. All four of them moved towards the door, making polite parting noises. Adam took his mother's arm. Yeoman took Penny's.

'I'm looking forward to hearing you sing,' Penny called, as the Curteis-Squires disappeared into the warm evening. Adam laughed.

Penny and Yeoman found a Chinese restaurant in the High Street that still had an empty table. It also had big blow-ups of Hong Kong's waterfront all round the walls, and eight-sided lanterns with red tassels hanging from the ceiling. One of the tassels got caught in Penny's hair as she sat down. The place smelled of monosodium glutamate. Or yellow bean-curd. Or something. Most of the diners were not Eastern, but hidden away in corners were two or three elderly Orientals using chopsticks to shovel rice into their mouths with the kind of ferocity more usually seen in game reserves.

A solemn child gave them a menu printed in Germanic script. Her two front teeth were missing.

34

'Chinese Gothic's a new one on me,' Penny said.

'There's a lot of it about,' said Yeoman. In the reddish light, his eyes were almost black. They were pretty full of lustful esteem, too. It was one of those things Penny recognised as soon as she saw it. 'There's a lot of you about, too. Lucky I've got a good head for heights.'

'I'm sure that's not all you've got that's good,' Penny said.

An older version of the solemn child brought a bottle of soy sauce and put it with infinite care in the exact centre of their table. Across the aisle from them, a man in a grey suit was haranguing his wife about utilitarian radicals. She didn't look as though she liked being harangued. She didn't look as though she gave a toss for utilitarian radicals. She didn't look as though she was too keen on being his wife. When he mentioned George Grote, she dug viciously into a spring roll, which shunted across the table and disappeared into her husband's lap.

A bird-boned girl came and took their order. She murmured words they could not understand. When they spoke of No 97, she giggled and went away.

'Is there a Mrs Charles Yeoman?' Penny asked.

'Not that I've noticed.'

'How come?'

Yeoman turned down one side of his mouth.

'Don't feel you have to tell me, if you don't want to,' said Penny.

'I don't.'

There was a pause.

'So how come?' said Penny.

'The only lady I'd like to fill the position,' Yeoman said, blinking round the room, 'is unfortunately unable to do so.' He moved his eyes back to Penny. He scanned Hong Kong's waterfront as though picking out a place to tie up next time he arrived by ocean-going yacht.

'I'm sorry.'

Yeoman moved his lips upward. Something seemed to have happened to his smile. It looked as if it might slip off his face and shatter on the table. He put up a couple of fingers and set it straight.

'No hope?' Penny asked.

'Nope.'

'Gee, Yeoman. That's just terrible.' Penny leaned forwards and put a hand on his arm. He put a hand on her hand.

'I know,' he said. He tried for a don't-give-a-damn look. He didn't make it.

'Can you talk about it?'

'Sometimes.'

'Now?'

'I'd rather not.'

'Right,' said Penny. She wondered what the problem was with Yeoman's girl. Was she in love with someone else? Married to someone else? Or maybe the victim of some debilitating but not mortal disease that put marriage out of the question? Poor Yeoman.

A lot of activity began to take place. Solemn people, some with all of their teeth, began unloading hot plates. Dishes were put on to them. Things steamed. Other things smouldered. An eye stared crossly up from the head of a whole deep-fried fish. Penny thought she'd probably feel cross if she'd been deep-fried.

'Any family?' she asked. 'Brothers? Sisters?'

'Absolutely none,' Yeoman said. He spoke very definitely, as though he knew several people who, given half a chance, would sneak up on his nearside and pass themselves off as his siblings. 'What about you?'

'Just me,' Penny said. 'Don't believe there'd be room for more than one of me in a family.'

Yeoman ran his finger lightly over her knuckles. 'I never ate a Chinese meal with a black girl before.'

'For all my dirty hide, I am white, clear white, inside.'

'That wasn't a racist remark, if that's what you're thinking.'

'Neither was mine. I got nothing against whitey. Nothing at all.'

'John Stuart Mill,' the man across the aisle said loudly. 'Harriet Taylor. The Reform Bill of 1832.' He wagged a finger argumentatively. His wife looked as if she'd like to bite it off.

Penny was doing well on the chopsticks tonight. Sometimes

36

she didn't. But so far, there'd been no need for the jab-and-spear routine she'd worked out as an alternative for the off-days. Tonight, she could even have coped with a sleeve-dog as well. Yeoman was working away at No 97 like a professional. He certainly had the air of a man who could tell his arse from a bean-sprout. Penny preferred men who knew what they were about.

She thought again about Yeoman's girl. Perhaps she had suffered a mental breakdown. Or been severely injured in an accident. She wondered if he would tell her one day. She wondered if there would be a one day. Poor Yeoman.

An apple-fritter or two later, they strolled back towards the Abbey. People were crowding into the Great Court through the gatehouse, heading for the cloisters. There were ribboned boaters wherever you looked. There were parents in after-six wear they hoped wouldn't make their children throw up. There was a bishop. There were two tall Nigerians with bedspreads wrapped round their heads.

Lights shone from Penny's hotel. And from Maunciple's oriel window. Nothing within the precinct walls was very far from anywhere else. The cloisters were within spitting distance of the various school Houses, yet cut off from the rest of the town. It was all exceedingly snug.

Penny caught sight of Peter Corax talking to Marius Knight. So he'd arrived safely. He was wearing his Prince of Wales checked suit. Someone would have to tell him about the yellow stain near the crotch. Someone would have to make him take it to the cleaners. She wished it wasn't going to be her. She wished someone had taught him to catch the drip.

She saw the thin jogger. He'd changed out of his running shorts. He wore a denim bomber jacket with a CND sticker over the shoulderblades. The ends of his dark hair were damp. There was a gold ring in the lobe of one ear. No one would ever mistake him for a parent. He was talking to a girl who had a waterfall of mousy hair down her back. She must have been at least thirteen. He was using a lot of body language to express himself. Much more than he needed. Across the heads of the crowd, his message was clear: 'I'll swizzle the bubbles out of your champagne just any old time. Baby.'

To her surprise, Penny also noticed the Frenchman. He must have sent his teenaged charges back across the Channel without him. Perhaps he was a madrigal freak. He had added a Harris Tweed jacket to his ensemble. It had leather patches on the elbows. The Continental idea of what an English gentleman went around in. It made him look very unauthentic. Behind him, Kenneth Sumnour stared about, looking for someone.

Stringed instruments were tuning up in the cloisters as Penny and Yeoman found a corner of lichened gravestone that was still free of middle-class rumps. Possibly because it was thick with pigeon-droppings. More and more people were crowding into the enclosed space, pushing up against each other, spreading rugs on the dampening grass, laughing horsily. Kenneth Sumnour was still looking round, one foot possessively marking out his territorial imperative. She saw Margaret Curteis-Squire lurking behind a stone column. Her dark face was made even darker by the shadows. Under the arched pillars of the quadrangle, a choir of young people watched them with grave faces. Other young people sat with their parents in the audience and watched them back. Music stands stood about like neglected herons.

Spotlights were focused on the Abbey buildings. The air held a piece of silver moon. Anticipation quivered. Not of the concert, but of what lay ahead, once this almost-finished term was over. For many of the kids there, life would never again be as nearly-perfect as it was now, at this very moment, with the stonework glimmering apricot and primrose against a darkening sky, the smell of crushed grass in the air, and violins echoing from ancient stone.

An oboe blew a soft pure note. Yeoman held Penny's hand. A woman in front of them said in a whisper: 'Jessica's had four puppies. Isn't that marvellous, darling?' Darling was a thin boy with glasses. Darling thought it was really super. Darling asked if one of them could be called Kierkegaard. Darling sounded a bit of a prat.

A man with a great deal of grey hair lifted a baton. The choir drew in a deep collective breath. The oboist stood up. The concert began.

38

Max Maunciple sat in the big bay of his first-floor sitting-room. He'd had to be more than usually manipulative to obtain these grace-and-favour lodgings after his retirement from the History Department, but the effort had been worthwhile. The hanging window jutted right out into the Great Court, supported on black oak uprights over a fine front door. It gave him such a comprehensive view, that almost nothing taking place in the quadrangle could escape his attention.

Through the open window, he heard the young voices of the school's Madrigal Society.

'*Awake, sweet love, thou art returned*,' they sang.

'*My heart, which long in absence mourned,*
Lives now in perfect joy.'

Sweet love, he thought. Long in absence mourned. He'd seen Margaret that very afternoon. For a single mad moment, returning from the town, he'd almost thought she was there in his rooms. He smelled her perfume. The ghost of a remembered fragrance had hung about the passage, bringing her sharply to mind. Music, when soft voices die, vibrates in the memory, he told himself. Something like that. Margaret hadn't seen him. Nor had any intention of doing so. Not that he could blame her. He hadn't decided whether to tell Marius she was here or not. The boy was a fine-looking lad. He rather thought Marius didn't know about the boy. Nor ever had. He would soon.

He opened the door of a cabinet of inlaid satinwood that stood against one wall. So elegant. So right. Part of the pleasure it gave him derived from its beauty. A much larger part lay in knowing that it rightfully belonged to his cousin, Peter. Only that evening, prior to the concert, Peter had once again demanded its return. To no avail. He took out a bottle of gin. More than three inches had gone from the top. He wondered when he'd drunk that. He knew he'd finished a bottle last night, because his cleaning woman had taken it away with her usual look of moral superiority, clicking her teeth and muttering as she took it downstairs to the dustbin. He didn't remember starting on a fresh bottle. Oh well. There were eight other bottles, seals unbroken, standing on the shelf. They represented eight more evenings to be profitably passed. He picked out his favourite glass from a collection of antique goblets and filled it almost to the rim with gin. He splashed in tonic from the family-size bottle he'd gone out specially to purchase earlier in the evening.

He sat down at the table in the centre of the room and opened his briefcase. He took out a manuscript and arranged it in front of him, smiling slightly. The eighth Max Maunciple thriller. Two hundred and seventy-two pages of tautly-written fact, masquerading as fiction. His latest hostage to fortune. Well, not fortune exactly, since publishers were a mean lot of sods. But to a reasonable competency, certainly.

He ran his hand over the top page. Chapter 1. He experienced the frisson he always felt at seeing the finished manuscript. Creatively finished, that is. It still had to be copied out. Tomorrow he'd take it to the typist, who would produce a fair copy. It was playing with fire to have only one copy, he knew. But as a one-finger typist, he couldn't be bothered with carbons. He swallowed a draught of gin that would have knocked out a dray-horse. First he had to think of a title. He savoured the various choices in his mind. From his briefcase he took another piece of paper and stared at it. Five titles. While any one would have done, none had quite the note of malice that he prided himself on achieving. He thought for a moment, leaning his head on his hand.

A note propped against a bowl of oranges caught his eye. What a frightfully affected hand Dominic Austen had, all

40

downward flourishes and elaborate curlicues. '*Came to collect my humble scribblings. Will call back later.*' Mock humility. He opened his briefcase again and pulled out Austen's poems. No sane adult could expect to be taken seriously if he produced work in a folder with some kind of pink feline on the front of it. As for the so-called poems, humble scribblings was rating them far too highly. What a heap of tripe they were. Nothing but belly-aches about the poet's physical functions. Good God: the man could scarcely pass stool without writing a poem to celebrate the fact. And he'd had the impudence to suggest that he, Max Mauncible, might write a letter of recommendation to that place in the States he was trying to weasel his way into. Well, he'd come to the wrong place. He'd told Austen he did indeed plan on writing to the school in question. But merely to state that in his considered opinion, Dominic Austen was the very last person to employ in a place of that sort. Visiting Poetry Tutor, indeed. The man wouldn't recognise a poem, not a proper poem, if it stood on his foot. And a school full of nubile women? The idea was absurd. Especially American ones. They all seemed to be more or less permanently on heat. God, how he hated American girls. All churned out from the same sausage machine, with the same size hips, the same size busts, the same hideous lacquered hair-dos. He swallowed the rest of his drink. Christ. Those perfect teeth parted for ever in a friendly grin. Those pure whites to their innocent wide-open eyes. Those banal and pea-sized brains.

How different from the tall black creature who'd driven him over from Deal. Cousin Peter's unlikely landlady. Not a lass to be trifled with. There'd been more than a smattering of the transatlantic about her speech-patterns though not about her accent. That was pure Sloane Ranger. Hadn't Peter said she was Helena Hurley's daughter? The information sidled into his gin-hazed brain and he snorted sardonically. He remembered Helena from the old days, when her father, Lord Drumnagowrie, as he now was, had still been working his way up through the diplomatic hierarchies. Trust Helena to fall for a fuzzy-wuzzy. Always liked to shock, did Helena, though they

41

said she was the perfect diplomatic wife these days, over in New York. She'd sent him a stinking letter after *Taffy Was A Thief* came out. Was he to be blamed for the fact that Huw Williams had been dipping into his company's till? And was fool enough to live so far above his ostensible income? He couldn't really be held responsible for Huw doing himself in. It was typical of the man's flamboyance that he should jump in front of a Tube train in the rush hour wearing a dinner jacket and a white carnation.

He poured himself another gin. He shoved a couple of drops of tonic into the space still remaining in the glass. Gin was not a gentleman's drink, but then he wasn't a gentleman. He'd been bred as one, but he'd always refused to behave like one. It was not being a gentleman that gave him his power. People could never believe he was as much of a cad as he was.

Looking about him with a smugness he had no right to, he saw three books on a shelf near the door. They hadn't been there earlier. Perhaps Marius had brought them round while he was out. He looked up at the superb ceiling. The chandelier over the Regency table had once hung in the British Embassy in Paris. The flocked wallpaper of a most subtle green was handmade and priceless. His bookcases were of polished mahogany and had once belonged to a minor member of the aristocracy who was a far better man than he himself would ever be. Editions of *A Passionate Man's Pilgrimage* were prominently displayed. His other books he kept on a bottom shelf in his bedroom. He wasn't exactly ashamed of them – they'd brought in far too much money for that – but their lurid covers clashed with the elegance of the room. He wished he felt as passionate now as he had when he wrote it. Nothing seemed worth the effort, these days.

He added more gin to his glass. The glands under his ears were beginning to swell, the first sign that the spirit was doing its stuff. It was all he knew of orgasm now. All he really wanted to know. My dancing days are done, he thought.

> '*And if that now thou welcome be*
> *When thou with her dost meet,*
> *She all this while but played with thee*

To make thy joys more sweet,'

sang privileged youth in the cloisters, unaware that golden lads and girls all must as chimney sweepers come to dust. Well, he played with Margaret once too often. And Margaret's husband. He'd never welcome be if they should meet. He wondered why she was here. She hadn't come in previous years. It must be because it was the boy's final term. What did it matter, anyway? What did anything matter? His broken toe throbbed. He looked down at his shoes. God, they were frightful. Must have been pissed when he bought them.

He filled his glass again. He thought about the French teacher who wasn't French and wasn't a teacher. Only that morning he'd seen him wandering round the Great Court with his camouflage, and again in the afternoon, with a different lot. He'd told him earlier that he knew all about his little game. Seeing the damned fellow there, leaning against the souvenir shop, the Abbey shop, for Christ's sake, he'd been just about to tell him to clear off if he didn't want to be immediately exposed when the wretched Sumnour had waylaid him. Was it his fault that two years ago Jeremy Sumnour hadn't done himself justice in the examinations? Had failed to get into the university of his choice? Such an inelegant boy, he'd been. Such a lumpish, frumpish boy. Like father, like son. He should really have given the youth the extra coaching he'd asked for. That was why the school employed him, after all. But the Sumnour boy had sniffed. Perpetually. No sensitive man could have stood for it. His brother James had the same irritating habit.

Deep in his gut, Max Maunciple felt a tremor of fear. The trouble with day boys was that their parents were always much more in evidence than the parents of boarders. All his life he'd avoided physical violence. So crude, when there were other more elegant ways to score a point. The thought of Mr Sumnour's beefy fist smashing into his face was an unpleasant one. He fingered his overlarge nose. He very much hoped that James Sumnour had done better in his A-Level than he thought he had. Sumnour was the type who could fell an ox with a single blow. Always supposing he wanted to . . .

43

Daguerre. That was it. The Frenchman's name. According to David Marriner, anyway. And damned shifty he'd looked about telling him, too. Not that he was a Frenchman. Daguerre. Obscene trousers he was wearing, too. Looked the violent kind. Those who live by the sword, shall perish by it. Or something. If he saw the fellow hanging about tomorrow, he'd call the Customs people. He told the fellow so, only a couple of days ago.

Maunciple pulled out a green morocco leather diary. He flipped through the pages. Not much garnered this year in the way of scandal. People were growing wary of him. But that business at Sumnour's place could prove useful, if the man became abusive again. A pile of pamphlets caught his eye and he got unsteadily up from his chair. It took more limb control than he expected to walk round the table. The proceedings of a French historical society that Marriner belonged to. He must have called in and dropped them here while he was out earlier. Typical of him to take so long. It must be at least two terms since he'd asked for them.

'*Not long youth lasteth,*
And old age hasteth.
Now is best leisure
To take thy pleasure,' sang the choir, out in the summer evening.

I'll drink to that, thought Maunciple. He tipped the gin bottle over his glass. A few drops splashed on to the table and he wiped them up with the sleeve of his corduroy jacket. He didn't bother with tonic. Outside, it was fully dark. The spotlit belltower floated in the sky, hanging against the stars as though no longer anchored to solid ground.

'*Not long youth lasteth,*' murmured Maunciple. His own youth seemed to have lasted one hell of a time, long after he'd gone down from Cambridge. 'I was so much older then. I'm younger than that now,' he told himself wisely. Who'd said that? Some American singer that Deborah was always playing. Until he'd threatened to break the disc across his knee. She'd cried, of course. She always did. Could he be blamed if she'd been an hysterical and immature brat? She'd

44

probably never even intended to kill herself, just to give her people a scare. How old had she been? Twenty? Twenty-one? Old enough to know better than to take him seriously. Good God, if he'd thought for one minute. Besides, a writer, a creative person, couldn't be expected to conform entirely to expected *mores*. 'I was so much older then,' he said again. Fellow called himself after some damned poet or other. Not that there were any poets worth the name these days. Look at Austen, for God's sake. What was it? Larkin? Gunn? Betjeman? Christ, no. Dylan. That was it. Bob Dylan. 'I was so much older then . . .' He'd rather liked that. Hadn't he read somewhere recently that the man had become a born-again Jew?

He poured another gin. The level in the bottle was below the quarter-full mark now. The doctor had told him at his last medical check-up that he should lay off the stuff, but he'd be damned if he would.

'*Let spare no treasure,*

To live in pleasure,' he grated, along with the invisible singers. And by God, he hadn't. Not spared any treasure at all.

He hoisted the glass to his lips. Having a certain amount of trouble with the motor functions these days, he thought. Especially after a glass or two of drink taken. With the first swallow, he reached the optimum amount of poison necessary to cause death. The person who had placed the poison in the bottle might well have hoped for some moment of consciousness before Max Maunciple died. Might well have wished for a second or two of realisation of what had been done to him, to repay him for all that he had done to others. But it was not to be. Max Maunciple died swiftly, relapsing into coma and death, the fingers of his left hand contracting round his glass, blood suffusing his face, his eyes bulging only fractionally, his right hand lifting towards his heart as his braincells were blotted out suddenly and for ever.

45

FOUR

'Penny.' The voice below her window was urgent. 'Penny.'

She leaned out into a scent of tobacco plants and a murmur of home-going voices. Peter Corax stood below her, staring up, almost within arm's reach. Not quite who she'd been expecting. She started to say so. Another figure came out of the darkness. Yeoman.

'Something's happened to Mr Maunciple,' he said. He put one hand on Peter's shoulder. 'Can you come?'

Peter started to babble. 'You must come. It's Max. Please come, right now, Penny. He's all that was left. Please.'

'Dead?' Penny said. 'What happened?'

'Looks like a heart-attack.'

'The doctor told him,' Peter said. He clasped his hands together. 'He told him he ought to cut down on his drinking. Come on down, Penny. Please.' His voice shook.

'I'll be right there.'

Out in the little courtyard full of flowers, she took Peter's arm and felt him tremble as they walked in silence towards Maunciple's lodgings. They were perhaps fifty yards from the hotel, the big bay window unmistakable even in the dark. Maunciple must have been uniquely placed to keep tabs on what went on in the enclosed world of school and quadrangle. It was a safe bet that he did so.

The Great Court was still crowded, although the concert had ended half an hour earlier. Parents chatted to boys. Boys chatted to girls who gleamed like moths, white-bloused, navy-skirted, in a feminine version of the school dress. Penny remembered Peter's apoplexy whenever he spoke of the fact

46

that girls were allowed to join the school in the Sixth Form, his insistence that England was going to the dogs. Useless to point out that it had been doing that for a long time now. And that Peter himself had been well in the vanguard of the going. She saw a boy with dark untidy hair staring enraptured at a girl with a thick brown plait who carried a cello. She thought she saw Margaret Curteis-Squire.

Yeoman led the way into the ground floor of the building. The door stuck and he kicked it a couple of times in order to get it open. He led the way upstairs and along a short wide passage. Its ceiling was timbered in square panelling. Small golden suns flared like pimples at each intersection. In the big room fronting on to the Great Court, light chased and tinkled among the tear-drops of a magnificent chandelier. French, Penny thought. Eighteenth century. A marble fireplace chilled one wall. Books and papers almost hid the chestnut gleam of a fine Regency table in the centre of the room. Some silver in need of cleaning stood in a corner cabinet. A smell of feet came from a walnut davenport. Old bachelors don't die, they simply rot away.

But not this one. This one still had some rotting to do. This one lay in a Victorian easy-chair upholstered in green velvet, looking as though he were slumped in drunken oblivion. Oblivion, all right. A terminal case. Penny bent over him. His mouth hung open. A cavity in the lower jaw needed urgent attention. Grey glinted in the fine stubble of his evening chin. His hand was rigid round a post-Jacobite goblet decorated with etched flowers and ears of corn. His horrible brown-and-white shoes were pointed inwards towards each other.

Penny sniffed. There was a faint smell, ginlike, yet not gin. She didn't think it could be Maunciple's aftershave. She bent her head closer and sniffed again. Definitely not gin. She picked up the almost-empty bottle standing on the table beside Maunciple's chair and smelled it. Nothing. Except gin. Yeoman was watching her.

'I called a doctor,' he said. 'And the police. I wasn't sure if I needed to, but the numbers were by the phone so I figured

47

it wouldn't hurt.'

Penny looked again at the corpse. She stifled her feeling of relief that no one expected her to give it the kiss of life. God had got in first, with the kiss of death. Moisture had gathered at the corner of Maunciple's twisted mouth, and rolled onto his chin. Post-mortem slobber was still damp on his shirt. She could see a line of grime around his open collar. Too late now to tell him that Persil washes whiter. An incongruous rosebud bloomed in his lapel. Grogblossom pink. Like his nose.

Who would grieve for him? Apart from his publisher? She wished she felt something. But she didn't. Beyond the usual shudder at so potent a reminder of human mortality and the frailty of the flesh. She went over and put her arms around Peter. She rested her cheek against his and felt the wetness of tears. She didn't speak. What can you say about the dear departed when the dear departed is a well-known piece of crud? What do you say to a man with tears on his face? You don't. Not if he's Peter Corax. You give him a stiff drink instead.

In the handsome cabinet against the wall, there were several shelves of old glass, two corkscrews, and a papier-mâché tray of Victorian vintage painted with a landscape of hills and overdressed shepherdesses. There were seven un-opened bottles of gin. Two different kinds of whisky, one blended and one pure malt. One bottle of the kind of vodka that as soon as you discovered it, made you realise how wrong you were to think Wan King was a town in China.

She poured Peter a generous helping of the pure malt. His palate was so deadened now by the cheap stuff he normally drank that he would probably not know the difference. But he did. He swallowed it with a peculiar gulping sound. He remembered in time not to smack his lips.

'Where's the guy's manuscript?' Yeoman said suddenly. He had been prowling quietly round the room, pulling open drawers and peering into cupboards. He picked up a folder of bright green cardboard. A pink panther pranced like a furry stick-insect across the front. 'Centralised the silken bone of need,' he said. 'Gashed with desire, the darkness stings. Jesus

Christ.' He put the folder down.

'Which manuscript?' Penny said.

'His latest book. He said it was in his briefcase. All ready to go to the copy-typist.' He pointed at the case, which stood open on the table. There was clearly no manuscript inside it. Nor on the table. Nor anywhere obvious in the room.

'He told me too,' Peter said. 'When I g-got here just b-before the concert.' His chin wobbled. He took a firmer grip on his glass.

'Perhaps he sent it off by post while we were at the concert. A school this big would have some kind of central posting outlet, wouldn't you think?'

'But it hadn't been typed,' Peter said. 'He was still trying to find the right title.'

'He told me there was only the one copy until the typist made another,' Yeoman said. He sounded sombre.

Peter made another curious noise that seemed to have been intended to come out through his mouth but in fact emerged from his nose. 'I didn't like him,' he said. 'Fact is, I hated him. Loathed him. He used to bully me. But he was my cousin. The only family I had left.' He looked pathetically up at Penny. He held out his glass.

Penny half-filled it. 'You'll need some water with it this time,' she said. By the door was a handsome games table with a series of inlaid boards set on top of one another. Max Maunciple seemed to have been playing himself at backgammon. And losing. She went out of the room and across the passage. There was a small dingy kitchen opposite which contained a lingering smell of some expensive scent. A large tin of Nescafé stood opened on the table. A teaspoon encrusted with dried sugar lay beside it. There was a refrigerator with dirty fingermarks all round the handle. She didn't feel strong enough to open it. A Busy Lizzie lay decomposing on the windowsill. A baggy pair of double-knit cotton underpants, size L, hung from a hook on the back of the door. The elastic waistband needed renewing. A side of Max Maunciple his admiring public would never see. The man behind the mask. The kitchen sink smelled faintly of drains and gin.

Penny filled Peter's glass up with water. Underneath the sink was an orange plastic bin. She trod on the white foot-pedal. The lid snapped upwards. The bin was lined with a white plastic bag. It was empty except for a green gin bottle. She went back to the big reception room, pausing to throw the dice on to the backgammon board. A four and a six. Maunciple was playing a running game. She ran, moving two of White's men.

The door opened just behind her and a man in an expensive blue suit came in. He wore a blood-red silk tie fastened with a gold pin. He had more gold round the little finger of his left hand.

'Doctor Webbe,' he said curtly. He set down his bag and began doing brisk things to Maunciple's body. Feeling its heart. Peering down its throat. Lifting its eyelids. 'Wouldn't you know. Angie Bannen-Jones is the best cook in Kent and I get called away in the middle of the asparagus soufflé.'

Penny didn't enjoy watching him. Instead, she lifted the cover of the pink-panthered folder to reveal a title-page. '*Carrion Kisses*,' by Dominic Austen. The name seemed familiar. It brought to mind reviews in *Time Out*. Poetry readings in Liverpool. Membership of the SWP. Hadn't he been the one who produced a book of writings by pupils at a Hackney comprehensive that had set ILEA by the ears? There seemed a certain dichotomy between Hackney and the bird-haunted cloisters of Canterbury. She leafed through a page or two. It was raunchy stuff. Not to say actionable. Dominic Austen seemed to go for very young girls.

Doctor Webbe stood and dusted his fingertips delicately together, as though death might be catching. 'I've been telling him for years,' he said. 'Told him again only last week when he came for his annual check-up.'

'Where's that manuscript?' Yeoman said.

'Drank like a fish, of course,' said the doctor. He stared at Penny. 'If he'd stuck to the same stuff, he'd be alive today. Nobody ever came to any harm drinking cod's wallop. Water, that is.' He laughed.

'Unless it was contaminated,' Penny said.

50

The doctor stared at her. He didn't look as if he knew much about polluted water-holes and cholera-infected stand-pipes. He glanced at the remains of Max Maunciple and shrugged. 'It was bound to happen sooner or later,' he said.

'He was only fifty-six,' Peter said. He gave a hopeless sigh. His eyes fell on the satinwood cabinet. He brightened.

'You'd have no hesitation in signing a death certificate, then?' Penny said.

'None at all,' said the doctor. He seemed fascinated by Penny's tits. 'Any man in his condition who regularly downs the best part of a bottle of gin in an evening is just asking for it.'

'Condition?'

'Angina. Not a disease that responds particularly well to the gin treatment,' said the doctor. He laughed, showing gold teeth. Penny supposed this to be what they call gallows-humour. It didn't seem particularly funny.

'Death is the cure of all diseases,' said Yeoman.

'How very true.' The doctor seemed about to ask Penny if he might palpate her breasts. She intended to refuse. There was a quick knock at the door and Marius Knight came in. He wore a green velvet jacket that might have been made from the remnants of Max Maunciple's upholstery.

'Oh, my God,' he said. 'What's happened here?' His voice filled the room with Bernhardtian tragedy.

'Max finally took one drink too many,' the doctor said.

Knight sighed. His expression was difficult to read. 'I suppose it's the way he would have wanted to go,' he said.

'No, it isn't,' Peter said. 'He would have wanted to have the last laugh. He wanted you and me to go before he did. He always used to say that.'

Knight went and stood beside him. 'I'm sorry, Peter,' he said. 'I'm really sorry.' He took a pipe from his pocket. He began to fill it from a tobacco pouch he took from another pocket. He had double-jointed thumbs. One of them was grey with ash from tamping down tobacco.

The door of the room opened again suddenly, banging into Yeoman's shoulder. The CND supporter in the bomber jacket

51

came into the room. He stopped dead at the sight of so many people. He seemed taken aback. His gaze fell on Maunciple and he smiled.

'Christ,' he said. 'The old bugger's kicked the bucket at last. Thank God for that.'

As an elegy, it had a certain forceful pungency. Penny hoped they'd manage to do better when her own turn came around. She wished Peter would stop looking so bereft.

'Austen, for heaven's sake control yourself,' Marius Knight said sharply.

'Quite,' said Penny. This must be the author of *Carrion Kisses*.

'Whatever his faults, Max deserves a certain decorum in death,' Knight continued.

'I can't imagine why,' Dominic Austen said. 'He observed none in life.' Penny couldn't pin down what it was she didn't like about him. Perhaps his hair. And she'd always distrusted men who had made careers out of their careers.

'Our Poet-in-residence,' Knight told her quietly. 'Part of an experiment by the English Department. It was felt that the right man could do much to stimulate and encourage creative writing within the school.' He obviously felt that Austen wasn't the right man. He sucked on his pipe, making a quiet gurgling sound.

'Cultural well-being,' Penny said. She nodded wisely.

'Exactly. We were following the lead set by the King's School, of course. They had a brilliant man. Quite brilliant. The expectation was that the boys could benefit from seeing how a working poet finds and handles his inspiration. In the case of King's, the experiment was certainly justified.'

He clearly wished he could say the same about Abbott's. He had a problem there. Judging from his work, as represented by the contents of the green folder, Dominic Austen had been finding most of his inspiration among the girls of the Sixth Form. And handling it, too.

'Seawards faints the cocktip of my heart,' Yeoman said gloomily. He was holding the typescript of *Carrion Kisses* in his hands. He gave the impression of someone anxious to wash his mouth out with soap.

Austen walked over and snatched the folder away from him. 'You can just get your nose out of there, old chap,' he said. 'Those are strictly private.'

'And likely to remain so,' Yeoman said. 'Young buds bloom above my skeleton, acid the thornbush in my skull. What exactly is that supposed to mean, Mr Austen?'

'Well, now,' said Austen. He put his hands on his slender hips. He raked sensitive fingers through his hair. 'A Yank that can actually read. Whatever next.'

'Perhaps you're making a personal statement about the destructive force of innocence,' Yeoman said. God, he looked hard. As though he'd kick Austen's teeth in at the drop of a metaphor.

'Come on, guys. Let's keep the Lit. Crit. for another time, OK?' Penny said. 'Someone just died in here.' She turned to Knight. 'By the way, I'm Penny Wanawake.'

'I imagined you must be,' Knight said. He closed both hands over hers. There was a considerable amount of light-coloured hair on his scalp, some of it melting into grey. His eyes were very kind. 'I've heard so much about you from Peter.'

They both glanced across to where Peter sat hunched over the table, all miserable and wizened. A real achievement, considering his bulk.

'It's a great pleasure to meet you at last,' continued Knight. 'Though the circumstances are hardly propitious.' He stared at his dead friend.

Any circumstance that had Max Maunciple permanently out for the count was probably going to be better than any circumstance that didn't. It wasn't Penny's place to point this out. She looked suitably po-faced. She shook her head solemnly. It seemed enough. No one else was even bothering to look mournful.

'When did you last see Mr Maunciple?' she asked.

'Earlier this evening. Just before I attended the madrigal concert. He invited me round here afterwards, so he and Peter and I could catch up on old friends.'

53

'You mean he actually had some?'

'Yes. Me.'

'Last time I saw him,' Penny said, 'he was having words with a rather angry gentleman in the Great Court.'

'Ah yes. That was Mr Sumnour. One of our parents.'

'He seemed a little aggrieved.'

'Yes,' Knight said. 'I know he blames Max – quite unfairly, in my opinion – for the fact that one of his sons didn't do as well as might have been hoped.'

'What does Mr Sumnour do?'

'I believe he's the proprietor of some sort of – what do they call them? Health farms? Health hydros?' Knight shook his head. 'Why people feel the need . . .'

Yeoman was still moving about the room looking into drawers. Now he turned to Austen. 'What brought you here this evening, Mr Austen?' he asked. He didn't sound too friendly. He stared at the green folder in a provocative manner. He wrapped one lip over the other as though keeping back rude laughter. 'Were you planning an in-depth discussion of your work with Mr Maunciple?'

'What the hell is the matter with you?' Austen said. He hugged his poems to his thin chest. Perhaps he thought someone might want to steal them. There seemed to be a certain amount of antipathy flying about.

'I didn't see you at the concert,' Penny said to Knight. Both of them avoided watching the doctor, who had undone the buttons of Maunciple's shirt and was looking in a dissatisfied manner at his chest.

'I was at the back.' Knight took his pipe out of his mouth and gave the sort of grin usually called rueful. 'At my age, you have to be ready to make a quick getaway if the occasion warrants. Especially after a couple of pints.'

'And did it?'

'What?'

'The occasion. Warrant.'

'As a matter of fact, it did.' Knight brushed at his corduroy lapels. 'Us old codgers.'

'Was Mr Maunciple all right when you left him?'

'Perfectly. It must have been very sudden.'

Doctor Webbe had been scribbling for some time on a piece of paper, dotting i's with the kind of vigour usually reserved for the blinding of Gloucester in amateur productions of *King Lear*. Now he picked up his bag and banged it shut. 'Gross liver abuse,' he said. 'Angina. No exercise. What more do you want.' He walked over to a mahogany-framed mirror and straightened his red tie. 'Old fool.' He looked at his gold watch. 'Someone did call for an ambulance, didn't they? Wish they'd get a move on.'

He sat down in the twin of the chair in which Maunciple lay sprawled and began to read a copy of the morning paper which lay on the floor. He seemed a sensitive fellow.

'Think I'll piss off,' Dominic Austen said. 'I'm knackered. Christ knows why I went to that concert. Madrigals.' He gave an uncultured laugh and brushed hair off his forehead. 'Do I look as if I go for bloody madrigals?'

After a short silence, Penny said, 'Do we look as if we give a shit?'

'What?'

'I said I'm running the Fatty Arbuckle Contest for Gross Behaviour and you just won first prize,' said Penny.

'Cervix of Futurity, the silver seed transcends,' Yeoman said. 'That really is a very profound thought, Mr Austen.'

'Up yours,' Austen said. 'I'm going, if nobody minds.' He looked round at them. No one seemed to, terribly. He left. They heard him clatter down the uncarpetted stairs. As he wrestled with the front door, he uttered a few words it would be untrue to describe as well-chosen.

'Isn't *he* a charmer?' Penny said.

'It's guys like that give poetry a bad name,' Yeoman said. He slapped his hand down hard on the table so that Peter Corax jumped, banging his glass hard against his teeth. 'Wish I knew where Maunciple's manuscript was.'

'Why? Think it could have something to do with his death?' Penny said.

'Hell, no. Why should it?'

'You ain't fooling me with that casual-type talk,' Penny

55

said. 'You must do, or you wouldn't keep going on about it.'

'Going on?' Yeoman spread his hands. His yellow button-down collar rode up towards his ears. 'Who's going on?'

'Surely you're not suggesting that there is anything in any way – uh – odd about Max's death,' said Marius Knight. His face seemed to have flushed. His teeth were clenched, making his neck look as if it had been carved out of bog-oak. He did something to his double-jointed thumbs that made them sound as if the central heating had just been turned on.

'Odd?' Doctor Webbe looked up. 'Nothing odd about it. He had it coming to him.'

'Don't we all?' said Penny.

'It's just kinda weird, it not being here,' Yeoman said. 'We ought to try and locate it.'

'Once he's got his teeth into something, he never lets up,' Penny said to Knight. 'They're like that in Detroit. Inexorable. Tenacious.'

'Sides, I'd guess his publishers'll scream if they don't get it,' Yeoman said.

'The bulldog breed,' said Penny.

Outside, flashing blue lights sent a series of sharp-edged shadows circling the room.

'I suppose a lot of people would have been dropping in on Mr Maunciple, wouldn't they?' Penny asked. 'Old boys. Parents. One of them might have taken it.'

Knight coughed. 'I – uh – I don't believe that would have been very likely. Max wasn't as – uh – popular as some people.'

'He went out earlier in the evening, didn't he? Someone might have slipped in then.'

'It's possible, I suppose. But he was only gone about fifteen minutes. Or so he told me. That foot of his was giving him trouble and he couldn't walk very far. He said something about getting some tonic water. Luckily, there's a shop right outside the gatehouse.'

Feet tramped along the passage. Doctor Webbe put down the paper. 'About time too,' he said. 'With any luck, Angie will have saved me some of the apricot mousse.' He went out

56

of the room. Two men in uniform came in, followed by two policemen. In very swift order, the policemen had written down a brief biography of Maunciple's life, added a medical record supplied by the doctor and gone, the body had been wrapped in some kind of opaque cling-wrap and carted away by the ambulance men, the doctor had departed mousse-wards, and Marius Knight had swept Peter off to Ashmole to spend the night in his guestroom.

That left Penny and Yeoman. They both avoided looking at the wet stain on the seat of the green velvet chair. The pink rosebud lay on the floor, an eloquent symbol of something. It was difficult to know quite what.

'Where are you planning to spend the night?' Penny said.

'Not here,' said Yeoman.

'There isn't a spare bed in my hotel room, fortunately,' Penny said. 'Otherwise, I'd have felt obliged to offer it to you.'

'Shucks.'

'There's only a double bed.'

'Pity.' Yeoman smiled. He slowly stroked the back of his earlobe.

'How are you on sharing?'

'Try me.'

'I was kind of hoping to.'

'I should warn you, I don't wear pyjamas,' Yeoman said. His eyes were almost navy-blue when you got right down to it. Which Penny fully intended to do.

'Who does?' she said. 'Except Chinese peasants.'

'And I'm not a virgin.'

'As long as you don't tell my mother.'

Penny went over to the backgammon set and picked up the cup. She rolled Black's dice. Double six. She blocked White, leaving several blots. She doubled. The art of backgammon lay in knowing when to take a risk. It seemed a safe manoeuvre here. No one was ever going to finish this game. The last time she'd used the doubling-cube had been in the Bahamas. Omar had agreed to a friendly game for £5 a point. She'd won. Omar hadn't been too friendly as he wrote out a pretty hefty cheque. She'd sent it straight off to her father's

57

friends in Africa. She knew they'd see it got to those who needed it.

'Could I just ask you something,' Yeoman said. He twisted his hands together shyly. 'See, my mom always says I shouldn't go with young girls.'

Penny patted his yellow hair. 'Relax, sonny,' she said. 'I'm well past the age of consent.' Twenty-six, to be exact. Next birthday, to be exacter. Oh Gaahd.

'Then let's shift ass.'

They did. As they walked to the hotel through moonlight and the scent of relaxed trees, Penny puzzled over several things. For instance, why Dominic Austen had come to Maunciple's rooms that evening. Who had poured gin down the kitchen sink. Why there was an empty bottle in the trash. Where Maunciple's manuscript was. Why Margaret Curteis-Squire had scars across her wrists.

FIVE

It promised to be another brilliant summer day. Penny sat on one of the window-seats, looking down at the green quadrangle below. Bells jangled through the countdown to seven o'clock. Somewhere close at hand, a trumpet stumbled softly through the first line of '*Do you know the way to Santa Fé?*' It was a line Penny thought she could easily tire of. A boy of Oriental extraction ran fast across the grass towards Ashmole, the school House presided over by Marius Knight. Penny tried very hard not to find it weird that he was wearing a top hat and a lavishly-caped cloak. An elderly clergyman emerged from the chapel with a prayer book in one hand and looked up at her without surprise. Perhaps he thought she was the answer to a prayer. Or a fertility symbol. Perhaps it would be better if she put something on. She got a towel and wrapped it round herself.

'What ya doin'?' Yeoman said from the bed. He had his hands behind his head. Barnaby had been perfectly right about him having an all-over tan.

'I'm trying to think inspirational thoughts.'

'Thought any yet?'

'Yeah.'

'Like what?'

'Aw, gee,' Penny said.

'Boy, I really hate ladies who don't share their inspirational thoughts,' said Yeoman.

'How about I can make you and you can make me but only God can make a tree?'

Yeoman sighed aesthetically. 'That's certainly one for the

anthologies,' he said.

'A poor thing, and not mine own.'

'Whyn't you come back to bed and we can see if it's true?' said Yeoman.

Penny went. It was. The first part, anyway.

Later, she stirred against his long hard body as chimes tumbled in the bright air outside. 'Guess we ought to see how God's getting on with those trees.'

'Wish I could figure out what happened to that freakin' manuscript.' Yeoman fiddled with the St Christopher medal around his neck. 'Somebody musta took it, that's for sure.'

'Any idea why?'

'Maybe someone didn't want the latest Max Maunciple to hit the bookstalls.' Yeoman pressed one of Penny's fingers against his throat. She could feel the vibrations as he talked. 'You know he had a reputation for destroying people, didn't you?'

'Sure did. How come you do?'

'I found out all I could about him before I made this trip. Read everything he'd written. Including that memoir.'

'Want to know what I think?'

'It's driving me crazy.' Yeoman touched her shoulder gently with his lips.

'I don't think Maunciple had a heart attack at all. I think someone got to him.'

Yeoman didn't reply immediately. Then he said, 'What makes you say that?' His voice was cold. He seemed very much cop and not much lover all of a sudden. His hand was hard on her breast. It occurred to her that it might not be much fun being interrogated by him down at headquarters.

'Various reasons,' she said. 'Most of all, because of the trash.'

'The trash?'

'The trash-can was empty. No tea-leaves, no eggshells, no bits of burned toast. So it must have been emptied since he ate breakfast. Yet there was an empty gin bottle in it.'

'So he tied one on at lunchtime,' Yeoman said. He kissed the underside of her jaw. She thought his behaviour was just a

60

little bit sexist.

'Listen here,' she said. 'Someone had also poured a whole heap of gin down the drain.'

'Musta been crazy, with booze the price it is these days.' Yeoman stroked her hip gently. 'Maunciple probably had an accident. Spilled a glass or something.'

'No.'

'Are you saying somebody deliberately poured drink away for some reason?'

'Yes.'

'Anyone with any criminal intent would have run the faucet to get rid of the smell.'

'They did. But not enough to fool me. I have a very acute sense of smell.'

'You don't miss much, do you?'

'Only when I'm playing darts.'

'So what you gonna do about it?'

'Thought I might ask a few questions. Poke around a bit. See what's going on round town.'

'Just tell me one thing, Miss Marple. Does anyone give a flying fuck whether the guy's alive or dead?'

'I should think those that knew him vastly prefer his present state.'

'So?'

'The truth shall make you free. I'm not being judgmental here. If someone helped him on his way, I'd be among the first to hand out medals. I just like to know, is all. Find out what's what.'

'Sounds like you done some finding out before.' Yeoman said thoughtfully.

'Certainly have.'

Monsignor Capet at Hurley Court, her mother's house, the amethyst in his ring winking in the sun as the swing in which he sat moved lazily to and fro, his eyes staring emptily. And Marfa, last year, blonde and beautiful, her face gashed by a psychopath. Morals didn't come into it. Vengeance didn't come into it. What was vengeance, anyway? No more than a cigarette after a screw. If you didn't smoke, you didn't need it.

61

It was simply that truth was better than obfuscation. Truth was one of the last absolutes in a world of changing values. Which was why it was important. In the blurred compromises of a society winding down from Victorian idealism, there was something satisfying about an absolute.

Yeoman kissed her belly-button. She could feel the bristles on his chin. He did it again. She wriggled. 'You sure got nice skin,' he said.

Penny walked two fingers down his sunburned spine. 'Like it, do you?'

'Like it? Man. That is nice skin. And when I say nice, you are talking to a skin-expert here.'

'I can feel that,' Penny said. 'Want to go jogging?' She laughed.

A while later, the phone rang. The skin-expert picked it up and passed it to Penny.

'Good morning, Mr Yeoman,' a voice said in her ear. A transatlantic voice. A reins-of-government voice. 'This is your President speaking.'

'Cut the funnies,' Penny said.

'Little bit of a time-lag there, I thought,' said the voice. 'Guess you must have been on the far side of the bed.'

'What do you want, Barnaby?'

'I just put fifty thousand smackers of our money on a horse and I'm feeling a little nervous about it.'

'You didn't choose it yourself, did you?' Penny said in alarm.

'For Chrissake. I'm not stupid. No. Antonia told me what to back. But I'm still nervous.'

'Don't be. She never fails. What's it called?'

Barnaby laughed. 'You're going to love this,' he said. 'Little Black Boy.'

'I intend to call the Commission for Racial Equality immediately.'

'It's by Golly That's Good out of Orange Marmelade.'

'Oh God.'

'Quite. So how'd the dwarf make out?'

'Why don't you go rob a bank? Or an Iranian?'

'Once I've put Antonia on her bus, that is precisely what I intend to do.'

Yeoman lay beside her, staring up at the ceiling. He was as still as a corpse. She knew Barnaby knew he was there. She knew he knew she knew.

'Barnaby,' she said.

'Present.'

'Don't try ringing me at Chelsea. I may stay on here for a few days.'

'Those madrigals really got to you, huh?'

'Peter's cousin died last night. Max Maunciple. I suspect that someone helped him do so.'

'From all accounts, it was high time.'

'I'll tell you something else,' Penny said emphatically. 'If I knew for sure who'd done it, I wouldn't even turn him in.'

Yeoman stirred beside her. He made a tiny noise. It could have been the cop in him, protesting.

'But you'd like to know who and how and why,' Barnaby said.

'Yeah.'

'I was really hoping you'd hang up your deerstalker after that Marfa business. Dammitall. You nearly got killed. What would I do if something happened to you?'

'You'd devote yourself to the business in an unavailing effort to forget me,' Penny said. 'Your heart would never heal, but boy, would they ever benefit back there in the Third World.'

'That's what I'd do, is it? I'm glad we got that settled.' Barnaby made a kissing noise into the telephone. 'Bye now. Give my regards to that tiny policeman.'

Penny lay back on the pillows and listened to the bells peal. Yeoman set about doing nice things to her. She thought about Miss Antonia Ivory, the spinster lady who lived in the basement flat of the house in Chelsea. Miss Ivory ran the R. H. Domestic Agency with a regard for the out-moded virtues of manners and breeding that was unashamedly snobbish. Miss Ivory only took girls from the very best homes on to her books, and then only after conducting searches into

63

their background that made the CIA look like amateurs. Which a lot of people thought they were. Miss Ivory ate Squashed Fly biscuits in bed and suffered with her indigestion. As the daughter of a former trainer, Miss Ivory knew all there was to know about form. Both equestrian and social.

She knew nothing about the secondary company – R. H. Enterprises Inc. – that her fellow director, Mr Barnaby Midas, MA (Oxon), had formed. Nor how this company gained its funding. She did know that Mr Midas liked to bet very heavily at fairly frequent intervals, and was delighted to lay her expertise at his disposal. She prided herself on never having lost a bet since a long-ago incident when a dubious salmon-paste roll had so upset her always-sensitive digestive tract that she had plunged and lost £5,000 of Barnaby's money on the wrong horse. She herself rarely risked more than 10p on a bet. It was one of Barnaby's nightmares that some enterprising punter would kidnap Miss Ivory and overload the system. Or even cause her bodily harm in order to lengthen the odds. She was an invaluable asset to the firm, and he had insured her as such at Lloyds. His own fingers were insured for the same reason.

It never occurred to Miss Ivory to wonder where Barnaby got his stake from. Nor what he did with the huge sums of money that he won. Miss Ivory had old-fashioned views about men. She thought they had their little ways. She frequently said so. She never seemed to make the connection between the placing of some well-bred girl in a well-to-do, nanny-needing household with the subsequent break-in that household suffered. But then she didn't know about Barnaby.

Penny did. And what happened to the money. Sometimes she carried it herself to Kandiville, capital of Senangaland, for distribution by friends of her father. More often, she entrusted it to Barnaby. Either way, the money was immediately channelled out across Africa to wherever it was needed most. Penny had seen too many children dying of starvation. Too many young mothers with dead babies at the breast. Too many fathers howling to the uncaring skies their grief for a lost son. Penny didn't like waste. If she sent £10 to feed a child in famine-country, she wanted to be sure that child received £10 worth of help. Not £6 worth. She wasn't interested in paying for advertising. She didn't want to line the pockets of the middlemen and distributors. She had no time at all for those who wished to divert aid away from the needy towards guns and bombs.

'Would I be right in thinking your heart's not in this?' Yeoman said. He lifted his head from her thigh and looked at her.

'Who's talking hearts? This is bodies, man.'

'It sure is.'

'Sides, we already had one meaningful discussion this morning. And I'm hungry.'

'So am I. Though it wasn't food I had in mind.'

'You won't starve to death,' Penny said, 'I promise.' She didn't want to think about the plenty she'd seen who had.

Yeoman worked himself up to the pillow beside her. 'Do you have a regular guy?' he said.

'A woman would ask that before, not after.'

'Well, for your information, *I* don't have a regular guy. Do you?'

'Sure I do.'

'Was that him on the phone?'

'Yeah.'

'Wouldn't he mind if he knew about – well, us.' Yeoman gestured at the bed and Penny's black body on the sheets.

'First off, he does know. Secondly, he's got no call to mind about me because I'm a free agent. So is he. Way I figure,' said Penny, propping herself up on one elbow, 'people are just plumb scared of showing each other affection. In case they get misinterpreted. Hell, we all need as much of it as we can get. If there was a bit more loving going round, there might be a bit less fighting. I'm just doing my bit for world peace.' She sucked in her cheeks so her dimple showed.

'Spread a little happiness,' Yeoman said. He winked one dark-blue eye at her.

'I like to spread a lot, sugar.'

Fifteen minutes later, she stood at the door of the hotel

65

dining-room, which was gloomily panelled in neo-Elizabethan fumed oak. Only one table was occupied, by someone reading *The Times*. Margaret Curteis-Squire. She didn't fool Penny. Nobody with two working eyes could have been that interested in a full-page advertisement in Arabic inserted by the Libyan National Army of Liberation. Unless they were Arabic. Penny would have taken any odds that Mrs Curteis-Squire wasn't.

'May I join you?' she said politely.

Margaret Curteis-Squire glanced pointedly round at the empty tables, but made no objection. Penny knew she wouldn't. Most people were too polite. It was easy to see why Max Maunciple had flourished. In most countries, rudeness like his would have been given short shrift. Here, people quailed at the thought of making a scene.

Margaret Curteis-Squire folded her paper and put it beside her plate.

'Of course,' she said. She had some beautiful opals in her ears, and a heavy gold bracelet of curious design hanging from her arm. It didn't hide the scars. 'Did you sleep well?'

'Yes, thank you,' Penny said. She looked round for the waitress. 'Once they'd removed Max Maunciple to the mortuary.'

'What did you say?' Margaret spoke slowly. She put a hand to her throat. Her bracelet dropped down towards her elbow.

'Poor man had a heart-attack,' Penny said. 'A terrible tragedy.' She didn't think Margaret would agree.

Margaret said nothing. She stared at Penny's left shoulder. She wasn't seeing the Giorgio Armani sweatshirt Penny wore. Giorgio would have had a fit if he'd known. She was looking back at another time. From her expression, she'd got acquainted with grief, and they'd become good friends.

The waitress arrived. She had a lot of bounce and an Antipodean accent.

'What're we hevving today?' she said.

Penny didn't know about anyone else. She looked at the menu, nicely printed in Gothic script. There seemed to be a considerable amount of gothicism in Canterbury.

66

'Rarse Crispies maht be narse,' said the waitress.

'I can't go along with that,' Penny said. She shook her head. She ordered half a grapefruit without any sugar, and a full fried breakfast of bacon, egg, sausage and tomato. It was included in the price of the room. She might as well take advantage of it.

When the waitress had bounced away, she said to Margaret, 'If you've not been to the school before, you probably didn't know Mr Maunciple, did you?'

'As a matter of fact, I did. Once. A long time ago.' Margaret lifted her coffee-cup to her mouth. Her lips were trembling.

'Did you know his cousin, Peter Corax. The novelist,' Penny said. 'He's a sitting tenant in my house in Chelsea.'

'Yes,' Margaret said.

'He's staying with Marius Knight at Ashmole,' said Penny. Monosyllabic replies had never bothered her too much. Not when she was fishing for information. 'You probably know him too, don't you? Isn't your son in his House?'

Margaret bit her lip. Her face seemed to crumple round the eyes. She put down her coffee-cup with a clatter. 'I haven't actually met him since Adam came to the school,' she said.

Penny could hardly hear her. The waitress brought half a grapefruit on a green saucer. It had a thick crust of sugar on top. Penny looked at it. She looked at the waitress. The waitress took it away.

'What did you think of the concert last night?' Penny said.

'I enjoyed it.'

'Me too. I thought the second half was better than the first, though. It had more, I don't know, more thrust.'

'Thrust,' Margaret said vaguely, as if wondering what exactly thrust meant. Penny didn't know either. 'Yes.'

'I was worried when Adam's music blew off his stand,' Penny said. 'Right in the middle of his solo. Good thing he knew the piece by heart.'

'Yes,' said Margaret. 'It was – uh – it was an anxious moment.'

The waitress brought half a grapefruit without any sugar and put it in front of Penny.

'We're reshed orf air feet,' she said. New Zealand rather than Australia, Penny thought.

'I can see that,' she said sympathetically. She looked round the empty dining-room. 'I wouldn't have your job for all the tea in China.' She shook her braids so that they swung against each other. The white beads made a tiny clicking noise. 'No, ma'am.'

'If Ar hed all the tea in Charna, narther would Ar,' said the waitress. 'It was tomaaders on toast nixt, wosnit?'

'It was the full fried breakfast next,' Penny said. 'You ever take one of those courses to improve your memory?'

'Yis,' said the waitress. 'Thet's hair come Ar remember so good.' She grinned at Penny. She bounced off.

'You're here without your husband,' Penny said. Pitiless in the search for enlightenment. It wasn't a question. Nonetheless Margaret answered it.

'He had to go to Singapore, so I came instead.' Penny knew she wanted to tell her to mind her own business. Penny knew she never would.

'He must be disappointed at missing this week, since it's Adam's last term.'

'He is. Very.' Margaret circled the rim of her cup with one finger. The opals on her hand shot sparks of light on to the cheap china. She clenched the inside of her lower lip between her teeth.

'Why did you choose this school for Adam?' Penny said. She dug at her grapefruit with a serrated spoon. 'Was it because of knowing Mr Maunciple?'

Aha. The worm began to turn. The worm sat up straight. The worm shook its head so that its opal earrings flashed, and leaned towards Penny. 'You're a very inquisitive young woman,' it said, in unwormlike tones.

'Oh, boy,' said Penny. 'Ain't that the truth.'

The waitress appeared. She put a plate down in front of Penny. It contained eggs, bacon and tomatoes. She also had a rack full of toast.

'No sausages?' asked Penny.

'Ar knew there'd be sumpun wrorng,' the waitress said.

'So did I.'

'Ar'll giddem.' She bounced slowly towards the kitchen where a bored-looking man in a soiled work-jacket was picking his teeth and watching Penny through a hatch.

'He was a nasty bit of work,' Penny said. 'Max Maunciple. Did you ever read his books?'

'I've read them all.' Margaret's teeth seemed to be stuck together.

'He seemed to use his friends and acquaintances for copy. Seeing that you used to know him, you must have dreaded finding yourself in one.' Penny parted her lips girlishly and leaned forward with an air of artlessness. She was quite good at artlessness, but Margaret didn't appear to buy it. She reached down and fetched up a big bag from beside her chair. A very old man in a dog-collar shuffled in and sat down at one of the tables. Penny could hear him humming Old Hundredth.

'No,' Margaret said. Very firmly. 'I didn't dread anything of the sort. You imply that there was something discreditable in my past for him to use. Well, there wasn't.'

'His latest manuscript has apparently gone missing,' Penny said. She did some more work with her dimples. The waitress brought two sausages and tipped them on to Penny's plate.

'Inything ilse?' she said.

'I seem to remember something about some tea,' Penny said. 'But that may have been last week. Or last month.'

'Tea.'

'And you needn't waste time warming the pot.'

'Tea.'

The waitress tapped her temple with one finger. She grinned. She went over to the ancient cleric and took his order down on her pad. It wouldn't have taken her much longer to carve the Rosetta Stone in triplicate.

'Missing?' Margaret said. The opals in her ears quivered. Deep in the heart of each one burned minute flashes of fire.

''Sright.' Penny began on her breakfast. 'Seems odd, doesn't it? Almost as though someone wanted to prevent publication or something.'

69

'How strange. Have his rooms been searched? Perhaps he – uh – perhaps it's been tidied away somewhere.'

'Charles Yeoman, whom you met last night, had a pretty good look round, but he couldn't find it. And he's a trained policeman.'

'Is he, indeed?' Margaret clutched her bag. She didn't seem too concerned. Was that the sign of a person who had covered their tracks too well to be worried? Or a sign that she was innocent? And if so, what of?

Penny was pondering this when Yeoman came in. He wore a blue sweatshirt and white jeans. Nautical but nice. He looked as if he had just stepped off a millionaire's yacht. Or was just about to step onto one. Really ace. Really fit. Maybe it was from all those vitamins she'd found ranged alongside her own toiletries in the bathroom this morning. All in little plastic jars. All labelled Leyland Pharmaceuticals. They certainly seemed to work.

'Hi,' he said. 'How're you?' He smiled at Margaret.

'Good morning, Mr Yeoman,' she said.

'I guess Penny told you about the trouble last night,' Yeoman said, sitting down at the table.

'She did. How perfectly terrible.' Margaret sounded quite cheerful about it.

'Mrs Curteis-Squire used to know Max Maunciple when they were younger,' said Penny.

'Is that right? You must be upset by the news, then.'

'I'm not in the least upset,' Margaret said, in a voice which had more than a touch of the Rock of Ages about it. 'Max was a pernicious devil. If I could have got away with it, I'd have killed him quite happily myself, long before this. He's done a great deal of damage to many people, including some who mean a lot to me. However, I would doubtless have been caught, and I had no intention of spending the rest of my life in jail on his account.' She sounded as though she had given the matter considerable thought. 'That really would have pleased him.' She pushed back her chair and stood up. Her black skirt was splashed with white roses. In the relative gloom cast by the oak panelling, her eyes were without

70

expression. The planes of her subtle hispanic face were flat and stark. Only her earrings had any life. If Macbeth had stumbled in with a bloody dagger, moaning about murdering sleep, no one would have been startled. She leaned one hand on the table and looked down at Penny and Yeoman. 'I'm glad he's dead.' She turned and walked away.

'Wow,' said Yeoman.

He and Penny watched in silence as Margaret moved between the chairs and tables towards the door. Her bag seemed very heavy. Her back was very straight.

'The attempt, and not the deed, confounds us,' said Penny.

'Thought it was supposed to be unlucky to quote *Macbeth*.'

'Only on the first night.'

'And we got past that, right?'

'With flying colours.'

'Wonder what Maunciple ever did to her to cause a reaction like that.'

'It might be interesting to find out,' Penny said. 'From the way she spoke about him earlier, it must have been a long time ago but she still hasn't really recovered from it.' She watched the waitress come in with a tray of tea things. She watched her unload them on to the clergyman's table. 'Damn,' she said.

'Got any plans for today?' Yeoman said.

'A few.'

'Need me to act as Doc Watson to your Sherlock Holmes? Otherwise, I could do things on my own.'

'Like what?'

'Like find the copshop and see what I can dig out. See if the boys in blue got the same idea you did. About Maunciple being murdered.'

The waitress appeared with another tray and began unloading it.

'Hey, is that my tea?' Penny said.

'Ar hurp so.'

'For a moment there, I thought I must have begun hallucinating.'

'Unliss it's corfee.'

'It better not be.'

71

'Thet's what Ar thought.' The waitress backed off. She grinned. She moved away.

Yeoman looked round the dining-room. The aged priest stared at him uncertainly and began sneezing. From his pocket, Yeoman pulled a piece of paper. 'Look at this,' he said. 'I found it among Maunciple's papers last night. Could lead us to a thief. Or even a murderer.'

'So you think I'm right. Someone wasted Max.'

'I'm not saying that. But it's a place to start looking, if you are.'

'You're a real bet-hedger, you know that?'

'It's what makes me so irresistible.'

Penny stretched out her hand and Yeoman gave her the paper. It was crumpled and she smoothed it out. It was a list of titles written in an elegant Italic hand. On the right-hand side of the page was a circle of initials.

'*There Came a Big Spider*'
'*Beauty is Skin Deep*'
'*Told By An Idiot*'
'*Far Above Rubies*'
'*Time's Eunuch*'

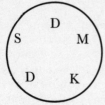

'Hm,' said Penny. 'What do you think it means?' In themselves, the words were harmless, but behind them lay a malice that provided a multiplicity of twisted significances.

'Speaking as your everyday flatfoot,' Yeoman said, 'I'd imagine they were possible titles for his latest book. And the initials could stand for whoever was likely to get hurt most, depending on which he chose.'

'Who are they?'

Yeoman shrugged. 'Could be just about anyone. But since we have to start somewhere, what about with people close to him, here at the school. After all, if he *was* deliberately killed, it's more likely to have been by someone who knew about the concert last night, and realised that it gave him a good chance to get on with the job without being observed.'

'D could stand for that poet. Dominic Austen.'

'Could do,' said Yeoman. He stared at her across the teacups. She wouldn't have sworn that he saw her. 'We'll just have to see what we can shake out of the trees.'

'*Beauty Is Skin Deep*,' said Penny. 'I saw someone laying into Maunciple last night who actually runs one of those beauty resort places.'

'There you are then.'

'It's somewhere to begin.'

'So we go our separate ways today,' Yeoman said.

'Different strokes for different folks.'

'I'll see you back here later.'

Penny felt her brain switch on. 'Absolutely,' she said.

SIX

The pedestrian area in the middle of Canterbury was crowded. From the way people stared, it was obvious that six-foot black girls in Guerilla Chic trousers didn't often blow into town. Penny gave them their money's worth. Big eyes. Big smile. If you've got it, flaunt it. It seemed to make some of them perk up a bit. Men, mostly. Trudging about with plastic bags full of plastic food was a hell of a way to spend a summer morning. There seemed to be a lot of dogs on leads. And even more toddlers. Marks & Spencer were doing a roaring trade in lambswool cardies. A girl in gold-rimmed specs sang Schubert Lieder with her hands clasped in front of her stomach. Another girl accompanied her daintily upon the clarinet. They weren't making much headway against a group of kids three yards off who were body-popping themselves senseless to UB40 on a ghetto-blaster.

Near the car-park, a short man with a beard approached Penny. 'How would you like to go dancing with me tonight?' he asked. He didn't sound too hopeful.

'You only come up to my crotch,' said Penny.

'That could make it interesting,' he said.

'For whom?'

She watched him shamble away. A bunch of sneering French adolescents was kicking its way along the pavement. Three of them wore T-shirts that said KEYCUTTERS DO IT WHILE YOU WAIT. The Frenchman she had seen yesterday was being carried along in their midst. His moustache seemed smaller. Perhaps it was moulting. She wondered if he put up at a hotel and met them each day off the

74

boat at Dover.

She drove out of Canterbury into the countryside. High
summer. Richness. Lushness. Ripening apples and compli-
cated tangles of hops. Oast houses lurked charmingly among
thickets of ancient trees. Lych gates led inexorably past
leaning gravestones to shaded Norman church porches.
Everywhere there was a smug sense of values retained in the
face of anarchy. It made her want to fling beercans and crisp
packets out of the window.

A sign appeared in a hedgerow studded with red blackber-
ries. HOLKHAM COURT. For Health and Beauty. Props:
Mr K. Sumnour. Mrs D. Sumnour. She turned in between
wrought-iron gates. High banks of something green hid any
vista there might have been. She had an impression of
spacious grounds and elderly trees. The drive led her to an
imposing Victorian country house. There were crenellated
battlements, ideal for pouring boiling oil from. Penny hadn't
remembered the Victorians going in for that much. There
were architraves and mouldings. There was a tower. If you
had a sheep handy, there was a porch big enough to roast it in.
To the right, there were tennis courts. To the left, a horse
contemplated some grass.

The drive widened to curve around on either side of a
sculpture depicting two intertwined and despairing ladies.
Health and Beauty, perhaps. When Penny put her brakes on,
a lot of gravel flew up. She got out and peered at her
paintwork. No visible scratches. If there had been, she'd have
had something to say. Certainly would. Even to the woman
built like a nursing-bra who was watching her from inside the
glassed front-doors with a watering-can in her hand.

Penny loped up a flight of shallow steps flanked by a couple
of stone Christmas puddings on plinths. When she had pushed
open the doors, the woman spoke.

'We don't normally cater for people like you,' she said.
Daunting. Not one of the approaches Dale Carnegie would
have recommended.

'How do you feel about Jews and Catholics?' Penny asked.

'You don't appear to be either overweight or unwell.' The

75

woman spoke in a voice that made Penny feel guilty for being able to breathe without the aid of an iron-lung. 'What did you want?' She frowned.

'How far back do you want to go?'

The woman stared at her. She clearly didn't recognise grammatical ineptitude. Penny sighed. 'I'd like to see Mr Sumnour, please. If he's available.'

She looked around. They were in a long, glass-fronted hall which ran most of the length of the house. Green palms huddled in corners. Low tables held magazines which displayed bodies far beyond the reach of those desperate enough to spend a small fortune on a week at Holkham Court. There were a great many basket-chairs. A swag of curtain broke the line of an arch leading somewhere healthy. It only needed Noël Coward to come on in his dressing-gown, waving a cigarette holder, to make you realise how old the Bright Young Things must be today.

'Who was it wanted him?' the woman asked.

'I've no idea,' Penny said. 'If you mean, who am I, the name is Wanawake. Penny Wanawake.' She hoped, for Mr K. Sumnour's sake, that this wasn't Mrs D. Sumnour. She'd never seen iron-grey hair with a pink rinse before. The woman looked like a soap-filled Brillo-pad.

'Mr Sumnour's busy,' the Brillo-pad said. She didn't attempt to make it ring true.

'Suppose I said I have seventeen overweight and unhealthy sisters and I've come to discuss a block-booking.'

'He'd still be busy.'

'People who tell lies get boils on their tongue.' So, at least, Nanny Simpson had always maintained.

Penny advanced across the floor of elaborately-patterned tiles. Several of the basket-chairs seemed to be occupied by turtles whose necks creaked as they turned to watch her go by. Their eyes stared unblinkingly from little leathery faces. A big slogan across the archway proclaimed that this was Holkham Court for Health and Beauty. Penny thought they could get the owners under the Trade Descriptions Act. They might be healthy turtles but they sure as shooting weren't beautiful.

76

'Perhaps you'd care to come back later,' Mrs Brillo-pad said sternly.

'No, ma'am. Don't think I'd care to do that at all,' Penny said. 'Mind if I stick around a little?'

The woman said nothing, although she clearly did. Penny studied the inspiring mural behind the reception desk. It showed an amalgam of bronzed limbs vaulting tennis-nets and cleaving turquoise waves. She examined a noticeboard on the wall. There was to be a talk on *Arthritis and Acupuncture* the following evening. Sounded like fun. A range of costume jewellery by Gemco was on display in the Library. What to wear in the sauna. A Mrs T. Woolfson was requested to report to the hydrotherapist before lunchtime. The pressure was obviously merciless.

'Mr Sumnour won't want to be disturbed,' the Brillo-pad said, after a while.

'Depends who's doing the disturbing,' said Penny.

A girl in a white overall clattered pertly across the hall. Creak, creak, went the turtles. If she was wearing knickers, Penny was a Dutchman.

'Mr Sumnour's with his – uh – accountant,' said the Brillo-pad.

'Perhaps you'd care to rephrase that.'

'Why?'

'If that's his accountant, I'd love to see his bank manager,' said Penny.

Kenneth Sumnour was walking towards them with the pert girl, who now held a tray full of small paper cups. He carried a package done up in pink paper. The turtle necks creaked. It was as good as Wimbledon.

Sumnour wore a thin yellow sweater of some man-made fibre, and pale checked trousers of the sort usually seen holing out in golf-bunkers. He had an Emperor Nero haircut that badly needed washing. His face looked worse than it had yesterday.

'Hi. I'm Penny Wanawake.' Penny put out her hand. Sumnour took it. His fingers were very cold. His shoes were highly polished. He smelled of onions.

'Ken Sumnour.' He narrowed his eyes. 'What exactly can I do for you?'

'I was hoping we could talk.'

'What about?'

'Max Maunciple.'

Sumnour glowered. His cheeks reddened. He looked at his watch. 'You'd better come into my office,' he said. He ran a professional eye over Penny's hips. He turned to the Brillo-pad. 'Marge, bring us two coffees.' Penny wished he didn't have a large boil on one cheek.

Marge appeared to debate asking him to make that one coffee, one arsenic. She smoothed down the steel wool on top of her head. She looked as if all her lampshades were made of human skin.

'Very well,' she said, 'Kenneth.' Whatever their relationship, they needed to work on it.

The turtles were making reptilian noises over the paper cups, which probably contained monkey-glands. Or royal jelly. Penny followed Sumnour into a room full of sunshine, with arched windows reaching from ceiling to floor. There was a view of parkland studded with cedars-of-lebanon. The sunshine showed up the bare threads of the carpet, and the scuff-marks on the paintwork. Some up-to-date gadgetry involving a screen and a keyboard stood on a table. An impossibly vibrant female person waved from a photograph on the wall. She wore black shorts and looked about a hundred years old. Penny knew she ought to recognise her. She was a terrific advertisement for the place. Spend a week at Holkham Court and you too can be impossibly vibrant, however old you are.

Outside on the lawn, two plump women carrying tennis racquets had stopped beneath one of the cedar trees. Their faces were racked with hunger. One patted what was undeniably a triple chin. The other tried to span her waist with both her hands. No way, lady. Gog and Magog, working together, might have made it. Not her.

Sumnour sat down at a shabby flat-topped desk, its scratched surface bare except for a pile of car-stickers, a photograph of two small boys, and a vase of flowers. He tore at the pink paper round his parcel. A cloth frog with a fringed yellow collar fell out. There was a string protruding from its neck. It was the first time Penny had realised that frogs had necks.

'What do you want to tell me about Max Maunciple?' Sumnour asked.

'He's dead,' Penny said. 'From a heart-attack. Last night, during the concert.'

Sumnour pulled the frog's string. A scratchy voice spoke from inside its body. 'Stay cool, fool,' it said. It had an American accent.

'May I quote you on that?' Penny said.

'Dead,' said Sumnour. 'Bloody good thing too.' He fingered the boil on his face.

'You don't seem surprised, Mr Sumnour.'

'The only thing that surprises me is that he didn't die a bloody sight sooner.'

'I take it you weren't all that fond of him.'

'Fond. Fond of bloody Maunciple. Don't make me laugh.'

'I wasn't trying to.'

Sumnour stood up and went over to one of the windows. Penny twisted her head sideways to read the top one of the car-stickers. A GRAPEFRUIT A DAY KEEPS THE INCHES AWAY. Put out by the Citrus Fruit Marketing Board. It seemed to her that the Holkham Court health hydro was just a little run down. And Kenneth Sumnour was no advertisement for his own wares. She picked up the frog.

'If it wasn't for Maunciple, Jeremy – that's my other son – would be here now,' Sumnour said. 'Where he belongs.' He came back to his desk and sat heavily down. He put two fists on the desk-top in front of him. His yellow sweater was snagged.

'Instead of where?'

'Drinking himself to death in bloody Rhodesia. In the company of some fat black whore and a pack of noisy children. Not,' Sumnour said, 'that I'm prejudiced or anything.'

79

'I can see that.'

'Thanks to Maunciple, Jeremy never realised his potential, did he?' Sumnour said. His face was getting very red. Reliving old grievances can do that to a person.

'Why was that?'

'Failed his A-Level, didn't he? Couldn't get into the university to study history, could he?'

'And you blame Max Maunciple.'

'Bloody right, I do. Old fart refused to give him extra coaching. Strung him a line about him not having any problem getting the right marks. Then what happens. Before we know it, he's chucked it all in and joined the Rhodesian police, hasn't he?'

'Has he?'

'That's what I'm saying. Throws everything up to go and live with a bunch of nignogs.'

'I'll bet they were thrilled.'

'Not that I've got anything against blackie,' said Sumnour. 'Next thing we know, Jerry's been kicked out of the force for persistent drunkenness. My Jeremy. Straight a lad as you could hope to find. Takes up with this – uh – coloured lady. Lot of little bl – little bastards. Sunk right down.'

Sumnour looked away. He tugged at the boil on his cheek. Penny hoped it wouldn't come off in his hand. She pulled the frog's string.

'Get lost, biscuit brain,' snarled the frog. Penny put it back on the desk.

Sumnour leaned his head on his hands and stared despondently at a deep gouge on the surface in front of him. 'I know I'm not much,' he said. 'Not got much culture and that. And this line of work doesn't suit me. It was the wife. Trained as a beautician before we were married. With the garage doing so well, she had this idea we could make a mint out of a place like this. Give the kids the kind of background we never had ourselves. Better than a concrete forecourt on the by-pass, she said. Her brother came in with us and it all seemed to be merry as a marriage-bell. Now. Well, I don't know.' He pointed at his blemished face. 'This thing with Jeremy's got me all messed up. I mean, look at me. What in Christ's name do I look like?'

'Hell,' said Penny. There was no point pretending otherwise.

'Never used to,' Sumnour said. 'It's only since Jerry went off the rails. What kind of an advertisement is it for a place like this when the man in charge looks like a spotted dick?'

'A spotted what?'

'Dick. You know. Plum duff. Steamed pud.' The description was horribly apt. The sides of Sumnour's jaw were flushing again with angry blood. His spots stood out like sultanas. The smell of onions was strong.

'Surely you can't blame Mr Maunciple for all that,' Penny said. Freudians would argue that the seeds of dissolution were sown long before Jeremy got into the History Sixth. Looking at Sumnour's face, she didn't think she'd bother pointing this out.

'I most certainly can,' Sumnour said. 'I've been up to Harley Street. The Middlesex. Places like that. They all say it's psychosomatic, brought on by stress. I've spent a ruddy fortune on quacks. Including the wife's brother. Clever bloke, old Barry. Started from scratch and got a chain of chemist shops now, up Northampton way. I've tried every bloody ointment he's got but nothing does the trick.'

'I see.'

'The real question,' Sumnour said gloomily, 'is how do I get rid of it?'

'Keep off fried food,' said Penny.

'Fried food.' Sumnour stood up again. He walked around the room, his mouth puckering. When he spoke, it was in an angry shout. 'There's not enough fat in this place to grease an elbow, let alone a frying-pan.'

The door opened. The Brillo-pad came in with a tray. She had a distinct air of the female impersonator about her. Better than Dustin Hoffman. Not as good as Jack Lemmon. Perhaps it was a trick of the light. She plonked the tray down on Sumnour's desk.

'Your coffee,' she said, 'Kenneth.'

81

'Thank you, Marge.' Sumnour pulled up his sleeve and scratched a large inflamed patch on his arm.

'Coffee,' cried Penny. 'Golly, Marge. That's really kind of you.'

For two pins, Marge would have locked her in the sauna and turned the temperature up to maximum. She didn't say so. She just looked that way.

'Anything else I can do?' she said. 'Kenneth.' She almost wore through the enamel on her teeth getting it out.

'No, thanks,' Sumnour said.

'Goodness, isn't this fun,' said Penny. 'Shall I be mother?'

'If there's nothing else,' Marge said.

'Don't think so, Marge.' Sumnour waited until Marge had left the room, then sat down again behind his desk. Penny poured him a cup of coffee.

A lavish gentleman with large ears pranced past the window. He had the kind of embonpoint that made Henry VIII look like the victim of a wasting disease. A crowd of equally well-built men followed him. Some of them wore dressing-gowns.

Kenneth Sumnour looked out at them with loathing. 'I hated that fat bastard. Maunciple. I hate all fat bastards, come to that.'

'Could be the secret of your success,' Penny said.

Sumnour picked up his coffee-cup and drained it viciously. He yanked at the string in the frog's neck, which came flying out. The frog made a faint transatlantic objection. Sumnour threw it down. 'A present from my wife,' he said. 'The bloody business is going downhill at a rate of knots. I've got psychosomatic leprosy. One son's a drunk and the other's a junkie. And all the wife can do is spend my money on bloody talking frogs. Said she thought it would take my mind off.' He made an uncontrolled honking noise through his nose.

'Junkie?' said Penny, keen as mustard.

'How else do you explain the way he behaves?'

'We're talking about – uh – James?'

'Acts like a bloody sleepwalker half the time. Staring off into space. Mouth hanging open. Doesn't eat. Up all night long with the stereo blasting away.'

'Sounds like normal adolescence to me.'

'What would you know?' Sumnour demanded violently. 'Jeremy was never like that.'

And look where he is today, Penny might have said. She curbed the impulse. Instead, she said, 'Are you suggesting that drugs are available at the school?'

'Stands to reason, doesn't it? Half these bloody public schools are pushing it, aren't they? There was one in the paper only the other day. Had everything, far as I could make out. Drugs, drink, blue movies, the lot.'

'And you think there's something similar going on here?'

'Headmaster's wife was a pin-up,' Sumnour said.

'Surely not. Abbott's is a religious foundation. And isn't the Headmaster a cleric?'

'At this place in the paper,' Sumnour said impatiently. 'Not here. Of course not.' He scratched his cheek. He stared at Penny as though hair had suddenly started sprouting from her ears. 'What are you, anyway? Why am I bloody talking to you?'

Penny had been wondering that herself. 'I'm not sure,' she said.

'From the local rag, are you?'

Penny adopted a non-committal air. She saw again the spiky italic writing: *Beauty Is Skin Deep*. And the initial S. She wondered if Kenneth Sumnour might have an interest in suppressing Maunciple's next book. Or in suppressing Maunciple.

'Did Mr Maunciple ever come out here?' she asked.

Sumnour stood up again. He scratched the back of his neck, dislodging a small shower of dried skin. 'As a matter of fact, he did. Bloody nerve, considering I'd already given him the rounds of the kitchen over young Jerry's examination result. And told him what I thought of his sodding books, too. Load of old wotsit, aren't they?'

Although she didn't want to, Penny could see the outline of his navel. 'What did he come for?' she asked. 'To have – uh – treatment?'

83

'We had an Open Day. The wife's idea, not mine. The usual bloody cock-up. It's not as if I haven't got enough to cope with as it is, without a bunch of busybodies tramping about all over the place, poking their noses into my private affairs, mucking about with my computer, switching the ultra-violet lamps on in the sun-parlour. Christ, I thought Mrs MacVane would sue. Talk about lightly grilled on both sides.' Sumnour laughed, but not as if he thought the world would laugh with him.

'I wouldn't have thought an Open Day at a health-farm would have been Mr Maunciple's scene.'

'Only came to cause trouble, didn't he? That was his speciality. I even caught him monkeying about in my office. Bloody looking through my files, if you please.' Sumnour slumped back in his chair. He brooded.

What could Maunciple have been looking for? What, in a place like this, needed covering up? Was Sumnour the Mr Big of the grapefruit racket? Dealing fraudulently in high-fibre options? Involved in the illegal immigration of Swedish masseuses?

'Was there anything in them to see?' Penny asked.

Sumnour gazed at her hard for a moment. Then he lunged towards her, his eyebrows twitching. 'Here, what is this?' he shouted. 'What are you getting at?'

Penny sat her ground. She bunched her fists and squared her jaw. She looked invincible. It didn't seem to have any deterrent effect whatever.

'Anything to bloody see. What's that supposed to mean?' Sumnour shouted.

'Perhaps he was looking for copy,' suggested Penny. 'Perhaps he was planning to set his next book in a place like this.'

'Christ, I hope not.' The banlon sweater sagged. Beneath the imperfect surface of his face, Sumnour looked sick.

'Why not?' Penny said. She gave a phony little laugh. 'It seems rather a good place for a crime novel.'

'He wasn't here for bloody copy, believe you me,' said Sumnour. 'It was just after that business with the East End

84

Jewboy, he snorted.'

Penny smothered the fury this phrase aroused in her. Her throat was suddenly dry. 'Business?' she croaked.

'You remember. Your bloody paper had people snooping round here for weeks. Nearly drove the wife round the bend.' Sumnour stood up again and came round the edge of his desk. He looked kind of mad. 'Here. You are from the *Kent Messenger*, aren't you?'

Penny swiftly reached the same conclusion as Max Maunciple. Given an ox needing felling, Sumnour was your man. Whether that was the same temperament as the one that could doctor a guy's booze was another matter. She rather thought not. She too stood up.

'Because if bloody not, why are you asking me all these questions, like you owned bloody Scotland Yard?'

Penny had no satisfactory answer.

A lady appeared on the other side of the glass overlooking the grounds. She wore a short white tunic that revealed thighs as dark and hard as old mahogany. Bionic thighs. You could have stuck drawing-pins into them if you wanted to keep your stockings up, and felt no pain at all. The lady threw her arms above her head. She bent from the waist and peered closely at the lawn. Shifting slightly, Penny saw that about a dozen other ladies, considerably more bountiful in their proportions, were imitating her. They had the intent strained expressions of chronic constipatees.

Penny drooped her eyes meaningfully, the way people did in B-grade detective movies. 'We have reason to suspect that Max Maunciple's death was more than a simple case of heart-failure,' she said. It sounded impressive. Even official.

Sumnour seemed to buy it. He scratched the flesh under his chin with a paper-knife. He looked thoughtful. 'I see,' he said. His eyes were briefly inward-looking. 'Yes.'

It seemed a good time to leave. 'Thank you so much for talking to me,' said Penny. She really meant it.

In the hall, the turtles were shifting slowly about in their basket-chairs. One had actually risen fraily to its feet and was making off towards the curtained archway. Perhaps it was planning a sneak raid on the lettuce-patch. The rest turned their elderly necks as Penny walked across the floor. Creak. Creak. She waved at Marge, who definitely did not wave back. She flicked a finger at a palm and watched the dust-motes rise.

She hoped there wasn't less in Kenneth Sumnour than met the eye.

SEVEN

A boy of about fifteen with a fuzz-sprouting upper lip was walking across the grass at the foot of the school chapel. He wore pin-striped trousers and was whistling the violin part from the first movement of the Trout Quintet. He looked the weedy sort, who might be interested in writing poetry. Penny accosted him.

'I'm wondering where I can find Dominic Austen,' she said.

'Who?'

'The Poet-in-residence.'

'Why?'

'Because I've just translated *Vile Bodies* into Urdu and I thought he might like to read it.'

The boy didn't blink. 'How interesting,' he said. 'My father speaks Urdu. As a matter of fact, he's a world expert on the languages of the Indian sub-continent.'

'Dynamite,' said Penny. 'What about Dominic Austen?'

The boy shook his head. 'As far as I know, he doesn't speak a word,' he said. The hairs on his lip moved faintly as though some small insect was passing through. She couldn't decide whether he was having her on or not.

'Look, kid,' she said. 'Just give me the guy's address, OK?'

'I'm afraid I disapprove of poets in general, and this one in particular,' the boy said coldly. Jesus. Was this how schoolboys came these days? Penny felt it said something for her own education that she was able to refrain from sinking her teeth into his neck. She shook her braids menacingly.

'I know nothing about him, anyway,' the boys said. 'I'm on the science side, not the arts.' He fingered his upper lip in a bold manner.

'Let's see if bribery will work,' said Penny. 'I'll let you use my Philips Ladyshave if you tell me how I find out where Mr Austen lives. Is it a deal?'

'Ask one of the girls,' said the boy. 'They're all making fools of themselves over him.'

'Well, thanks. You've been a terrific help.'

The boy sauntered away. When he was out of arm's reach, he began whistling the solo part from Mozart's Flute Concerto in D. Pure bravado, of course. Boy. If there was one thing Penny wished she could do, it was whistle.

Two youths in dark trousers, their shirtsleeves rolled up to the elbows, went by carrying a couple of celluloid eggs big enough to store a whole battery of hens. A minor canon shuffled past, clutching a tin of Steradent. Some girls came out from a side door of the chapel. They wore navy-blue skirts and white blouses. They were discussing the Flowers of Evil. From the animation on their faces, Penny felt pretty certain they were talking about the group, not the translation from the French. She stepped in front of them.

'Austen,' she said. 'I'm trying to find Dominic Austen.'

'So's my father,' one of them said. They all laughed.

'Keen on contemporary poetry, is he?' Penny asked. 'Or just contemporary poets?'

'Contemporary virgins, actually,' said the girl.

'He read a couple of Dom's recent poems and he's convinced Dom's been groping Helen,' explained another girl.

'And has he?' Penny said. So it was Dom, was it? Helen was eminently gropable. They all were. Bright-eyed. Bright-haired. Bright, period.

'Of course not,' Helen said. She made a disgusted face. She shook back hair that she'd obviously spent hours combing to look as if it was uncombed. 'I'm not into geriatrics, thanks.'

'Yecch,' said Penny. 'I know what you mean. He must be all of thirty.'

'I know,' said someone else. 'Can you imagine? I bet he's got a little pot belly.'

'And sagging nipples, like my father's.'

88

'Revolting corns on his feet.'

'Yuk.'

Penny felt she ought to ring the Voluntary Euthanasia people. Or lay in a roll or two of Baggies. At the very least send away for brochures on retirement homes. She'd be twenty-six soon. Well over the hill.

'Love your hair,' Helen said. 'Those braids are heaven.'

'You look like Nefertiti or something,' said another girl. 'Wish I was black.'

'Cleopatra,' said someone else.

Penny felt younger, and much more beautiful. She turned her head this way and that. The beads in her hair clashed. 'The future is black,' she said. 'For the present, where might I find Mr Austen and his sagging nipples?'

'He's got a room in Prebend Street,' said Helen. She pointed to the far end of the quadrangle, where an arched gateway set into flint walls gave onto some roses. 'Go through there. Prebend Street's just across Broad Street.'

'Number 23,' added another girl.

'Thanks.'

Penny watched them walk away, waving at a group of boys with books under their arms. It seemed delightfully free and easy. Very different from her own cloistered, all-girls school. Even if it had been attended by the children of Royalty. Or perhaps because. She'd left it totally ignorant of what they now called life-skills. Which, at the time, had meant sex. Still did, for that matter. Though she was far from ignorant now. Her nine months in Africa had been more than a gestation period. They had given her time to learn. Time to see. Time to give birth to the few firmly-held tenets that now ruled her life and style. Which wasn't to say she didn't have a great deal more to learn and see. A great deal more birth to give.

At the edge of the busy main road, she waited for a break in the traffic. Elderly Americans were descending from an air-conditioned bus, commenting on the state of their knees. Many of them carried raincoats over their arms. Elderly Americans all knew that it never stopped raining in England except when a peasouper fog obliterated everything except victims of Jack the Ripper. Today must have been a real disappointment. The sun blared down from an immaculate sky. Heat mirages writhed above the tarmac. English reserve was cracking like ice-floes in the unusual warmth.

Penny passed a blank area of glass and concrete. Car-hire firms. Petrol stations. Double-glazing showrooms. Insurance company offices. The towers of the cathedral hung above the city walls, solid as faith. The town-planners couldn't manage total destruction, though they'd had a damned good try.

Prebend Street was narrow and grey. Any evidence of a greater force than Man's had been kept to a minimum. The only animate object in sight was the mould in a milk bottle on a windowsill. Mean little houses gave straight on to the pavement. Handy for evicting drunks and dustbins. Penny dared not swing her arms for fear of smashing in someone's front window.

Number 23 had a mud-coloured door which was loosely connected to the jamb by a Yale lock. No self-respecting burglar could have passed it by, except that no self-respecting burglar would have been caught dead in Prebend Street. The door had a knocker on it in the shape of a lion with a ring in its mouth. Penny hit it hard. Who'd ever seen a lion going round with a ring in its mouth? Lions had no reason to. Ever. Dogs sometimes had rubber ones. Bulls had them through their noses. And pigs. So did punk rockers. But not lions. She hit it again. Before she could move back, the door had opened and she was standing cheek to cheek with Dominic Austen.

'Bed any good looks lately?' Penny said. It was a rotten pun, but it made Austen step back. Today he was wearing maroon dungarees over a khaki shirt from Dickie Dirts. Pinned to them was a badge that said SAVE THE BAT. He had an apple in one hand.

'Who the hell are you?' he said. A nicely-brought up lad, you could see.

'The Wife of Bath, honey.'

'Odd,' said Austen. 'Chaucer doesn't mention that she was black. Or have you had a total skin transplant?' He took a bite of his apple. His eyes were amber-coloured.

'A bit of each, I guess.'

'What do you want?'

'I've read some of your work,' Penny said, 'and I was particularly struck by the penetrating, if you'll pardon the expression, nature of your poetic vision. If you can spare the time, I thought it might be interesting to discuss one or two of the more meaningful insights.'

Dominic Austen grinned. 'Are you kidding?'

'Yes,' Penny said sincerely.

He stepped backwards. He gestured her inwards. 'Come in,' he said.

After last night, she was surprised. She hadn't exactly been Little Miss Manners. But then neither had he. She could have done without the shocking-pink feather which hung from one of his ears.

'I'm Penny Wanawake,' she said. 'We weren't introduced last night.'

He nodded. 'Dominic Austen. You'd better come up to my room.' He indicated a flight of stairs so steep you needed crampons to get to the top. He went first. If he fell backwards, at least he'd have a soft landing. On her. Great.

At the back of the house, a door slammed. Before it did so, Penny heard a voice say triumphantly, 'Told him I might as well be a kangaroo. Know what I mean?'

'I just rent this place,' Austen said over his shoulder. 'But Mrs – uh – Thing has been good about letting me furnish it in my own way.'

'Is she one of the Hampshire Things?' Penny said. She'd been taught that it was a basic courtesy to remember people's names.

'She's called Mrs MacGonagall, actually.'

'No relation to the talented William, I suppose.'

'I haven't asked.'

'What a coincidence.'

Dominic Austen didn't ask why. Penny had a feeling he knew that William MacGonagall was considered by many to have been the worst poet in the world. He flung open a door at the end of a passage carpeted violently in green. He did it with unnecessary vigour. The room was long and light. The floorboards were bare. Books lay everywhere, piled with poetic abandon on tables and floor and the arms of a sagging Chesterfield big enough to house a Pakistani family. A Styrofoam head with glittery eyelashes held a silk opera hat. Marilyn Monroe with her arms pressing her boobs together smiled from one wall. Che Guevara in a sinister beret looked moody on another. A Blondie record sleeve was lying on the floor beneath a mobile made of pieces of tin sharp enough to scalp a Mohican.

Since Mrs MacGonagall couldn't provide a garret for Austen to starve in, he'd done his best to create one. A smell of German salami hung in the air. Or was it synthetic midnight-oil? It only needed Mimi to come whingeing in about her chilblains to complete the illusion of Bohemia.

'Fierce,' said Penny. 'I mean, this is fierce. I just love creative squalor.'

'What are you,' said Austen. 'Freelancing for *House & Garden*?'

'Not today,' Penny said. 'Today I'm looking for a stolen manuscript.'

'The only manuscripts here are mine.'

'I can understand that,' said Penny. After all, nobody in his right mind would want to steal Austen's stuff. She looked away from the enormous photograph pinned to the wall. A blow-up of what were probably Austen's private parts, since he couldn't surely want to look at someone else's. Unless he was queer. Which she definitely didn't think he was. He seemed very well hung.

'I suppose you'd like a drink, would you?' Austen said.

Penny looked at an elephant's foot beside the Chesterfield. It held a couple of dirty glasses and a bottle of Glenfiddich. Starve in style, that was the ticket. Someone had painted the elephant's toenails scarlet. 'Only if you've got a clean glass,' she said.

'I was thinking more on the lines of coffee.'

'If you mean that instant muck, forget it.'

Austen lifted the bottle of Scotch and stared at it. 'This stuff

92

costs a fortune, you know.'

'Sorry,' said Penny firmly. You had to know when to put your foot down.

Austen sighed. He produced a clean glass. He poured an under-generous tot and gave it to Penny. He added water to his glass from the pink basin set into one corner of the room.

'I appreciate this,' Penny said.

'Not as much as I would have done,' said Austen. 'What's all this about a stolen manuscript? And why come to me?' He sat down on the sofa.

Penny removed an ashtray from a grubby armchair. It had three stubs in it. She recognised a joint when she saw one. Even on a weekday. She too sat down.

'The typescript of Max Maunciple's latest novel seems to have gone missing,' she said. 'Several people saw it in his room earlier in the evening. After his death was discovered, the manuscript was no longer there. We're wondering why.'

A slow grin began to spread across Austen's face. He put his glass down carefully on a pile of running magazines. He leaned back on the Chesterfield, which rocked slightly. Penny saw that it was missing one of its ball-feet and had been propped up by a pile of paper and a softback of *Baghavad-Gita*.

'Am I reading you right here?' he said. He shook the pink feather. 'Are you actually suggesting that the old pervo might have been bumped off?'

'I'm enquiring into the possibility, yes.' It always amazed her that people so rarely questioned her right to do so. Not because some are born leaders, but because most are born followers. That was what it amounted to. Hit them with enough authority, and they'd follow you anywhere.

Austen adjusted the strap of his dungarees. Maroon, for God's sake. Dungarees, with a pair of £50 running shoes. What a pseud. 'Any idea how it was done?' he said. He raised his eyebrows. He ducked his head to one side. If he was trying to look cute, he should have removed his feather earring first.

'We aren't even sure it was.'

'If it *was*, any idea why? Or how?' Austen reached for a small Toby Jug containing a couple of dozen yellow pencils.

'Once we know who took the manuscript, we might be able to come up with a motive,' Penny said. 'That's why it's so important that we find it.' Who was this 'we', anyway? She hoped Austen wouldn't ask. 'As you may know, Mr Maunciple tended to use real-life situations in his books. Perhaps he picked the wrong fall-guy this time. Someone with too much to lose.' She leaned forward with a forbidding wrinkle of the brow. 'Someone, Mr Austen, very much like you.'

'Me? What the hell are you . . . *Me*? You don't know . . . You're talking balls.' As a pantomime of derisive surprise, it was pretty good. But not quite good enough. Panic stared out of his satyr's eyes.

'Got a weak bladder, have we, Mr Austen?' Penny said. Very Dixon of Dock Green.

'A weak bladder?' Austen scrunched up his face. 'I'm not exactly senile yet.'

'I noticed you gave the Dowland a miss last night. Doing a bit of skul, were we?'

'A bit of skul?'

'Skulduggery, Mr Austen.' Penny didn't think she could keep this up much longer.

'I was having a pee, for Godsake.'

'Where did you have it?'

Austen looked round the room with a half-smile on his face, like a quiz-show host about to bring out a witty riposte. 'I fail to see that my habits of micturation have anything to do with you, Miss – uh – '

'Wanawake.'

'Wanawake. But there happens to be a gentlemen's convenience all of a minute's walk away from the Cloisters. Placed there by a thoughtful Abbey Preservation Society for the use of the general public. Perhaps you've noticed it.'

'Must have been busy in there last night. I already know of two other people who were in there at more or less the same time as you.'

'For more or less the same reason, I bet.'

'Perhaps one of them could vouch for you.'

'I passed Marius Knight, if that's what you mean by

vouching. Look, what is this inquisition? You can't possibly
. . . No, you don't really . . .' He threw himself back again on
the Chesterfield, which rocked with more zest than last time.
He laughed. It didn't sound entirely carefree. 'You can't
seriously think I killed Maunciple, can you?'

'Why did you come to his room last night, after the
concert?'

Austen stood up. He placed himself in front of Penny with
the air of a man determined to hide nothing from you, even if
you didn't want to know.

'I gave him some of my work earlier in the term because
I've applied for a really cushy job at a girls' college in North
Carolina. Free board and lodging. Free heating bills. Free
food. I could save a packet, and get on with my work, too. I
hoped that Max might give me some sort of a reference.'

'I can just imagine what sort it would have been.'

'The States is where it's all happening, these days,' Austen
said. 'God, I really want that job. I thought a reference from
someone as well-known as old Max might clinch it for me.'

'About as effective as shaking your prick at a polar-bear,'
said Penny. 'I mean, Mother Teresa he wasn't. Did you really
think he would treat your poems kindly?'

'I can't pretend he was entirely complimentary, the few
times I asked him about them.'

'Perhaps you couldn't stand the ridicule and killed him out
of wounded pride.'

'Perhaps I didn't.' Austen kicked at a table. He projected
thwarted genius. He poured more Glenfiddich for himself.
And some for Penny, as though he could hardly bring himself
to do it. 'The damned fool accused me of being some kind of
sexual pervert, actually.' He twiddled the badge on the front
of his dungarees. He looked earnest. So did his hair. 'I happen
to believe in the Wordsworthian theories about poetry,' he
said.

'All that jazz about commotion recollected in tranquillity.'

'Emotion.'

'Same thing.'

'I meant the spontaneous overflow of powerful feelings.'

'Hey, boy,' said Penny. 'Way I read it, you been doing more than your fair share of spontaneous overflowing.'

'What?'

He seemed puzzled. So was Penny. 'Do you ever read your own poems, or do you just write them? Anyone would be forgiven for assuming you were making out with most of the girls at the school.'

'*What?*'

'Or is it all metaphorical?'

'You can't seriously think I'm slipping it to the English Sixth, can you?' Austen looked outraged. He lifted his chin and gave Penny a two-second burst of his powerfully pure profile.

'Say, were you born like that or did you have plastic surgery?' she said.

'They're professional virgins, every last woman of them.'

'Come on, Austen. You don't seem to have written about anything else since you got here.'

'I may write about it. That doesn't mean I actually do it. A man has a right to dream.'

'Try dreaming something else. I don't know how it'll go down in North Carolina but they'd certainly ban it in Boston.'

'People like me are always out of step with the times,' Austen said. The thought seemed to cheer him up.

'Different drums, huh?'

'I couldn't have put it better myself.'

'That may be your problem.'

Austen leaned back once more, so that the sofa lifted clear of the copy of *Baghavad-Gita*. Penny could see a big dent in the cover. If he leaned back often enough, the sofa would eventually tip over. Penny hoped she'd be around when it did. Austen wrenched his mouth down. He pressed his temple with three sensitive fingers. Life had obviously given him a raw deal. What he'd hoped for was a da dying of lung-rot after a lifetime at the pit-face, and a mam who'd been forced to take in washing to keep body and soul together. What he got was a semi in Wandsworth and a public school. No use being magnificently unprepared for the long littleness of life if you

96

come from Wandsworth.

Penny watched him watching her. She knew about him because she'd gone to the Public Library in the High Street after returning from Holkham Court. She also knew his middle name was Hubert. She felt sorry for him. She shifted slightly so her long legs were where he couldn't miss them. She watched him take in their ebony burnish. And the Kurt Geiger sandals on the ends of them. He cleared his throat. He ran one of the yellow pencils lightly along the grooves in the bleached wood of Mrs MacGonagall's G-plan coffee-table. Penny presumed it was hers. Austen didn't look like the G-plan type.

'So we're basically agreed,' she said.

'Are we? On what?'

'That you have an excellent motive for murdering Max Maunciple.'

The pencil lead snapped, leaving a small black mark on the table. Austen gave some kind of chuckle. Shaky was the word that did it most justice.

'Have I?'

'Sure.' Penny bent forward. She fixed him with a significant stare. Hawkeye Wanawake. Always gets her man. 'You desperately want that job in the States, right?'

'I don't know about desper – '

'Maunciple announces his intention, let's say, of writing to the North Carolina people and saying you're not fit to be let loose in a ladies' seminary. You see your future career in ruins, so you doctor a bottle of gin and leave it where he's sure to find it. Perhaps you opened it and poured a couple of slugs out, to make sure he didn't go for one of the unopened ones in his cabinet. Then you slip away from the concert to see if it's had the desired effect. Finding him dead, you empty away what remains in the doctored bottle, wash it thoroughly and stick it in the trash. Then you get another fresh bottle, empty most of its contents away and set it beside Maunciple's armchair. No one the wiser. It will simply be assumed that Max overdid it one too many times. North Carolina, here I come.'

'I poisoned him, did I?'

'Someone did.'

'Put it in the booze, did I?'

'We're waiting for the lab analysis now,' Penny said. Sometimes she wished she weren't such a good liar. It wasn't a talent she'd inherited from her parents.

'What're they analysing, if I've poured it all down the drain?'

'Stomach contents,' Penny said briefly.

'And I stole Max's typescript as well, did I?'

'Uh-huh.'

'Why?'

Why *did* he? 'We're working on that.' Penny said.

'I could have left my own poems there, of course, in order to have an excuse to return later to the scene of the crime,' Austen said thoughtfully. He smiled, lifting the planes of his narrow face into something less posed, more attractive than previously. 'Mind you, I bet I was pretty damned disconcerted to find so many people there when I showed up.'

'I bet.'

'The nervous tension of it all undoubtedly made me behave in an uncharacteristically boorish fashion,' continued Austen. 'In my momentary panic, I got right up your nose, thus causing you to become suspicious and making it harder for myself.'

'Harder,' said Penny. 'Yeah.' She had the feeling she had lost something. The initiative, perhaps.

'However, now I've had time to think, I realise you can't pin a thing on me, and my attitude is almost, well, insolent.'

'Right. Insolent.'

'So how about coming out for a drink with me this evening. It might help you in your – you know – enquiries.'

'You know enquiries. What sort are they?' Penny thought rapidly as she said this. She didn't think she liked Austen. On the other hand, she might learn something useful from him. No self-respecting amateur gumshoe would pass up an opportunity like this.

'Will you?'

'Will I what?'

98

'Come out for a drink tonight.'

'Why?'

'Because frankly, Miss Wanawake, I think you're pretty stunning.'

'I'm also impervious to charm.'

'Will you?'

'Isn't the school play on tonight? I want to see that.'

Austen groaned. 'Oh God. Not that modernistic crap. You'll hate it. A lot of intellectual flummery. Christ meets the anti-Christ, or something.'

'I want to go.'

'Well, after that, will you?'

'All right,' Penny said. 'But may I ask you a very personal question first?'

'If it has to do with genital warts, the answer is, no, I haven't.'

'I just wanted to know if your nipples sag.'

'Perhaps after our drink, you could take a look and see.'

EIGHT

'How did you make out today?' Penny asked that evening. She sat on one window-seat, watching Yeoman sit on the other. He seemed preoccupied. One finger endlessly rubbed up and down the windowpane. He'd go right through, if he wasn't careful.

He straightened his shoulders. He grinned. 'Do you mean before or after breakfast? Before was really – '

'After.'

'Oh, after. I went down to the precinct-house. Nosed around a little.'

'We say police-station.'

'Whatever you call it, I nosed around it. Introduced myself. Got friendly with a couple of the guys.'

'What did they say?'

'That they had absolutely no reason whatsoever to think that Maunciple's death was anything more than it appeared to be. Heart-failure.' He stared across at her. 'I'm inclined to agree with them.'

'What?' Penny frowned. She pulled her feet out from under her and stood on them. She put her hands on her hips and shook her head from side to side until the white beads on her braids clicked violently together. 'Why, Charles Yeoman. I declare. That is utterly and entirely despicable.'

Yeoman held up one hand. He hit his forehead hard with the other one clenched into a fist. 'Don't tell me,' he pleaded. 'It'll come. It's – it's Vivien Leigh in *Gone With The Wind*. Am I right?'

'What's with this "inclined to agree" shit? This morning you gave me the distinct impression that you agreed with me there was something not quite jake about the way Maunciple died. Especially with his manuscript gone.'

Yeoman looked away. 'Actually, hon, I think maybe we were making too much out of this whole thing,' he said.

'*We* were? It's you that's been making a big deal out of the manuscript, not me.'

'So I'm big enough to admit I might be wrong.'

'I'll never be that big,' Penny said. She bunched her lips up angrily and stared out of the window. The sky was moving towards evening, darker than daylight but not yet night, a mussel-shell, fairytale blue. The Abbey buildings were beginning to glow as the spotlights deepened. Leaves stirred, exquisitely green. A single bird called somewhere. 'Besides, there're too many things that don't add up.'

'When I added them up, they came to exactly zero,' Yeoman said. 'Incidentally.' He reached into the wardrobe and pulled out his hold-all. He tossed it onto the bed. It looked like diversionary tactics. He took a blue shirt on a hanger out, and held it up against himself. 'What do you think?'

'*Tailor & Cutter* want you to model their spring suiting and you're wondering if blue is really your colour.'

'No.'

'Your arms shrank in the shower and you'd like me to take tucks in the sleeves.'

'No.'

'Jesus, Yeoman. I don't know. You're wondering whether they'd take it in part-exchange for a microwave oven.'

Yeoman took out another shirt. And his pink suit. He put them on the bed beside the hold-all. 'The desk-clerk downstairs told me there's an unexpected vacancy, and I can have it if I want,' he said.

'An unexpected vacancy.'

'Right. And being a dedicated cop, I found out, through discreet questioning, who it was who had gone.'

'I don't need to guess. It was Mrs Curteis-Squire, wasn't it?'

'Ten out of ten. Shall I pack my stuff and move into her vacated room, or not?'

101

'Not,' Penny said.

Yeoman began to hang things back in the wardrobe.

'I wonder why she left,' Penny said.

'Mysterious creatures, women.'

'What do you reckon the chances are that she had that manuscript in her bag this morning?'

'Who can say?'

'Think she murdered Maunciple for it?'

'I told you,' Yeoman said, his back to her, 'I don't think Maunciple was murdered.'

'But you do agree that his latest book's gone missing. You do agree on that one, huh?'

'Maybe. Maybe not. It could be somewhere perfectly innocent. I didn't give his apartment a thorough going-over last night.'

'I can't figure you out.'

'Just being cautious, lady. I seen too many people take a toss by jumping to conclusions without enough evidence to support them. We've got absolutely nothing says Maunciple was murdered.'

Penny tapped her elegant black nose. 'Except this. It's all I need.'

'Wouldn't stand up in a court of law, honey.'

'I just hope you are not going to chicken out on me, Charles Yeoman.'

'Convince me, then. Give me one good reason why the Curteis-Squire dame should lift the manuscript.'

'Because she didn't want it published.'

'Uh-huh. And what do you think she wants to hide?'

'Could be anything. An illegitimate child. An affair. Something discreditable from her past that she doesn't want raked up. If she knew Maunciple way back when, he probably knows quite a bit about her. He might even have been keeping tabs on her and found out something recent that she doesn't want revealed. I wonder where she was between, say, seven o'clock and seven thirty yesterday. I'll have to check up on that.'

'She your only suspect?'

102

Penny splashed bourbon into two glasses and gave one to Yeoman. 'No,' she said. 'There's Dominic Austen. He's certainly got some kind of a motive. He's after a job in the States, and Maunciple was about to see he didn't get it. And there's Mr Kenneth Sumnour. I went to see him this morning. His place certainly didn't look as if it could take much adverse publicity. On top of which, he apparently blames Maunciple for the mess his first son has made of his life, and is afraid his second son is going the same way.'

'This stuff doesn't taste the same without ice, does it?' Yeoman said. He went into the bathroom and came back with a handful of vitamin pills which he swallowed wholesomely.

'They're wising up, though,' Penny said. 'I actually saw icecubes on sale in a supermarket recently. Outside London. Amazing.'

'Ten years behind us,' Yeoman said. 'Yes, sir. A good ten years.' They were both briefly silent, contemplating the primitive lifestyle of the average Brit.

Yeoman spoke again. 'To restore your lost faith in me,' he said, 'I found out something helpful. When I mentioned Mr Kenneth Sumnour down at the copshop, it rang all sorts of bells, so I checked him out at the local newspaper office. Do you know what I found?'

'No.'

'About a year ago, a Mr Leon Goldman died while taking a cure or whatever they do, at Sumnour's place. At the inquest, the coroner suggested there had been contributory negligence. Maxie might have thought it would make a good story. Sumnour would have considerable interest in suppressing that little item, wouldn't he?'

'If it's been splashed over the local papers, any damage must already have been done.'

'Not necessarily. Newspapers have to tread on the right side of truth if they don't want to get sued. And they can't theorise too much, either. A novelist can write what he likes and suppose what he likes, all in the name of fiction.'

'Very interesting,' said Penny.

'Takes the heat off Margaret.'

'Maybe. There's also Marius Knight. He told me last night that he'd slipped away from the concert for a few minutes. Austen said he'd seen him, too. That would put him right on the scene of the crime. And he's ideally placed for planting the gin beforehand.'

'It's all a bit tenuous, isn't it?'

'Not if you take those initials into consideration.'

Yeoman shook his head. He gazed at his feet. 'You and Agatha Christie,' he said. 'Perhaps they all clubbed together to buy the gin. Perhaps they each added a drop of this mysterious, undetectable poison, and carried it together to the guy's room while he was out. Jesus. I've heard of imaginations running riot. Thought it was just a figure of speech.'

Penny walked over and stood looking down at the top of his head. There was an endearing sort of lock standing up on the crown. She made herself not be endeared. This was the guy who was stabbing her in the back.

'Stay cool, fool,' she said. Very froglike.

'Are we going to this play tonight?' Yeoman said. 'It's about some guys hatching out of eggs and wrestling for the world's soul. Or something.'

'Christ.'

'And Hitler, so I believe.'

'I already saw the eggs. Isn't that enough?'

'If you had any idea what a culturally deprived life I lead, back in Motor City, you wouldn't deny me this one small treat,' Yeoman said.

'Can you guarantee a treat?'

'If it wasn't, you being there would make it one.'

'Hard to stay adamant after that,' Penny said. 'OK, I'll come, but first I must whip down to Ashmole and see how Peter's bearing up under his sad loss.'

Some three hundred yards across the Great Court stood Ashmole. It was a four-square Queen Anne house, approached via a set of tall ruined arches. Wings on either side of the house enclosed a large area of gravel. Handy for parental parking. Awful for walking across in high-heeled shoes. It was one of the times Penny felt there was something to be said for those sandals handmade out of a single piece of leather you could buy from the back of the *Guardian*. Not much, but something.

The parking space was empty except for a small crimson car parked so close to the front door it was almost inside it. The last rays of sun brightened the white paintwork of the top storey. Boys in shirtsleeves flitted to and fro inside the rooms like virile butterflies. The Pastoral Symphony slammed out of one window at a decibel pitch loud enough to penetrate even Beethoven's ears. Satie flounced and suggested from another. From a third, Marianne Faithful used four-letter words to get her simple message across.

A boy wearing lipstick came out of the house as she reached the front door. Unless it was a girl. You couldn't always tell. Both sexes of that age had the same basic expression. No longer innocent, yet still uncorrupted. And the same haircuts.

Inside the door, a boy with eyes like brown pansies showed her to Marius Knight's study. He was standing in front of a fireplace full of bulrushes, smoking a meerschaum and talking to Peter Corax. Penny had expected to find Peter prone to tears. She found him merely prone. He lay on a sofa with a carved back, a glass resting on his chest, a smile resting on his mouth. It seemed superfluous to ask how he was.

'We were reminiscing about old times,' Knight said. He busied himself with an icebucket. His beautiful voice rasped like a jeweller's file on Penny's chestbone.

'And about poor old Max,' said Peter. He raised his glass and tried to drink from it. Quite a lot of liquid spilled over his neck.

'I see they didn't go so far as to proclaim a day of national mourning,' Penny said. She took a pistachio nut from a dish and cracked it between her teeth. She loved pistachio nuts. 'You have to lift your head, Peter, as well as your glass.'

'I keep hoping for a change in the laws of physical science.' Peter bared his teeth at her.

Penny examined the room. It was furnished on a giant scale. There was a large mirror over the mantel. Three large sofas. A large desk covered in papers. A large sideboard covered in bottles. A large TV set rolled away into a corner. A large number of photographs. None was of anything female.

She wished she could remember what Peter had told her about Knight. Peter's friends all led lives of such scandalous debauchery that when he spoke of them she automatically half-closed her ears. Protecting herself against what amounted to aural pornography. Was Marius Knight the one who had been caught *in flagrante* with a yak in the Taj Mahal? Or the one someone had photographed naked, beating the chairman of a House of Commons sub-committee senseless with a cattle-prod? Or the one who had thrown up at the altar-rail of St Margaret's, Westminster, during his daughter's wedding to a Yugoslav transvestite? Or someone else?

Peter had dropped an icecube and was fishing ineffectually for it with one unsteady hand. 'Honestly,' Penny said. 'You really are a disgusting old man.'

'My dear, I *know*. But it's such *fun*.'

Penny put her hand inside his shirt. She could feel his heart beating hard against her palm. She retrieved the icecube and dropped it back into his glass.

'Thank you, dear child,' he murmured.

Peter had been a sitting tenant when the house in Chelsea was put up for sale. And was therefore one of the reasons why she had been able to afford it. Along with Miss Antonia Ivory. On his own admission, he had been kicked out of more of England's venerable institutions than most people had even heard of. It said a lot for England that he had been allowed into them in the first place. He wrote the kind of clever novels that reviewers dared not pan in case they had missed the point. He was often tipsy. He sometimes brought men back to the flat he occupied on the top floor of the house. Large, brutal young men in Doc Marten's and tattoos. One day, one of them would probably beat him to death. Penny was sure he peed in the washbasin. He was always in demand at parties because he could be relied upon to do something unspeakable. She loved him.

'I saw her,' he said now, obviously going back to whatever he had been saying before Penny arrived. 'I really did,

106

Marius.' He said 'shaw'. He sounded as if any moment he would fade into drunken sleep. Penny knew this meant he was at his most malicious. In his youth, he had looked like a marble cherub, with curls and apple-shiny cheeks. Now, after years of excess, he looked like a marble cherub that had fallen far too often onto its nose.

'Who?' Marius said, as though he could not remember what they had been talking about. He sucked in on his pipe. Nothing much happened since it had gone out. He began the elaborate routine that relighting it involved.

'Margaret. Margaret,' Peter said, pronouncing all three syllables in Gerard Manley Hopkins style.

Penny's ears grew an inch. 'Margaret?' she said. She did her piccaninny beam. The one no man could resist.

Knight was evidently made of granite. 'Take no notice of Peter,' he said. He said it in the sort of voice that dares you to bring up the subject it has just closed.

Penny took him on. 'I've never heard you say anything about a Margaret before,' she said to Peter. She dimpled prettily. Girlish as hell.

'That, my dear, is because there is nothing to say about a Margaret,' Knight retorted. He took her elbow and steered her over to one of the large sofas. He sat her gently down beside him. He tamped down tobacco with one dirty thumb.

'I tell you, it was she,' Peter said. 'It may be nearly twenty years since I last saw her, but I couldn't be mistaken. She's hardly changed. Large as life, she was. Beautiful as ever, too. More so, if anything. Walking through the Buttermarket with a lad I'd have swum the Hellespont for. A member, I may say, of this very school, unless the wearing of boaters has become the mode among the young bloods of the town.'

Knight appeared not to have heard. 'That most charming young American came to see me this morning,' he said to Penny. 'He seemed to be a great admirer of Max's.' His voice massaged her eardrums.

'He read the *Passionate Pilgrim* book, and it fired him to spend his vacation here.'

'So he said. I love that transatlantic earnestness, don't you?

107

It's a trait I fear we irreverent British are sadly lacking.'

'Opals big as gramophone records in her ears,' Peter said. 'That's why I noticed her in the first place. You remember how Margaret always loved earrings.'

Knight did something noisy with his thumbs. It sounded like a neck breaking. He twisted his mouth. 'Your friend seemed deeply concerned about the fact that Max's latest book seems to have been mislaid,' he said to Penny.

'I know.'

Knight laughed gently. 'I couldn't quite concur with his remark about it being a sad loss to literature.'

'Yeoman said that?'

'Something very similar, certainly.'

'He's a police-detective, back home,' Penny said, as though that might explain why someone who had majored in nineteenth-century literature could have made such a crass remark.

Knight nodded. 'He told me. I presume it was his police, rather than his literary training that caused him to search my room so diligently.'

'Yeoman searched your room?' Penny was beginning to feel like a parrot.

'Odd, isn't it? I left him here alone for a few moments to attend to some matter, and he gave the place a thorough going-over. One of my monitors was passing the door and happened to observe him.'

'I wonder why.'

'Presumably because he thought I might have taken it and hidden it here.' Knight smiled. 'He may have read the *Purloined Letter*. What better place to hide papers than in a room already full of them.'

'*No mask like open truth to cover lies,*' Peter said from the couch where he sprawled like a badly-dressed porpoise. '*And to go naked is the best disguise.*'

'Someone with your build should think of other ways,' Penny said.

'Not me,' Peter said. 'Margaret. She was making no attempt to hide herself.'

108

Marius closed his eyes. Penny thought that one of the saddest things you could hope to see was a middle-aged man looking like a heartbroken child. Something was going on between the two of them and she wanted to know what.

'Naturally I dashed after her,' Peter said. 'However, by the time I had pushed my way through *hoi polloi*, she had disappeared into Boots. I searched diligently for her through pyramids of disposable nappies and positive mountains of sanitary towels, but she was gone.'

'She probably saw you coming,' Penny said.

'The clincher, the real clincher, Marius my old friend,' Peter said, slurring his words unnecessarily, 'What made me *know* it was her, was that bracelet thing you gave her. Remember?'

'*Amor Vincit Omnia,*' Marius said quietly. He sounded very tired. He sounded as if he hadn't slept for twenty years. He laced both hands behind his head and leaned back into them with his eyes shut. Penny wondered what pictures he saw.

'That's the one,' Peter said. '*Amor Vincit Omnia*. Love Conquers All.' He liked to remind people that he had once been among the foremost classical scholars of his generation. 'What an extraordinarily incorrect statement that has always proven to be.'

'Only in your cynical world, Peter,' Knight said. 'Not in mine.'

Peter drew in a long breath through his snub Socratic nose, considering the words. At a personal level, love had conquered a tremendous amount in its time. Particularly incompatibility. Of breeding, of brains, of sensitivity, of age. A tremendous amount, yes, but not everything. Decidedly not everything. However passionate his feelings had been for the many beautiful boys who had passed through his hands, love had never succeeded in conquering the remorselessness of maturity, in bridging that hideous gap which lay between lovely stripling and coarsened man.

'Perhaps you're right,' he said. He thought one or two Horatian thoughts about heaped rose-leaves and Persian splendours. '*Obscurus fio,*' he murmured.

Penny looked at Knight. He sat staring rigidly at nothing. He held his pipe so tightly she thought it might snap. She spoke coldly to Peter. 'You've got a mouth as big as the Amazon,' she said.

Peter simulated distress. He attempted to lift one unkempt eyebrow. 'Penelope, what kind of talk is this?' he asked.

'It's button-your-lip talk, Peter. Now, why don't you go check out the gargoyles on the chapel or something.'

'Do they need checking out?'

'No.'

'Then I shall stay here. I'm perfectly comfortable as I am.'

'I'm bigger than you are,' Penny said. 'And meaner.'

Behind his half-closed lids, she could see his eyes, bright as bullets. She loved him, yes. But she didn't think he was a credit to the human race. In fact, she knew that despite his enormous charm, he was quite the opposite. A cheat, a liar, a bully. If he could get away with it. When she was around, he couldn't. Sighing heavily, and grumbling, he levered himself upright. His belly hung between his legs. The fly of his trousers was imperfectly zipped. With much protesting, he went.

Penny went over to the fireplace. On the mantel above it, in a litter of pipes and tobacco-tins and red plastic golf-tees, was a photograph mounted on cardboard with a double line of blue ink framing it. It showed Marius Knight sitting among the current crop of Ashmole boys. Juniors in front. Middles behind. Seniors level with Knight. The boy sitting next to him wore a magnificent royal-blue gown, heavily gathered at the shoulders. He was clearly the most senior boy of all. He was clearly Adam Curteis-Squire.

'I've met him,' Penny said, pointing to the firm jawline and golden curls.

'Adam? Ah yes,' Knight said. 'One of the best Heads of House I've ever had. We shall miss him next term.'

'I suppose he's going to university.'

'Indeed, yes.' Knight sounded as proud as if the boy were his own son. 'Cambridge. He gained an Open Scholarship in Natural Science.'

110

'His mother was staying at my hotel,' Penny said.

'Really? I've never actually met her, though I'd like to. It always helps to place a boy if you can meet the parents. His father usually brings him down at the beginning of term, or picks him up. Donald Curteis-Squire. Nice man.'

'For a moment,' Penny said, giving a trilling laugh, 'I thought she might be the Margaret Peter and you were talking about earlier.' The trilling laugh sounded awful. She thought she'd better work on it before she used it again.

Knight frowned. 'Absolutely impossible,' he said. He dropped his pipe. It fell onto the carpet, spilling ash everywhere. He rubbed it in with his foot. He'd obviously read somewhere that ash was good for rugs. Unless he just couldn't afford a vacuum-cleaner.

'How do you know?'

'Miss Wanawake, you have been acquainted with Peter for some time now, I believe. You will therefore be aware of his – uh – penchant for what I can only call mischief. Particularly when he has had a little too much alcohol. I know you have something of a reputation for ferreting solutions out of mysteries, but I can assure you there is no mystery here. The Margaret he referred to is someone we both knew a long time ago. In mentioning her at all, he was merely trying, in a somewhat unpleasant fashion, to make me react, to make me rise to the bait.'

Penny thought he had probably succeeded. This was a man who had lost his cool, if only temporarily. She watched him bend down to pick up his pipe. When he stood up, his face was red. He flexed his dirty thumbs. He stared sadly into the fireplace. He looked as though he could be pushed around.

'It's just that Mrs Curteis-Squire is called Margaret,' Penny said.

She wished she hadn't. Knight's face was suddenly not merely red, but deeply flushed. The colour spread downwards below the collar of his shirt, and upwards into his eyeballs. The muscles of his mouth were white around the stem of his pipe. He looked murderous. It was a startling transformation. It defied all expectation. Like opening an oyster and finding

111

an Oxo cube inside. Or biting into an apple and cutting your tongue on a razor-blade. She'd obviously been wrong. Nobody was going to push Marius Knight around.

She had planned to add that Adam's mother had been wearing opal earrings. She looked at Knight's double-jointed thumbs, at the knuckles of his fingers. She imagined them round her throat. She decided not to.

Out in the Great Court, she could see Peter being deliberately pathetic under an oak tree. She had intended to ask Marius Knight a searching question or two. Now she decided that the devil she knew would probably be a better source of information than the devil she didn't.

An elderly-looking boy stuck his head round the door. 'Sorry to disturb you, sir. My parents are here and would love to have a word.'

'Not when they've heard the word I'm going to give them, Williams,' Knight said. His hands were trembling.

The boy laughed. 'Oh, sir,' he said.

'It's been awfully nice talking to you,' Penny said. She moved towards the door. There was a sword-stick lying on top of a bookcase. She didn't like the look of it. Dangerous things, sword-sticks. She'd seen one go right through a man's body once. Easy as slicing a banana. Before she could do a thing about it, he had fallen dead in front of her. She wondered why Marius Knight had one. She waved at him.

'See you around,' she said.

NINE

The school play probably had a great many things to recommend it. Offhand, Penny couldn't think of a single one. She found herself irrationally annoyed by the Speedo swim-suits inexpertly covered in feathers which both the main characters wore. One of them had hair and a moustache like Hitler; the other, a Nazarene beard. She didn't like the way they spent most of the time curled up inside the two celluloid eggs, being symbolic or figurative or some damned thing. She hated the rouged extras who clomped round the floor on platform soles, doing an inordinate amount of fretting and strutting. Abstract notions about genesis and dissolution flew around like bats. Religious and political significances winged their way towards the low vaulted ceiling of the sepulchral cellar in which they were seated. She failed to be absorbed. She felt oppressed. The effort not to yawn made her eyes bulge. She hoped she didn't look as much like Idi Amin as she felt she did.

A man in the row in front of her had given up the struggle to follow the action. He was asleep. Every now and then, he snored. When he did, his wife would rouse herself and nudge him cruelly awake. Across the tiny auditorium, Dominic Austen's eyes gleamed as he sat with folded arms and an expression of contempt. He was watching her. She wished he wasn't. Partly because she half-suspected him of murder. Partly because, in spite of this, she couldn't help rather liking him. He gave the impression of one who could think of better ways to spend an evening. That made two of them.

She could also see Adam Curteis-Squire, who kept looking

113

at his watch. There was no one else she recognised. Except Yeoman, seated at her side, and looking deeply enthralled. He had to be putting it on. She wondered how much longer he'd remain in Canterbury. He'd already overstayed his schedule. With all the other places he had to see, there was a lot of shrine-visiting still to do. She wanted him to stay. And not just because of his all-over tan.

When the audience was finally released, Dominic Austen was waiting for her outside. If the play had purged him of pity and terror, it wasn't immediately obvious. His goatish eyes narrowed at the sight of her. He drew breath in through his nostrils. She was reminded of the great god Pan, doing his thing by the river. She wondered if, inside his £50 trainers, his feet were cloven. When Yeoman materialised at Penny's side, the smile on his face suffered from something akin to brewer's droop.

'You joining us?' he said. It was about as far from being an invitation as it could get.

Yeoman shook his head. 'Sorry. Got something I have to do.'

'Are you sure?' Austen was being pretty open about the pleasure Yeoman's announcement gave him.

'Absolutely. It's gotta be done tonight.' Yeoman kissed Penny lightly on the forehead, gazing hard at Austen as he did so. Establishing territorial imperatives, probably. In the darkness, the flecks in his eyes were invisible.

'See you,' Penny said.

'Hey, babe,' Yeoman said. 'Almost forgot. Can I borrow your car?'

'Sure.' Penny felt around for her keys. 'Just so you don't drink and drive.'

'*Moi*?' said Yeoman. 'I'm a cop. I show respect for the law.' He stuck his hand out to Dominic Austen. 'If you feel the urge to get something down on paper,' he added cordially, 'resist it.'

'Screw you,' Austen said.

'Not me, you won't,' Yeoman said. 'Because I'm straight, man. I want you to know that.' He winked at Penny. 'Have a

114

good time, folks.' He strolled off, none knew where, though Penny wished she did. He was up to something, and including her out.

Austen took her arm in a grip the wrong side of sadistic and hustled her out through the Abbey gatehouse and into the town. By night, Canterbury looked far seedier, an amalgam of blowing fish-and-chip wrappers, skulking cats, half-lit alleys, bemused tourists looking hopelessly for some action. Penny wanted to tell them that everything went on hold after six, but they wouldn't have believed her. Provincial towns did their best to live down the reputation of the Swinging Sixties, but it was uphill work. Shop windows contained reject china and secondhand books and thin gold rings mounted on Perspex cubes. The planners had turned the ancient High Street into the usual banality. Boots. Dewhursts. W. H. Smiths. Woolworths. A Norman arch here and there was the only reminder of piety.

Three people with spiky pink hair slouched past. Between them, they must have been carrying about five hundredweight of metal studs attached to their leather jackets. No wonder their shoulders were so round. Further along, Austen followed them in through a door made of stained-glass and dark wood set with iron bosses. The illusion of antiquity was unnerving. Judging by the mass of people wedged inside, antiquity was a big crowd-puller. More dark wood criss-crossed the ceiling. A hauberk or two hung from the walls. No one in there was more than thirty except the glittery lady behind the bar. She had a long thin nose and even longer thinner earrings. Had she put her head on one side she would have drawn blood.

Austen stood tapping a one-pound coin on the bar top. The bar-lady seemed reluctant to take his order. He'd changed into a tweedy jacket and flannels since the afternoon. He hadn't forgotten to transfer the badge. He must really care about bats.

Penny hoped the pound wasn't all he was proposing to spend. 'Please do not ask for credit as a refusal often offends,' she said.

'I suppose you want something expensive,' said Austen.

115

'I was wondering what it was I liked about you.'

'Well?'

'I'm still working on the answer.'

'I mean what'll you have?'

'Jack Daniel's, please.'

The lady with the thin earrings blinked at them. Austen quickly ordered a Ruddles for himself and bourbon for Penny. He called the bar-lady Annette. It didn't seem quite right, somehow. With a glass in his hand, he grew less dour. He drank deeply. 'Well, now,' he said. Penny couldn't think of a single reply.

He tilted his pint mug again and swallowed its contents. He looked at Penny as though hoping she wasn't going to do the same. He ordered another.

'Nice little place they've got here,' Penny said. She wasn't expecting to be taken literally.

'It's not marvellous,' Austen said. 'But the best of a bad bunch. I think I've tried every damned place in town and they're all hopeless.'

He put one finger in the small of Penny's back and began pushing her through the smoke towards a door in the far wall. The room beyond was lit by three blue lamps. A small stage framed by shiny red curtains took up one end of it. A coloured light moved nervously across them as though searching for enemy fighters. There was a number of small tables and smaller chairs. There were pews around the outer perimeter, most of them fully occupied.

A girl in a leopard-skin body-stocking and a huge quiff of blue hair was shrieking something on stage. Behind her, three other girls dressed in gold foil snarled at a mike. There didn't seem to be room round it for all their teeth. A hand-lettered sign at the side of the stage announced Edie Puss and the Gilt Complexes. Penny was quite glad she couldn't make out what any of them were saying.

As she and Austen sat down at a table, she could feel her pupils working overtime to adjust to the gloom. After a while, she could even see into the corners of the room. In one of them, what she saw made her eyebrows go up and down a

116

couple of times. The nonchalant Frenchman. He appeared to be staring at her. It was probably an illusion caused by the superfluous sunglasses he wore. Perhaps his eyes were blue-light-sensitive.

Austen suddenly took hold of her hand and started telling her she walked in beauty like the night. At least he had the sense to turn to a real poet when he wanted to do a spot of chatting-up. Penny watched the Frenchman. He was talking to a boy who sat at the table opposite him. He had a yellow Bic pen in his hand and a book open in front of him. An account book. Although she personally felt that very little harm would be done if cannabis was decriminalised, Penny was very sure she didn't much like the implications of what she was seeing. The boy stood up. The wandering spot caught his hair, turning it swiftly green, then purple, then red. Adam Curteis-Squire. She liked the implications even less. Adam leaned on the table. He said something vehement. The Frenchman laughed. Adam didn't. He spun round and came towards her.

'I would have thought the school would make places like this out of bounds,' Penny said to Austen. 'At least to boarders.'

Austen had got to the bit about all that's best of dark and bright. He sounded annoyed at being interrupted. 'At this time of year, nobody gives a fart,' he said with his usual elegant turn of phrase. 'Half the boys are with their parents, anyway. If they choose to come in here, that's their business.'

One of the Gilt Complexes did a curious shuffle at the back of the stage and moved her head rapidly backwards and forwards. A few people clapped. It wasn't easy to see why.

As Adam passed her, Penny reached out and pulled at his sleeve. He looked down at her, frowning, clearly not in the mood for polite conversation with recently-met strangers. Eighteen years of expensive education warred for a moment with natural inclination. Breeding won out. A charming smile replaced the irritated frown.

'Why, Miss – uh – Wanawake,' he said. He batted his gold-tipped eyelashes. 'What a surprise to see you here.' He peered

117

closer into the blue darkness. 'And Dom, too. Mr Austen.'

Up on the stage, Edie screamed an expletive into the microphone which hung around her neck. She tore it off. She goose-stepped around for a while, chanting a single obscenity over and over again. Her boots seemed to be made of solid gold. Her lipstick was black.

'Join us,' Austen said. He pulled out a stool that was wedged under their table. He'd obviously decided to postpone the Byronic chit-chat for a while.

Adam hesitated. He looked over towards another table some distance from theirs. A girl with the pale bland face of a madonna was watching him. She suddenly screwed up her face and made all the signs of someone about to suffer a severe attack of projectile vomiting.

'Well, I – uh – ' said Adam. He clenched his teeth together. 'I really can't.'

'I only wanted to ask if your mother was all right,' Penny said. 'I heard she'd checked out of the hotel.'

'How kind of you to enquire,' Adam said. 'Your American friend wanted to know, too.'

'Did he indeed?'

'I told him she'd gone to stay with friends.'

'Where?'

Like his mother, Adam was too polite to tell Penny to piss off. 'In a village just outside Canterbury,' he said.

'But she'll be coming into town again, won't she?' Penny said. She hadn't finished with Margaret Curteis-Squire by any means. On the other hand, she wasn't quite sure she had the amount of boldfacedness needed to ask outright for the address of the friends. Not without an excuse. And for the moment, she didn't have one.

'I certainly hope so,' Adam said. 'Speech Day's coming up, and since I've won a prize or two . . .' He smirked modestly.

'It's diabolical,' Austen said. He slapped the table with the palm of his hand. His SAVE THE BAT badge fell off and bounced onto the floor. 'This whole elitist notion of competition. Labelling people . . . under-achievers . . . success-orientation . . . prizes, for Pete's sake.' He sounded incoherent. 'The private sector should be done away with. Will be, too, next time we get a proper government.'

'The public sector can't afford Poets-in-residence,' Penny said. 'Where would you be then?'

'Anyway, sir,' said Adam. 'If you abolish the public schools, you'll be denying future generations the chance to rebel against their upbringing. The way you have, sir.'

'What?'

'Weren't you at Oundle, sir?'

'Listen to me, you little bugger,' Austen said. He rose from his chair and reached across the table as though planning to take Adam by the throat. Halfway through the movement, he subsided. 'Under the socialists, there won't be any need to rebel,' he continued equably. He slumped in his seat, gazing at his empty glass.

'Who're you kidding?' Penny said.

'Anyway, I didn't come here to talk politics.' Austen stood up. 'I need a refill.'

'I'll pay, this time round,' Penny said. She found her wallet in her bag. 'It's the duty of the privileged classes to sponsor creative endeavour, don't you agree?'

'Thought you blacks were an oppressed minority,' Austen said.

'Uh-huh.' Penny shook her head. 'Maybe once. But these days, it isn't enough just to be black. You got to be a single parent and lesbian and crippled. And Welsh. I don't qualify.' She handed him a fiver.

Austen used an undulatory movement of the hips to move between the tight-packed tables to the door. Adam remained nervously at Penny's side, ignoring the madonna, who now looked as though she were shaping up for an epileptic fit.

'That man over there,' Penny said, nodding at the Frenchman. She tried not to notice the golden glow of Adam's face, nor the hair curling over his collarless grandad shirt. 'Who is he? Do you know his name?'

'He calls himself Daguerre,' Adam said.

'What do you call him? The Candyman?'

Although it was an American term, Adam seemed to

119

recognise it. He flushed. Then paled. The qualities that had once made England great were very much in evidence as he said evenly, 'I call him Daguerre.'

'Get stuffed,' Edie screeched into her mike. She twisted from side to side as though her ribs itched. If she'd ever had any pubic hair, she didn't have now. There wasn't room inside the body-stocking. She had at least fourteen gold studs pushed through the rim of her right ear.

'Thanks,' Penny said.

'I have to go,' said Adam. He moved quickly back to his own table. The madonna clutched his shirt when he was near enough. She appeared to be mad. She banged her eyes open and shut at him several times. Whatever happened to the idea that to be young was very heaven?

Penny got up. She walked over to the Frenchman's table. His corner seemed darker than the rest of the room. She rolled her eyes a bit so he could see the whites. She was afraid she might otherwise be invisible.

'Is this a Daguerre I see before me?' she said.

The Frenchman looked at her. His sunglasses were opaque and jet-black. Very unnecessary. Very sinister.

'*Très amusant*,' he said.

'*Droite*,' said Penny.

'I'll bet you tap-dance too,' he said. He didn't sound very French when he said it.

'You aren't French,' exclaimed Penny. You couldn't put much over on her.

'I'd be the first to agree with that.'

'So how come you got that French haircut and always go round with that bunch of French kids?'

'How come you're asking?'

'I couldn't live with myself if I didn't find out why you wearing shades, man.' Penny clicked her fingers in an ethnic sort of way. 'I mean, there ain't no sun in here.'

'I'm blind,' Daguerre said.

'No shit? Where's your seeing-eye dog?'

'At the oculist.'

Daguerre lifted his hand and slowly removed his glasses.

120

Without them, his eyes were light-blue, chockful of clarity and truth. Just showed how deceptive appearances could be. He put his elbow on the table and leaned his head on it, thumb under chin and one finger each on cheekbone and jaw. He smelled of Eau de Monsieur Cardin. Insouciant as hell. 'If you're looking for a fist down your throat,' he said conversationally, 'keep right on talking.'

This was a real mean guy. 'They quit writing scripts like that the day Sidney Greenstreet died,' Penny said. 'Anyway, you wouldn't hit a woman, would you?'

'Wouldn't I?' said Daguerre. Tough as hell. Old boots had nothing on him.

'What are you pushing?' Penny said. 'Just pot? Or the hard stuff as well?'

'I'm pushing extra tuition in French, is all,' Daguerre said. 'At a discount.'

'Your clientèle being drawn from the well-heeled sons of those who can afford to pay for a public-school education?'

'And daughters. Nothing sexist about me,' said Daguerre. He barely moved his lips when he spoke.

'What happened to the French master at the school?'

'He choked to death on a snail.'

'Daguerre,' Penny said. 'That's a good old French name. But you sound more like an American.'

'Don't I though.'

'Are you French-Canadian?'

'Vive Quebec Libre,' said Daguerre. His candid eyes were as hard as pebbles. He pressed the nipple of his Bic pen and put it into the pocket of his shirt. Penny had never cared deeply for men who wore pens in their shirts. The pocket-cuff of this one had a little monogram on it. BAD, embroidered in fancy machine-stitch. His initials? Or a descriptive adjective? Either way, it placed Daguerre firmly on the North-American landmass. No other group of people in the world had such impeccable bad taste.

A boy walked quickly past the table towards the rear wall, then quickly back again. He bit his lip as he passed.

'Looks like someone wants to book a French lesson,' Penny

121

said. 'I'll leave you to it.'

'Wise move,' said Daguerre. He clasped one hand in the other and placed them both on the closed ledger in front of him. His moustache twitched. He made the muscles of his neck suddenly stand out.

'God. I wish I could do that,' Penny said.

'Who are you?' Daguerre's voice sounded as though someone were grating nutmegs in his throat.

'Penny's the name and sleuthing's the game,' said Penny. That'd be something for him to sweat about. She gave a pretty significant wink. He didn't seem to notice. She did it again. He put his sunglasses back on. She walked away, trying to indicate that there was a knife taped to her calf and she was prepared to use it.

Austen was waiting for her with two drinks in front of him. He was watching Edie without any visible sign of enjoyment. Edie was soaking wet. Her boots glittered.

'Alone at last,' he said cheerlessly as Penny sat down.

'See that kid over there,' Penny said. She nodded towards Daguerre's table. The ledger was open again. The French lesson appeared to be in full swing.

'What about him?'

'Is he from the school?'

'Could be.'

'Do you know his name?'

'James something,' Austen said indifferently. 'How should I know? I only come into contact with a handful of them.' He took Penny's hand again. 'Look. Where had we got to?'

'Meets in her aspect and her eyes, was it?' Penny wondered what Margaret Curteis-Squire's friends were called, and whether she ought to get out there. Her indifference to Austen's poetic seduction was so overt that he abandoned the attempt. Just as well.

'The thing that really amazes me,' he said, eyes alight with insincerity, 'is the small impact Maunciple's death has made.' He evidently expected his own demise to shatter worlds.

'As ye sew, so shall ye reap,' Penny said. It wasn't all that easy to say. 'Nobody liked him. *Ergo*, nobody misses him.'

'How terrible, to die unmourned,' Austen said. 'Still think he was murdered?'

'Yes.'

'What do the fuzz say?'

'Oddly enough, they prefer to accept that it was heart-failure.'

'How blinkered of them.'

'Quite.'

'I imagine that lets me off the hook,' Austen said. 'Whew. The relief of it.' His yellow eyes gleamed. Not entirely with amusement. If you had something to hide, Austen's face was a good place to hide it behind.

'Oddly enough, I prefer to accept that it wasn't heart-failure,' Penny said.

'And you won't rest until you've brought the culprit to book.'

'Got it in one.'

'Proof?'

'I'll find it.'

'In that case, I ought to confess that I popped into Maunciple's rooms early in the evening to ask for my poems back. He wasn't there so I left a note. I'd hate you to find my fingerprints lying around and come to the conclusion that I was the guilty party.'

'What time?'

'Around seven.'

'See anyone else?'

'Not that I remember. There was an awful lot of coming and going.'

Penny looked over at Daguerre's table again. 'That boy. Is he called James Sumnour?'

'I don't know. I told you, I don't know the whole school by sight.'

'Seen the bimbo with the shades before?'

Austen squinted into the blue-lit gloom. He shook his head. 'I couldn't say for sure.'

'How about me, baby? You can have me tonight,' Edie whispered. The Gilt Complexes nodded. 'Yeah, yeah,' they said. Their hair quivered like pampas grass. Some of the audience was rocking on a bit of floor, arms held at stiff angles. A girl in a lumberjack's shirt fell to the ground. As far as Penny could tell, she didn't get up again. It was breathlessly hot.

The boy at Daguerre's table stretched out his hand and took something from him. It didn't look like a reflexive verb. Not from where Penny was sitting. The sunglasses turned briefly in her direction. *Très* chilling.

'Is there much of a drug-problem at the school?' she asked.

Austen shrugged. 'A certain amount. It's inevitable. Especially in a school that's so near the town centre, and has such a large proportion of day-boys. Even the boarders have a lot of freedom to wander about.'

'Any masters involved?'

'Could be,' said Austen slowly. He lounged in his seat, relaxed as a rubber glove. Except that the hand holding his beer mug was white-knuckled and his carelessly-crossed leg rigid. It was tight-ass time all right.

'Are you ignorant? Or loyal?'

'Just cautious.'

Crafty was probably nearer the truth. Penny could almost hear his braincells tumbling over one another. If I give her a name or two, it'll get her off my back.

'I expect you smoke the odd joint yourself, don't you?' She knew damn well he did. She'd seen the stubs in his room earlier that day.

'From time to time.'

'Hell, who doesn't,' said Penny. She lifted one shoulder and gave a crooked grin. Very woman-of-the-world.

'I wouldn't want it loudly publicised,' Austen said. He moved shiftily about.

'Where'd you get your stuff,' Penny said.

Austen didn't answer. She wondered what he'd been up to. He didn't look like a murderer. But no one ever did. Except in a passport photograph. He'd probably done nothing worse than blow the minds of a girl or two in the English set. Copped a cheap feel, perhaps. Why did he look so worried.

124

'You scratch my back, I'll scratch yours,' Penny said.

'My back doesn't need scratching.' He hesitated. 'What's involved, if it did?'

'A name. If you know one. And in return, I'll let you read me your poems.'

Austen wasn't listening. He bent down and picked up his badge from the floor. He tapped it against his teeth. In the weird blue light, they had a charnel-house glow. She saw his braincells whizzing round and reaching an almost audible halt. Must have come up with three pieces of silver in a row.

'David Marriner,' he said.

'Who's he?'

'Modern Languages Department at the school. Not my type, I'm afraid. Nor yours, I imagine.'

'If he's a pusher, he certainly isn't.'

'He's ex-Army, and it shows. Much too hearty for my taste. He's one of those people whose tracksuit has tapes under the feet. Always leaping about in a peaked cap.' Austen brooded. 'God. I hate men who wear yachting caps. Especially when they're standing at the wheel of a small boat with spume and whathaveyou blowing in their faces.'

'You speak with feeling.'

'You can say that again.' Austen shuddered. He pulled at the front of his hair and brought a lock of it down to lie in lyrical disarray across the front of his head. 'He's got a boat.'

'Very suitable, with a name like that.'

'What?' said Austen. 'Oh yes.' He shuddered again. 'I was fool enough to go sailing with him once. Christ. There was a gale-force wind blowing and that maniac kept rabbiting on about the way I'd tied some knot or other.'

'This Marriner sails a lot, does he?'

'A fair bit. Hops over to France and back before you can say Uffa Fox.'

'France, huh?' Penny felt as though she had KER-DOING!! written above her head.

'It's only twenty-one miles away,' Austen said. 'I mean, honestly. Do *you* know the difference between a granny and a reef?'

125

'As a matter of fact, I do. I was in the Girl Guides for four years.'

'Well, I wasn't. You'd think I'd just assassinated the Pope. I suppose that's what comes of growing up in a place like Dartmouth. It gets into their blood.'

'What does?'

'The sea. To someone like Marriner, sailing across the Channel is as easy as nipping down to the local for a quick one.'

'Where does he keep his boat?'

'Dover. He's got a flat there, too, so it's very convenient. Not that he's all bad,' Austen added hastily.

'Just bad in parts.'

The red curtains staggered across the stage, obliterating Edie Puss and two of the Gilt Complexes. The third jumped down onto the dance floor and gyrated with puppetlike movements of her spine. The blue lights suddenly went out. Nothing much happened for several minutes, except the sound of chairs scraping against the floor. Some red bulbs lit up the room. In the lurid dimness, people began groping their way to the door.

'He brings back a lot of wine,' Austen said. 'And we get the benefit in the staffroom.'

'I see,' said Penny.

She really thought she did.

TEN

The only other living creature visible in the precincts of Canterbury Cathedral was a lecherous sparrow. Penny knew he was lecherous because he'd spent some ten minutes indicating as much to a series of indifferent lady sparrows. When he flew in her direction, she got up from the bench where she'd been sitting and went into the cathedral by the great West Door. Black shadows crowded the corners behind the huge arches. Washes of colour lay over the rows of rush-bottomed chairs and the grey flagstones. There was a smell of damp holiness.

Behind a table, a plump old lady knitted a very small cardigan in white angora wool. As Penny approached, she pushed at a couple of pamphlets about Life After Death and the Way Through Sin, as though it might make them more inviting to a prospective purchaser. It didn't. Nothing could. Not if the purchaser was Penny. There was too much life to be dealt with before death for her to worry about what came after. Not her own life but the lives of others. Young others. Innocent others. Others who had nothing and expected nothing. As for sin, she hadn't much against it. Nothing at all, in fact. Not against the fun kind of sins the Church frowned on, anyway. If they ever came out strong against indifference or starvation or war, she'd be right in there rooting.

She sat down in the choir and gazed up at the East Window.

Was it possible that Maunciple had stumbled across some kind of drug-ring centred at the school? Was it too much of a coincidence that Marriner and Daguerre both had interests on each side of the Channel? Was there some kind of local French Connection?

It was feasible that Maunciple had found out about it and used his information in his latest, and now missing, novel. If he named names, pointed fingers, showed causes, it was also feasible that Daguerre and Marriner would have had to silence him in order to keep their partnership going. If indeed, they had a partnership going. She had no evidence at all that either knew the other. No evidence at all against Marriner, except Austen's reluctant mention.

She got up and strode round the cathedral, past tablets of stone commemorating long-dead pillars of the Church, past brass plates erected by his fellow-officers to glorify the Colonel of the Regiment, past marble urns and anguished cherubs. *Hic jacet*. Sorely missed. In Loving Memory. Emotion compressed into unfeeling by the stonemason's chisel. Not many women seemed to have been remembered. By their fellow-officers or anyone else. She walked up the steps towards the carved rood-screen and looked back down the long nave. The soles of her feet tingled. Henry II's four sidekicks must have come rushing in through that door, clanking and jingling, calling for the Archbishop, waving their swords. Becket would have known he was a dead man as soon as he saw them. Here, he must have come forward to meet them with all the might of the Church behind him. Here, confronted them. Here, died. Violence still lingered in the air despite the quietude. The right deed for the wrong reason. Or so Eliot said.

Further on, she came across the tomb of the Black Prince. She wished that most of what she remembered about English history couldn't have been written on the head of a pin and still left room for a whole formation-team of dancing angels. All those years at school, plus a year at a Swiss finishing place, a year at the Sorbonne, a year at Stanford, and she still didn't know exactly what the Black Prince had been famous for. Except it wasn't for being black. No, brother. The dude sure hadn't been blood.

Something was scuttling about in front of the altar. An officious man in a black dress. She could see he was dying to tell her she wasn't allowed to be where she was. In Penny's experience, there were only two kinds of verger. That kind. And the kind that has just locked up the vestry and gone home for lunch.

His disapproving jowls had shattered her mood of matutinal calm. She emerged into the precincts and walked slowly back to Abbott's through the pale sunshine. In the main quadrangle, a portly gentleman of middle height, sub-fused into gravity, was strolling across the grass in a panama hat. His head was bent as though he searched for cigarette stubs. Or early worms. He wore a clerical collar.

'Hi,' said Penny. In view of the fact that this was hallowed ground, she dropped her eyes shyly and gave her Sunday-morning smile.

'Good morning.' The man smiled at her yellowly. He tipped his hat. Penny liked that very much. 'Enjoying the sanctuary of the Abbey?'

'Sure am,' said Penny. 'Gimme that ol' time religion.'

'Ah. A fundamentalist, I see.'

'Guess you could say.'

'It appears that we are to have another glorious day,' the man said.

With one of those intuitive leaps at which women are supposed to be so good, Penny asked herself if this could possibly be David Marriner. Admittedly he wasn't wearing a yachting cap. Admittedly he didn't look as if he'd ever taken the Queen's Shilling. But anybody about at this early hour was more likely to be connected with the school than not.

'A nice day for sailing,' she probed, cautious as a rabbit.

'You may well be right.' The cleric settled his hands behind his back. He looked profound. 'I'm not much of an outdoorsman myself,' he said. 'Besides, I'm kept too busy with my many commitments. A school like this doesn't just run itself.'

'Hey,' said Penny. 'Don't tell me you're the chief honcho himself.'

'If, as I infer, you mean the Headmaster, I'm afraid that, for my sins, that is exactly what I am.' He gave a tiny bow. 'The Reverend John Shepherd.'

'Well, howdy, Rev,' Penny said. 'From what I've seen,

129

you're doing a great job here.'

'You have an – uh – interest in the school?'

'Kind of. Right now, my interest lies mainly in a guy called David Marriner.'

The Headmaster turned distinctly chilly. 'I see.' From the way he said it, he could have been sucking on a lemon. He implied that far too many people were interested in David Marriner. All of them the wrong sort.

'Know where I could find him?' Penny was aware that she had just been given the big freeze. She thought she could handle it.

'You could get hold of his address from the school office,' the Reverend said, doing a great imitation of an iceberg. 'Except that it's not open until this afternoon.'

'Oh dear,' said Penny. She did a great imitation of someone whose crest had just fallen.

It seemed to work. 'I believe he occasionally frequents a gymnasium not far from here,' said the Headmaster. He looked at his watch, which had black Roman numerals and liturgical hands. 'What day is it? Yes. He might well be there today. Now.'

'You really are sweet,' Penny said.

If the Reverend John Shepherd was unaccustomed to being called sweet by big black girls, he didn't let on. 'I hope you find him,' he said. He made as if to move on, but Penny shifted around on the grass so he couldn't.

'What a terrible blow it must have been to have Mr Maunciple die so suddenly,' she said.

'Uh – yes.' The Headmaster made a grab at a Christian response. 'Yes, indeed. We shall miss him most dreadfully.'

'Do you have much of a problem here with drugs?'

The Headmaster reared up. He plucked at his panama hat. It had what might have been a moth-hole just above the black ribbon band. Penny hadn't know that moths ate panama hats. 'In a school this size,' he said, 'there is bound to be an occasional lapse from the high standard of conduct that we expect from our pupils. Which we, indeed, encourage both staff and parents alike to foster in the younger generation.'

130

'Give it to me straight, Rev. Do you or don't you?'

'I won't deny that a small number of boys have been asked to return home prior to the end of term. And certain others are under close observation.'

'What about masters? Any of them involved?'

'Masters. Certainly not. A school like ours does not employ staff of anything but the highest probity. We would be failing in our duty to both pupil and parent if we were to relax our standards in any way.'

'Attaboy,' said Penny. 'So Marriner pumps iron, does he?'

'Pumps iron?' Shepherd made it sound like some unspeakable sexual deviancy.

'Lifts weights. Works out.'

'That is correct. One could wish that Mr Marriner spent more time on his spiritual and less on his muscular development.' Shepherd parted his lips to allow a gleam of daffodil dentistry to emerge. Penny guessed he was probably making a joke.

'You've been most helpful.' She smiled and patted him on the shoulder. 'Keep up the good work. You're a credit to the school.'

The Headmaster looked startled. 'That's awfully kind of you,' he said uncertainly. Surely those were his lines, weren't they? Something was wrong somewhere. He tipped his hat again and carried on looking closely at the grass verges.

As Penny hurried towards the hotel, a small crimson car hurtled towards her at about 110 mph. It was being driven by an extremely saintly man in a dog-collar. Was it her imagination or were his eyes tightly closed? She didn't waste time checking it out but swerved quickly on to the forbidden grass. She had nothing against clergymen, though she wouldn't want one to marry her sister. But she definitely preferred them to drive with their eyes open.

Yeoman was still asleep when she got back to their room. She changed into a leotard. The sound of her doing up her tracksuit zip woke him. She leaned over him. His eyes really were of a most startling blue. The black flecks shimmered.

'Where'd you go last night?' she said.

131

'What'll you give me if I tell you?'

'It's what I'll give you if you don't that matters.'

'When you put it like that . . .' Yeoman struggled upright. He plumped a pillow behind his back. 'Make me a cup of coffee before I keel over and die,' he said. 'Please.'

Penny plugged in the electric kettle provided by the management. She tore at a small packet with her teeth and emptied its powdery brown contents into a cup.

'Well?' she said.

'I went to see Margaret Curteis-Squire.'

'Oh.'

'I wanted to find out for sure whether she had that manuscript or not.'

'And did she?'

'I'd say not.'

'What did she say?'

'Not much.'

'Why not?'

'She wasn't there.'

Penny contemplated him. Big shoulders. Big biceps. Big everything, when you came to think of it. Big nerve, too. 'Are you saying you searched the house where she's staying?'

'Something like that.'

'You actually broke and entered.'

'I entered. I didn't have to break because they'd left the side-door unlocked.'

'Jesus. Thought you said you respected the law.'

'You wouldn't want me to waste all that gas for nothing, would you? Don't you care about the way our natural fuel resources are being squandered? It seemed logical to go ahead and take a look, seeing as I was on the premises.'

Behind Penny, the kettle began to leap about and thrust its lid up and down. Steam rose in little bursts from its spout. 'How did you know where she was staying?' she asked.

'I'd rather not reveal my sources,' Yeoman said. 'Every good cop has his own stoolies.'

Penny poured boiling water onto the coffee granules. A scum swirled around the surface of the resultant liquid. She

132

wondered whether Raleigh would make the connection between it and the beans he had brought back from the New World. She took it over to Yeoman and held it above him. 'A cup in the hand is so much nicer than a cup on the balls,' she said. 'How did you find her address?'

'I *can* reveal,' Yeoman said quickly, 'that before you went off with that bullshit artist last night, a certain golden youth appeared. It didn't take too much to persuade him to tell me where his mother was hanging out.'

Penny gave him the coffee. 'So you're back with me again: you think Maunciple was murdered.'

'No.'

'Then why this obsessive compulsion to find his book?'

'All those years of staring through a magnifying glass, I guess,' Yeoman shrugged. He winked at her. He set his head sideways and smiled so his crooked tooth showed.

'If you're trying to disarm me,' Penny said, 'you're failing.'

'Shucks. It worked with the Venus de Milo.'

'I've been thinking about you,' Penny said. She sat down on the side of the bed. 'You're trying to kid me that you don't think Maunciple was murdered so that you can sneak around finding proof that he was. I think you're bucking for promotion back home in Detroit. Creep-arsing your way into the Lieutenant's chair. Solving a murder in England won't do your rep any harm at all.'

Yeoman turned the corners of his mouth down. 'Hell,' he said sadly. 'The cynicism of modern youth.'

'I'm right, though, aren't I?'

'I'm not saying you are and I'm not saying you aren't.'

'What are you saying, then?'

'I'm, frankly, at a loss for words.'

Penny took one of his hands. ''Fess up,' she said. 'Deep down, you do really think Maunciple was murdered, don't you?'

Yeoman hesitated, as though weighing up the pros and cons. Then he said, 'Yes. I guess I do.'

'And you do agree that two heads are better than one, if we're going to find out who did it?'

133

'Depends on the heads. But yes, in principle.'

'So no more trying to steal a march, all right?'

'Right.'

Penny didn't believe him. Difficult to say why. But an ambitious man was often an unscrupulous one. He was using her. And who could blame him? She wished she didn't like him so much. She tied up the laces of her track shoes.

'I'm going to work out for a bit at the local gym,' she said. It was the truth, if not all of it. Two could play at that game. 'Want to tag along?'

'Hey. What a terrific idea,' Yeoman said. He raised a finger to his forehead. 'Just wish I didn't feel quite so lousy. Must have forgot to take my vitamins. I think I got a touch of spring fever or something. Nothing that bedrest won't cure. Why don't you go along without me, and I might join you later, huh?' He gave a brave smile.

Penny laughed.

She left the Abbey and walked towards the centre of town. In the cobbled Buttermarket, the open space in front of the cathedral, she looked about her. The aged crone scrubbing the steps of the Olive Tree public house wasn't likely to know much about gyms. Nor was the distinguished-looking gentleman hunched in a doorway, wearing an overcoat tied round with string. She went into a phone box. In the Yellow Pages she found Gymnasia: see also Health Clubs. She looked up Health Clubs. See also Saunas and Solaria. She just loved the Latin plural ending. It showed that civilisation hadn't entirely succumbed to the barbarians. She found a gymnasium with an address no more than five minutes away. The odds were high that because of its nearness to the school, this was the one Marriner would use.

The Aquarius Fitness Centre, when she reached it, proved to be a shabby set of rooms above a former travel agency. A lithe person lounged behind a small counter made of plastic tongue-and-groove. He wore an off-white T-shirt featuring a bowed figure carrying a water-jug on its shoulder. Penny guessed that off-white hadn't been the T-shirt's original colour. Behind him, there were shelves of fruit-juices and

134

several pictures of men doing alarming things with their bodies. A heart-shaped poster warned her to be fit, not fat.

'Mr Marriner here?' she asked the lithe person.

'Nope,' he said. He continued to stare at a body-building mag.

'But this is where he works out, is it?'

'Yep.'

Penny paid for an hour. There were several people already in the gym, although it was still early. A man wearing a leather belt around his waist, and a lot of sweat on his chest, grunted ferociously as he lifted giant bar-bells towards the ceiling. Three ladies, blonde, brunette and redhead, stood around discussing a fourth who'd gone into hospital for an operation. A man in a grey sweatshirt ran like hell on a jogging-machine. He gasped for breath. He clung to the handrail. He had a pink towel round his neck. Another man did bench-presses in a torn vest.

Penny did a hundred lateral twists. She did a hundred leg-lifts. She did a hundred free squats. Jane Fonda would have cried out in admiration at the way she was going for it. The blonde lady lay face down on a padded board and vigorously exercised her thigh muscles. The brunette pulled up and down on the lat machine and groaned a lot. The redhead examined a split in her Gitane-blue Lycra tights and said she'd take them back to the shop, she'd only just bought them. Penny did a hundred sit-ups, keeping an eye on the door. No one came in. The redheaded lady lay slowly down and did some bench-presses, her face contorted. Penny snuck a look at the amount she was lifting. It wasn't very much. The brunette said she thought her period was starting and she wasn't going to overdo it. The blonde lay on a slanted board and did some ferocious pull-ups with her hands behind her head. Very stylish. Penny did some too.

The door opened and two youths carrying Adidas sports bags came in. They smelled of meat. Perhaps they were butchers. They didn't look remotely like an ex-Army man who taught modern languages in the private sector. The man in the grey sweatshirt lay down on his pink towel and trembled violently for several minutes. The man in the leather belt dropped his weights on to the floor. He cursed. He shook his head. Sweat flew off it in all directions.

The door opened. An upright soldierly figure came into the room. He wore a navy-blue tracksuit with tapes under the feet. Penny lifted weights with her ankles and watched him. Did he, or did he not, have a seafarer's tan? The blonde lady cycled several miles very fast on the stationary bike, breathing through her mouth like a steam-engine. The brunette rubbed the back of her neck and said if it wasn't her period, she was coming down with a cold. The soldierly man came out of the changing-room and went through a routine of warm-up repetitions, his eyes fixed on the redhead's crotch.

The butchers lifted their legs off the floor an alarming number of times, their faces red with effort. The soldierly man leaned forwards on one knee like a discus-thrower and lifted a huge weight with one muscled arm. It wasn't Arnie Schwarzennegger, but pretty good all the same. Breathing deeply, Penny went over to him. Perspiration trickled down between her breasts. She put her hands on her hips.

'Wow!' she said.

'Today, Canterbury. Tomorrow the world,' said the man.

'Know anything about boats?'

'I'm not a shoemaker.' The man put down the weight and lifted it with the other arm.

'Boats,' Penny said.

'Oh,' said the man. 'No. Nothing.'

'You're not David Marriner.'

'I don't remember saying I was.'

'Shit,' Penny said.

'What did you say?'

'Shit. S-H-I-T.'

'That's what I thought.'

The man hefted an iron bar with several tons hanging from either end. His biceps bulged. So did his eyes. Little veins stood out like worms all over the visible parts of his body. Penny left before something burst. She worked out for a while longer. No one else came in. The blonde lady had dark

136

patches of sweat under her arms as she did leg extensions. The redhead stared dully at the speedometer on the jogging-machine. The brunette thought she might have slipped a disc. The butchers smelled.

When she had showered and changed, Penny went over to Mr Aquarius.

'Let me put it another way,' she said. 'Has Mr Marriner been and gone already?'

'Yep.' He turned over another page of his magazine, showing a fearsome creature, half-ape, half-man, caught in the act of popping muscles from all sorts of places where they were better kept hidden.

'Couldn't you have said so when I came in?'

'You din't ask.'

'Did he say where he was going?'

'Nope.' Mr Aquarius turned another page to reveal a lady who looked like an old tree. Gnarled. Knotted. Not the sort of person who'd be warming up the macaroni cheese when a man came back from work. If he was lucky. 'Said something about scraping his bottom.' He looked up at Penny. 'If you get my drift.'

'I do. Perfectly,' Penny said. 'Anyone who knows anything about boats would.' She went to the door.

The man said something. She didn't ask him to repeat it. It'd sounded like, 'Wouldn't mind scraping your bottom, then.' She didn't condone that sort of filthy talk. Not from men in off-white T-shirts, anyway.

ELEVEN

The sea beyond the harbour wall at Dover was so bright, it hurt. Sunshine glittered on the windows of the Regency buildings all along the seafront. Seagulls screamed above the funnels of the cross-Channel ferries tied up at the Western Docks. Way out to sea, a Hovercraft moved importantly from right to left in a burst of spray.

Penny parked behind a pub near the Easter-Docks. A black-painted notice told her the place was reserved for Customers Only. She figured that if she wasn't yet a customer, she might well be when she came back. Anyway, the pub wasn't open yet. She strolled along the esplanade. To her left, the Prince of Wales pier jutted out into the water. Fishing boats were tied up to it. Terns made a frightful row over bits of disgusting debris floating in the harbour.

She turned towards the Wellington Dock. On the other side of a stretch of water, the stone-built Customs house squatted like a garden gnome. There was a white-capped figure up in the glass observation room, staring keenly out to sea in case someone was trying to invade the country. There were several yachts making their way slowly out into the Channel. Words like 'spanking' and 'jaunty' and 'marlin-spike' sprang to mind. The wheel's kick and the wind's song. All that nautical jazz. It was enough to make even a Swiss banker break into a hornpipe.

'Good morning, miss.' A whiskery man in a navy-blue sweater stumped out of a little kiosk at the entrance to the docks. There wasn't a parrot on his shoulder but he managed to imply that was merely because the parrot was taking a tea break. He appeared to have only one tooth, set midway along his upper jaw. 'Can I help you?'

'I must go down to the sea again,' Penny said. She stared round the yacht-basin. There were an awful lot of masts.

'That's what they all say.'

'Actually, I'm looking for David Marriner.'

'Marriner? That would be the *Mary M*.' The harbour-master sucked air in past his clenched tooth. ''Fraid you just missed him. He locked out about ten minutes ago.'

'Oh, well,' Penny shrugged. 'I'll try again later. When's he expecting to be back?'

'Couldn't say, miss. Said he was going across today. Won't be back until sometime late this afternoon, I shouldn't wonder. All depends on the wind.'

'Across?' said Penny. 'Do you mean to France?'

'That's right.'

'Thanks.'

Penny walked back along the seafront. She went into the first phone box she found. It was amazing what intimate details you could find out about a person from a telephone directory. Like their telephone number. Like their initials. Like their address. D. G. Marriner was listed as living in Number 4, Nelson House. She could see it from where she was. A modern block of concrete flats, set on green stilts, overlooking the harbour. Large green letters spelled out the name across the third floor. NE SON HOUSE. She hoped the L hadn't hit anyone when it fell off.

She crossed the road and went into the entrance vestibule. In the concrete jungles of the States, there would have been security monitors. Armed guards. Slavering Dobermans. Not here. This was provincial England. This was still safe. She walked up to the second floor, using the concrete steps behind the lift. There was a green-painted handrail which felt damp to the touch. There were salt-stained windows offering a superb view of beautiful downtown Dover. There was nobody to be seen in the corridor. She rang the bell of Marriner's flat and waited. No answer. She rang again. Still no answer. She hadn't expected there to be. She inserted her American

139

Express card between the door and the jamb. She wiggled it about a bit. Nothing happened. She wiggled some more. She felt the card connect with the lock mechanism but the door didn't open. Damn. She'd never mastered that trick with a bit of plastic, though Barnaby had shown her how to do it countless times.

She took her manicure set out of her big white leather shoulder-bag. It had been Barnaby's Chrismas present to her. From Asprey's. Barnaby had had it specially personalised for her by a craftsman he knew in the Seven Sisters Road. The original implements were made of solid silver, with tortoiseshell handles. Now, each handle could be pulled off to reveal miniaturised tools designed to facilitate unauthorised entry. There was a lock-pick, a torque wrench, some magnets, even a flashlight concealed in the nail-buffer that gave out a beam no thicker than a needle. Until it was twisted. Then, the arc expanded to cover a 12-inch radius. All made of high-quality stainless steel. Barnaby's own tools included a CO_3 cylinder, soldering equipment, welder's goggles, an amplified stethoscope. Professional stuff like that. It made Penny's set look like a toy.

When Barnaby gave it to her, she had sucked in her cheeks and raised her eyebrows. 'Lord Peter Wimsey always got Bunter to do the dirty work,' she had said.

'I priced them out, but Bunters cost the earth at the moment,' said Barnaby. 'Let's wait until they start mass-producing them.'

He'd insisted she take lessons in the use of the tools from a colleague he'd met in Parkhurst. Joseph 'Faraway' Greenhill was a genial young man who wore horn-rimmed specs and pin-striped suits. He took his work very seriously and had therefore been very thorough. Besides, he didn't want to offend Barnaby. Not if he could help it. You never knew when you might not be doing bird again with the same blokes and Barnaby hadn't been known at Parkhurst as Duracell just because of his copper top.

Now, Penny leaned against the door of Marriner's flat and fiddled with the lock. So much easier than that credit-card

140

crap. Within seconds, she was inside. If anyone came round asking who she was, she could always claim to be Marriner's sister.

The flat was filled with space and light. Sea-green carpet thick enough to need mowing spread in all directions. The walls were painted white and hung with expensive-looking modern lithographs of the sort people bought at the Royal Academy Summer Show to indicate that they knew what they liked, even if they didn't know much about anything. One whole wall was devoted to the type of ceramic art only Bernard Leach could produce. Or the pottery-class at Featherstone Prison. There was a fairly nasty teak drinks trolly crammed with duty-free booze, and an even nastier coffee table made of teak and marble. In Penny's opinion, coffee tables were almost invariably nasty. Huge leather sofas faced the sea view. Stereo equipment and bookshelves covered another wall. Most of the books were about death. Either on a grand scale, as in *The Second World War*, by W. S. Churchill. Or on a miniature one, as in any number of crime thrillers. Including all the Max Maunciples. There were some superb pieces of Chinese armour on the walls of a tiny dining-room which also contained a luscious oak refectory table. The kitchen was what is usually described as dream. Penny often wondered why. Her own dreams featured things much more interesting than kitchens. A Juice-O-Matic stood on the counter, with squeezed orange skins lying beside it. An egg cup sat in the sink. She decided not to let the fact that David Marriner had carefully made a hole in the bottom of the empty shell influence her in his favour.

She searched the flat in the comprehensive way 'Faraway' Greenhill had taught her. After forty-seven minutes, she decided Marriner was either innocent or careful. He'd left nothing incriminating around. No small brown envelopes. No lumps of sugar on the bookshelves. No syringes or tobacco mixed with grass or spoons encrusted with strange white crystals. Not even a drinking-straw through which he might have sniffed coke. Nothing at all to suggest that he was in any way connected with illegal drug-running.

141

Behind the finger-plate on the bedroom door, she found fifty £20 notes. But hell. That didn't signify one way or another. Any cautious householder might do the same. There were fifty more inside the wrapping of a sealed bar of fabulous pink Camay in the bathroom cupboard. It proved nothing. Yet the flat itself was an indication of something. It seemed very unlikely that a teacher, however private the institution in which he taught, however high up the Burnham Scale he was, could command the kind of salary that had bought and furnished this place. Penny suppressed visions of trust-funds set up at birth by doting grandparents. Likewise legacies from dead aunts. The man *must* be illegit. He must. She needed him to be a villain.

She picked up a photograph album lying on the nasty coffee table. The photographs mostly featured what she presumed was Marriner himself. He appeared to be in his late thirties. Sometimes he wore Army kit. Sometimes a safari-shirt and shorts. Sometimes one of those Guernseys that people order out of the *Observer* colour supplement. In all of them, he had hair of the Clive James Brutalist school. Judging by his eyes, he also had a thyroid problem. He looked as though he were on permanent call by the SAS in case they needed help in storming an embassy. Alarming, in other words.

She stood at the window. The little yachts had fanned out across the sea beyond the harbour wall. France gleamed invitingly down on the other side of the water, so near she could practically smell the garlic, so near she could see cars on the coastal road out of Boulogne. A tanker moved slowly across the horizon. Fishing boats bobbed here and there, not doing anything in particular as far as she could tell. Cranes and heavy lifting equipment peered like rusty giraffes above the lines of lorries and trailers waiting to be impounded on the other side by angry French farmers.

A Sealink ferry lay tethered to the land and, watching it, she had a moment of insight, a flash of some sense that couldn't be called sixth, but might pass for tenth. She made a quick decision.

She was the last person on board the cross-channel ferry

142

Vortigern. Even as she set foot on deck, superfluously assisted by a jolly tar with tobacco-stained teeth, the longshoremen were pulling away the gangplank. A siren bellowed above her head. The gap between ship and shore widened.

She made her way aft. The air was hot and used. It smelled of pine air-freshener and last month's vomit. People sagged in rows of seats which all faced to the front, as though they were waiting for Dr Billy Graham to come and save them. Day-tripping school parties from places like Radlett giggled and preened in the passages. In the bar, she joined the queue. Crowds of horrible French children moved about in sulky herds. Many of them carried cardboard signs saying 'Carnaby Street'. Others clutched Buckingham Palaces under domes of glass full of water and fake snow. They shook them a lot. The word '*merde*' figured as often in their conversation as ''ckinell' did in the speech of their English counterparts. The number of Restricted Linguistic Codes would have brought Naom Chomsky out in a cold sweat of excitement.

As they drew further away from the land, a faint mist gradually obscured everything except the White Cliffs. They looked noble and as though they hoped Vera Lynn wouldn't start warbling some jingoistic nonsense about bluebirds. The sky was very empty above them.

Penny sat down by the window. She had a glass in one hand and a miniature bottle of bourbon in the other. Nearby, at a small round table, a woman sipped something pink and glowered at the adolescent French. One of them knocked a full ashtray on to the floor and laughed. The woman tutted.

'I blame the teachers,' she said. Her lips were sticky.

'They're no worse than our comprehensive kids,' her husband said.

'Except they're French,' said his wife. She moved about in her orange plastic chair. Her reasoning seemed to Penny to be faultless.

'Gives 'em a bit of fun,' said the man. 'Wish they'd thought of taking me on a day-trip when I was at school. Couldn't half of done with a visit to gay Boolong when I was a lad, I can tell you.' His eyes were full of suspender-belts and frilly knickers.

143

'Don't be disgusting.' The woman spun her glass round between her fingers. The rim had lipstick marks all round it. The man winked at Penny. She winked back. She opened the paper she had bought in Dover. Shortly afterwards, she closed it. Jesus Christ. It wasn't enough that half the world starved while the other half joined Weight Watchers. It wasn't enough to have butter mountains and milk lakes while children died from lack of food. Now they were feeding anabolic steroids to Third World starvelings to encourage growth. Give them liver cancer instead of bread. Man. That was really beautiful.

On the back page, a mournful man of Eastern extraction stared at her. He had just been robbed of several hundred thousand pounds worth of jewellery. Although the gems had been the property of his wife, there was no picture of her. Instead, there was a shot of his home. Pensbury Lodge. Near Andover. Not far from the famous golf-course, according to the caption. Penny folded the paper. She pulled out of her bag a copy of *The Caterpillar Cop*. She found Chapter Ten. She removed herself to Trekkersburg. There was no point looking for Daguerre. She knew he was on board. She knew she couldn't miss him when they disembarked. Where, after all, could he go, except over the side?

When the dunes of Boulogne appeared flatly to starboard, she got up. Gathered round the main exit point on Deck B was a mass of people. And crowds of schoolchildren. Two quite separate categories. In their midst, was Daguerre. His sunglasses turned towards her and away. If anything, he looked more insouciant than ever. The ship jolted up against the quay. Men in *bleu de travail* came aboard and began pushing through the crowd, plaintively shouting, '*Porteur.*' They left a strong smell of Gauloises as they passed. Penny always felt mean for not having seven pieces of matched luggage and a cabin-trunk for them to carry on shore.

An intercom voice implored all car passengers to rejoin their vehicles but to refrain from starting their engines or smoking on the car deck. The same voice announced that disembarkation for foot passengers would take place from Deck C. It took a few seconds for the crowd to register. Then

144

they shuffled and surged towards Deck C. Sometimes Penny thought the Chief Purser did it on purpose. She kept her eye on Daguerre.

Once on French soil, she walked along the covered passageway that led almost to the heart of the town. In the open air, the smell of fish was ammonia-strong. Small craft rocked at their moorings down in the harbour. Fish-scales glittered on the damp cobbles between the empty stalls of the fish-market. Boulogne backed away from her up the hill.

The English children made for the shops. So did the French ones. Daguerre no longer seemed part of them. He looked like anyone going about his gallic business. He carried a small black case with aluminium trim. He wore a sweater that might have been knitted up from his moustache-clippings, so closely did the two resemble each other in colour and texture. A coldish breeze blew in off the sea.

Penny followed Daguerre. They walked past smells from open shop doors. French smells. *Soupe de poisson. Chanel No 16.* Fresh-baked bread. Flowers. Pipe-tobacco. Daguerre walked purposefully and fast, heading for the modern part of town which swelled around and below the ancient ramparts. There were not many people about, most of the French being sensibly occupied with luncheon. It seemed like an awfully good thing to be occupied with. They reached a main road where traffic skittered dangerously about. Daguerre stopped at the edge of the curb, waiting for the lights to change. Penny stopped behind him.

'You're following me,' Daguerre suddenly said. He didn't turn round.

'Rats,' said Penny. 'I didn't think you'd notice.'

'What are you doing here?'

'Waiting for the Robert E. Lee. How about you?'

Daguerre moved his head so he could see her. Emotion slipped over his face like a stocking-mask. Even with his sunglasses on, Penny had no problem recognising it as anger. 'I'd advise you to get the hell out,' he said.

The lights changed. He set off across the road. So did Penny.

'Why?' she said.

'You're getting into something here that's bigger than you can handle.'

'Honey, ain't nothing too big for me to handle.'

'Don't bet on it.'

'I only bet on certainties. And one of them is that you're not giving lessons to anybody. In English or in French.'

'I'm not Sammy Davis, Jnr, either. So what?'

They were walking along a road lined with three-storey apartment blocks. Many of the metal shutters were closed to keep out the sun. It gave the street a dead look. A man in a three-piece suit sat on a bench beneath a plane-tree with a litre-bottle of wine at his side. Daguerre stopped abruptly.

'Look. Get off my back, will you?' he said. 'Keep your interfering nose out of my business.'

'Let me hang on that a minute,' Penny said, naive as the Virgin Mary. She made her dimples show. 'Then there *is* some business for me to stick my interfering nose into?'

'There sure is. And you just better butt out, is all.'

'Or else what?'

'Or else you'll be sorry.'

'You wouldn't take advantage of a poor coloured gal, would you?'

'I'd take advantage of my mother,' said Daguerre. He sounded as if he meant it. He sounded as if he already had.

'I take it we're not talking about conversational French any more.'

'We,' said Daguerre, 'are not talking about any damned thing at all.'

To prove it, he pressed a bell beside a pair of tinted plate-glass doors. They opened and he walked quickly inside. Before Penny could follow him, they slid shut again. Through the glass, she could see him talking to a fat lady sitting in a kind of kiosk. She wore a black dress and a brooch full of dead hair. She was a real tub of lard. Daguerre was pointing at Penny. The tub of lard was nodding her head and pulling in her lips. Penny could see she was saying things like over my dead body, and you can rely on me, Monsieur Daguerre.

Penny pressed her nose to the glass. Above the kiosk, there

146

was a ribbed black-felt board. It had names on it in white plastic letters. None of them was Daguerre. Well, that figured.

Daguerre disappeared into a lift. Penny pressed the bell. The tub of lard's voice sounded in her ear from a grill set above it.

'*Qu'est qu' y a?*'

'If you won't buy our lamb, why should we buy your letters?' Penny said.

'*Comment?*'

Penny went away. She reckoned she had about two hours to kill before Marriner could possibly show up. Plenty of time for a late lunch at Alfred's. She'd have the seafood platter. And *moules marinières* to start with. Or maybe *moules marinières* to go on with, as well. No. Better go for the seafood. Fish was good for the brain. And with Daguerre to cope with, she needed all the brain she could come up with.

Later, over a demitasse of Alfred's very strong coffee, and a glass of Cordiale Médoc, she pondered. The link between Maunciple and Daguerre was, as yet, tenuous. Nonetheless, placed as he had been, overlooking the Great Court, Maunciple could well have observed comings and goings that others might have missed. And, given his malicious mind, he probably had no difficulty in putting two and two together and striking gold. By why would Daguerre need Marriner? Was it Marriner's boat that was the attraction? Was Marriner bringing the stuff in, while Daguerre used the schoolchildren as cover to hide his frequent trips back and forth between France and England? It was obvious that Daguerre was the brains behind the operation. Whatever the operation might be. Penny had crewed for her mother often enough to know how easy it was to slip in and out of port with illicit cargo aboard. You tied up, raised the yellow flag and waited for the Customs launch to arrive. If they came, it was all won't you have a tot, officer, and this is my duty-free and the case of wine I bought from the *supermarché*, slightly over the top there, I'm afraid, ha ha. If they didn't, you hauled the flag down after two hours and Bob was your uncle.

Was there any link between the missing manuscript and the

147

Marriner/Daguerre set-up? Was there a set-up? She sighed. She had no proof. Not a shred. She wondered whether Alfred would care if she told him he made the only coffee she ever drank with pleasure. She decided he wouldn't.

She looked at her watch. Time for a stroll before she took up the role of idle observer of the passing scene down at the harbour. Did Daguerre seriously think he had warned her off? She wished she weren't quite so conspicuous. She walked round the ramparts. She strolled back down into the town and took an unexcited look at the little museum. Hard to believe the citizenry of Boulogne flocked here in their thousands to gawp at a shard or two of Roman pottery and some illegible medieval property-deeds. She went towards the *quai Gambetta* down the *Grande rue*, wincing past the furniture shops full of godawful tat. To think that France had once been the arbiter of taste for the whole of the Western world.

At the end of the jetty, she stared towards England. There was a lot of sea, much of it dotted with sails. Several of them were hovering round the harbour-mouth. Windsurfers zoomed in and out among them, looking dangerously fragile. Time passed. Slowly. She could have done with a straw to chew. She read some more MacClure, a sea-breeze whipping at the pages of her book. Next time she looked up, several small boats were entering the inner harbour. One of them was a Westerley Centaur. It had red spray-dodgers with a name picked out in white letters. *Mary M*. It featured a man in a yachting cap at the tiller. She couldn't see if he had a thyroid problem. He handled the boat with ease, bringing it past the ferries and alongside one of the pontoons. He made it look as natural as breathing.

Penny took her camera from her shoulder-bag and hung it around her neck. In case anyone was looking, she aimed it at a topless grandmother on the beach, who was holding the hand of a naked infant. She squinted at a beretted ancient entombed in sand by what she sincerely hoped were his relatives, not a hit-squad. She moved closer to the fish-market. Marriner was making everything ship-shape. And probably Bristol-fashion too. He adjusted the fenders. He stowed the sail. He pushed a

mop about. He went below and reappeared with a mug of
something steaming. His face was very brown. She rather
coveted his yellow seaboots with a lace all round the top of
them. There was a knife hanging from a lanyard around his
waist. He looked more alarming in real life than he had in his
photographs.

Daguerre suddenly appeared on the quay. He had taken off
his sweater and his sunglasses. She almost didn't recognise
him. She smiled. This was what she had come for. She
snapped him calling to Marriner. She snapped the English-
man waving back. She got the name of the boat in both times.
Perhaps it wasn't much use as evidence, the camera being a
notorious distorter of the truth. But it could be useful. And it
was the first hard indication that Marriner and Daguerre were
linked. She watched Marriner close the hatch and padlock it.
He came ashore and the two men walked quickly away into
the town. They were probably going back to Daguerre's
apartment. She saw Daguerre look back once before the shops
hid him. She didn't think he saw her.

Across the harbour, passengers were boarding the ferry
back to Dover. Many of them carried sticks of French bread.
Travel broadens the mind. Bread broadens the hips. Since
there didn't seem much else to do for the moment, Penny
walked across the bridge and joined them.

TWELVE

'Sounds pretty good to me,' Penny said. 'Those guys have a profitable drug-run from the Continent, with Daguerre handling the administration and sales this side, and Marriner using the *Mary M* as delivery-truck. Then Maunciple rumbles it. What better motive for murder could you want?'

Above her head, leaves stirred in a Bacchic sort of way. She and Yeoman were eating a cold supper in the glass-ceilinged annexe of a pub in the High Street. Vines and tendrilly things wreathed up stone walls and across trellises. A tap dripped mossily into a stone basin.

'But why steal the manuscript?' Yeoman asked. 'It couldn't matter to this Daguerre whether Maunciple exposed him in the novel or not, could it? He'd only have to shift his operational base somewhere else and set it going again.'

'It might have mattered to the other one. Marriner. The language teacher. He's not going to get very far in his chosen profession if he's doing time for drug-pushing, is he?' Penny wrinkled her face up then smoothed it out. It stopped an incipient sneeze. The stone walls were freezing. 'If it wasn't one of them, who do you figure took the manuscript?'

Yeoman looked like someone about to lay all his cards on the table. He shrugged. 'Anybody's guess,' he said. Penny felt pretty sure he'd kept a couple of aces up his sleeve. Hearts, probably, and spades.

'We haven't even established that either of them had anything at all to do with Maunciple's death,' she said.

'Honey, we haven't established that anyone except the Great Blunt Instrument in the Sky had anything to do with

150

Maunciple's death,' Yeoman pointed out. 'But let's say they did. Say this person planted the doctored bottle of gin, as posited by the Wanawake Theory. Say he comes back later, gets rid of it, replaces it with an undoctored one, creeps out and goes back to whatever he was doing, no one the wiser.'

'Or she.'

'What.'

'It could have been a woman.'

'Yeah,' said Yeoman. 'But it's quite possible that some entirely innocent bozo came in during the evening, wanting to speak to Maunciple and, seeing the guy's snuffed it, makes off with the manuscript. For whatever reason. See what I mean? The two could be entirely unconnected.'

'Could be.' Penny didn't think so.

Yeoman poked at a wet pink rectangle on his plate. 'Say, what is this garbage?'

'We call it ham,' Penny said. 'It's one of the triumphs of British cuisine.'

'I never knew pigs were amphibian. This stuff is actually oozing water.'

'Don't knock it, kid. It's a modern miracle.'

'Give me an old-fangled one any time. Like that water-into-wine trick. Now that's what I call a miracle.' Yeoman pushed the ham to one side. 'By the way. That Mr Chubbo came by. Said the funeral service is tomorrow and will you go with him.'

'Mr Chubbo.'

'Fat guy with curls. Seems to have problems with his zipper.'

'That's Peter.' Penny nodded. 'I'd better go. He'll need an arm to lean on.'

'Should I come too? It might be interesting to see who shows.'

'Come if you want. But if I'd murdered someone, the last place I'd be would be at his funeral.'

'Someone who commits murder isn't entirely rational, though. By definition. Isn't that the accepted thesis?'

Penny stared hard at him. 'Could be there are situations where murder seems the only rational – the only *right* solution.

151

Perhaps that's how Maunciple's murderer saw it, anyway.'

Yeoman blinked at her. In the greenery on the walls behind him, she could see bunches of tiny green grapes hanging in constipated clusters. They set her teeth on edge just to look at them. Yeoman leaned across the table. It didn't take much leaning since the tabletop was roughly the circumference of a cotton-reel. He circled her wrist with his fingers. 'Listen, sugar,' he said. 'Don't set too much store by this murder hypothesis of yours, OK? There's no one but you says the guy was done in. If you want my opinion, we're looking at two unrelated events here. One death. One theft.'

'Or two crimes, related or not. One murder. One theft.'

'If you're right, we'd have to find two criminals. A murderer and a thief. Or one who's both.' He smiled, showing his crooked front teeth. It was a superior, woman's-place-is-in-the-kitchen-sink-type smile. It made Penny mad. 'See. You don't have a whole lot to go on, do you?'

'Judas,' she said.

'Don't get bitter with me, babe,' Yeoman said. He smiled again. He probably got away with a hell of a lot more than he deserved to because of that smile.

'This morning you said you agreed with me about the murder.'

'I do, hon. I do,' Yeoman said. Not a bit as if he meant it. Much more as if he were stuffing a dummy into some kid's mouth to make it shut up. 'But you gotta come up with some good solid fact if you gonna convince a jury.'

He was right. 'I'm not all that interested in legal justice,' Penny said. 'Only in the truth. Whatever it was in Maunciple's gin, it was lethal. It was also, presumably, almost tasteless, or Maunciple wouldn't have swallowed it. And, by the same token, odourless. Know what fits the bill?'

Yeoman shook his head. His eyes were wary.

'A short-acting barbiturate. Like Seconal. Dissolves in alcohol. Leaves a slightly bitter taste, but the way Maunciple hit the bottle, he was probably past caring about the taste.'

'So now we're looking for a murderer with a sleep-problem. Is that what you're saying?'

152

'I'm not saying it had to be a barbiturate. For a start, doctors over here are reluctant to prescribe something that strong. But if there's one compound that would have worked, there'll be others.'

Yeoman started laughing. 'All this because you found an empty bottle in the guy's trash-can.'

Penny ignored him. 'The thing is, where would John Doe get hold of something like that?'

'We aren't fooling with no John Doe here. John Doe is Mr Average. This guy – if he exists – isn't. He'd have gotten away with it if it hadn't been for you. May still do so.'

'I figure he'd have to be a chemist of some kind,' Penny said. 'Or close to one.'

'The school would have some up-to-date labs, wouldn't it?'

'And some up-to-date chemists.'

'Perhaps your housemaster friend could give you the low-down on who'd have access to them.'

'Virtually everyone,' Penny said.

'So find a suspect who's also a trained scientist, or who has insomnia, and you could really be on to something.' Yeoman laughed again. Penny felt very close to hitting him. 'Unless it was a heart-attack all along.'

'It wasn't.'

Penny pushed back her stool. They stood up. She plucked one of the vicious green grapes and bit into it. Her mouth almost turned inside out. 'Gaahd,' she said. 'Makes you realise there's something to be said for *phylloxera* after all.'

They paid the bill. It seemed a lot for half a tomato and a slice of amphibian pig. They walked back towards the Abbey. The great door of the gatehouse had been closed for the night, shutting out secularity, and they had to step into the Abbey precincts through a wicket-gate. In front of them, the weighty mass of the chapel pinned Faith down long enough for the believer to encompass it. What other reason did men have for raising such monuments except to make tangible the intangible? It might be interesting to search out the necessary underpinnings of such an edifice. Find the unromantic foundations and relate them to the confident whole. If it was

153

possible. It probably wasn't.

'How about a romantic stroll by moonlight,' Penny said, staring up at the cascades of glowing stone which hung above them.

'Great idea. But first I gotta take a leak,' said Yeoman.

'There's a place just over there.' Penny indicated the public convenience provided by the Abbey Preservation Society.

'Yeah. But it closes at nine. Same time as they shut the main gate.'

'It does?'

'Guess I'll have to run into the hotel. Won't be long.'

'You got no music in your soul,' Penny said. 'Not a darn note.'

'When you gotta go, you gotta go.'

'Which is just what I aim to do. Straight to bed.'

'Now you're talking romantic,' said Yeoman. In the sharp-edged moonlight, his teeth shone. He put his arm round Penny's shoulders.

The following day, she drove Peter and Yeoman out to the small country church where Maunciple had apparently indicated he wished a few words to be said over his coffin before cremation. It seemed uncharacteristically sentimental of him. Peter had whisky on his breath. He sighed a great deal. He made remarks about Life and Death and the Meaning of Things in a voice full of profundity. The remarks probably were too, but because they were mostly in Latin, it was difficult to be one hundred per cent sure. He was wearing his Prince of Wales checked suit over a wrinkled shirt.

Apart from the three of them, there were several other mourners round the casket. Marius Knight. The Reverend Shepherd. Three or four colleagues from the school. A handful of uneasy boys and girls, the History Sixth detailed off to attend as a mark of respect. A woman carrying a wreath of evergreens and white roses. There were also a couple of dark-suited men with Hampstead haircuts, representatives of Maunciple's publishers, who made little effort to conceal their hope that they wouldn't miss the next train back to town. Margaret Curteis-Squire didn't show.

Penny had rather thought she might. Her dislike for the man had been very marked. It might be considered only human to come and gloat. To affirm that you were alive and he was dead. Perhaps Margaret was just nicer than most humans. Penny wondered if she really had been carrying Maunciple's manuscript in her bag the morning after Maunciple's death. Whoever had taken it, there was precious little chance of it still being around. It might help to know which of his possible titles Maunciple had settled for in the end. If any. On the other hand, it might not.

Peter did some cousinly gulping as the vicar of the parish read from the prayerbook. She squeezed his arm. The woman with the wreath sobbed. Marius Knight stood with head bowed, big hands clasped in front of him like a sporran. The Headmaster had evidently had a bad night. He kept yawning. Was he the insomniac they were looking for? It seemed extremely unlikely. Penny eyed him narrowly. Shepherd began with S. He might be worth looking into. Various birds about the place made a variety of tuneful noises. The smell of sunbaked leaf was strong. Willowherb sprouted prettily from old stone walls. Butterflies flitted. It was the kind of day that prompted people who were that way inclined to produce anthologies of pastoral poetry.

The clergyman finished his reading and moved ponderously towards the gate of the churchyard. Two men in sunglasses were lounging against the bonnet of a hearse, reading the *Sun*. They would be whisking Maunciple off to the crematorium at Barham for consignment to flames that might not be eternal but would certainly be all-consuming. The mourners looked at each other uneasily. What did one do next? Mr Shepherd settled it by briskly following the vicar. The woman with the wreath laid it tenderly on top of the coffin. There was a card attached to a rose-stem with a piece of green wire. It read: 'To darling Louisa. Always in my thoughts. Agnes.'

Nobody had suggested anything like a wake. After a word with Yeoman, Penny went over to Marius Knight. He turned a face full of sadness on her. His eyes were bloodshot.

'I shall miss him,' he said. 'He was always a good friend to

155

me.'

With a friend like that, Penny hoped he never made a bosom pal. She patted his sleeve for a moment. 'I'm so sorry,' she said.

She arranged with him to take Yeoman back to Canterbury. As they left, a small crimson car drove at enormous speed up to the gate of the churchyard. A saintly man hurried towards them. After a few words with Marius Knight, he ran back to the car and revved noisily away.

Penny told Peter she was taking him out to lunch. They weren't far from one of those East Kent villages that feature on 'This England' calendars. All weathered brick and diamond-paned windows groaning beneath chunks of wisteria. Guaranteed to bring a lump to the throat of an ex-pat at Christmas-time. The pub there put on the kind of lunch that was ideal for loosening the tongue. Especially if the tongue was already loose, like Peter's.

Having collected plates of home-made pigeon-pie from a man who stood behind a glass counter with a large aluminium spoon in his hand, they went outside and sat on a terrace of York stone that overhung a slow-moving stretch of river. If you wanted verdancy, you needed to look no further. Cows hung about at the water's edge. Reeds quivered beneath abundant willows. Swans swam snobbishly up and down. There wasn't a Mother's Pride wrapper as far as the eye could see.

Once Peter had stoked up, using a method based on the block-and-tackle, Penny went all out for the jugular. It was show-down time. The moment of truth. Or a version of it.

'Funny your old friend Margaret didn't come to Mr Maunciple's funeral,' she said. 'If you were right, I mean, and that *was* her you saw the other day in the town.'

'Course I'm right,' Peter said. He sounded truculent. After three whiskies, he was now getting stuck into a fairly choice Beaujolais.

'You'd think she would have, considering you were all once such good friends. When you were young. In the old days.' Penny lingered over the words. She tried not to despise herself.

When you got to Peter's age, and had drunk as much, phrases like that were real tear-jerkers.

'Friends,' said Peter. 'Not on your life. Margaret hated Max's guts. Absolutely hated him.'

'Why was that?'

'She always maintained that he'd deliberately engineered the breakdown of her marriage.'

'Her marriage has broken down?' Penny felt cheated. Were they not talking about the same Margaret after all? She'd been so certain that Mrs Curteis-Squire was the Margaret that Marius Knight had refused to talk about.

'Yes. To Marius.'

'To Marius?' Penny opened her eyes wide. This was pay-dirt. This was the Koh-I-Noor and the Great White Whale rolled into one. 'Marius Knight? And Max broke it up?'

'Mind you,' Peter said, removing a flake of pastry from his chin just before Penny thought she'd have to, 'those May – December marriages often have teething troubles. Margaret swept Marius right off his feet from the moment she arrived at the school, but there was, after all, fifteen years between them.' He gazed at the cows with his fork in the air. His face was knotted with concentration. A piece of pigeon fell on to his plate. 'What the hell was the name of that school?'

'Which school, Peter?'

'Where Marius and Max got jobs after Cambridge. Dammit. Can't remember the simplest things these days. What on earth was its name?' He looked like a Speak-Your-Weight machine trying to work out how many pounds there were in a kilo.

'And Margaret and Marius were actually married?'

Peter supped vigorously at his glass of wine and nodded at the same time. 'Max was as jealous as hell.'

'What did she teach?'

'Physics and chemistry, I believe,' said Peter. 'To the lower school, of course. They wouldn't have trusted a woman with a science subject in the upper school. Not in those days.'

'Physics and chemistry.' The Blackpool illuminations had nothing on Penny.

157

'Quite the little pioneer, was Margaret. For her time. Teaching in a boys' boarding-school. And what was traditionally regarded as a male subject. She gave it up, of course, once she and Marius got married.'

'So she'd know a thing or two about potassium permanganate and Boyle's law, would she?'

Peter grinned evilly at her. 'You know how seductive I always find your pretence of cretinism,' he said. He laid a hand on her knee. He rolled his globular eyes in a manner that might possibly have had results some thirty years back but was now merely obscene.

'Knock it off, Toots,' Penny said. 'I'm a girl. Or have you altered the habits of a lifetime?'

'Christ, no,' said Peter. He stared across the river. 'What was I saying? Oh, yes. Margaret. You see, Max always was a possessive bugger, and he couldn't stand the way this intruding woman had taken his best friend away from him. That's how he saw it, anyway. He told Marius that he'd regret the marriage. Said he was too old, wouldn't be able to satisfy a hot-blooded woman like Margaret. Not after a few years, anyway. She's got a lot of Spanish blood in her, you know.'

'I thought so,' Penny said softly.

'When that didn't work, he started on Margaret. Hung around her. Buttered her up. Drawing her fire, as it were, away from Marius and towards himself. Hoping to make Marius jealous. At first that didn't work either. Then she got pregnant . . .'

He paused, looking out over the water to where three drakes, their heads green as emeralds in the sunshine, were actively engaged in drowning a fourth. He stared rather sadly at Penny. 'So he tried a touch of the Othellos.'

'Not the old Embroidered Handkerchief Caper.'

'Yes.'

'And Mr Knight fell for that Iago shit?'

'I'm afraid so. You must remember that it's one of the oldest, but also one of the most effective tricks in the book. A jealous man is not a rational man.' Peter bit ferociously at a lettuce leaf, most of which fell to the ground beneath the table.

'Max as good as claimed the coming child was his. In view of the way he'd been hanging around Meg, quite a lot of people believed him. People that mattered. It didn't do Marius' reputation any good.'

'Who steals my purse steals trash, huh?'

'Exactly. Marius had always been what one might call an honourable man.' Peter sighed deeply. It was the self-satisfied sigh of someone who has been at great pains to be what one might call a dishonourable man. 'He felt tainted. He felt Margaret was, too. In the end, he told her he found it impossible to go on living with her. He sent her away. We all told him he was insane. Even the most junior boy could see he still adored her, and she him.'

'Poor Margaret.'

'Poor Marius.' Peter brushed at his shirt, where various small pieces of pigeon-pie had lodged in the wrinkles. 'I kept telling him it was only Max being his usual malicious, trouble-making self.'

'An honourable murderer, if you will, for naught he did in hate but all in honour.'

'My dear, how very apt. I think Max hoped that with Margaret out of the way, he and Marius would be able to return to the close friendship they'd enjoyed before she came on the scene.'

'But they didn't?'

'Not for a long time. Marius was shattered by the whole thing. It caused something of a scandal at the school. In the end, he went abroad, teaching for the British Council or something similar. He was in Alexandria, I do remember, because I visited him there. The street-urchins were simply too delectable for words.' He shook his head in reminiscence. 'And some unpronounceable place in Yugoslavia. And Russia. Madly dreary, I must say. The place teemed with Foreign Office drop-outs in ill-fitting suits. Marius didn't come back to England until about eight years ago. I always understood that Max helped him to get his present job at the school here. I say. They had some rather scrumptious-looking desserts inside, didn't they. Don't you think we might indulge?'

159

'When do you ever not?' Penny said. She followed Peter inside and watched him heap gooey things made of chocolate and cream and marrons on to a plate. She spoke censoriously of milk solids and emulsifiers. She mentioned the incidence of heart-disease in the West among males over the age of fifty. She talked of lecithin and reconstituted fats. Peter added something made of cherries and rum to his plate. They went out on to the terrace again.

'Did your cousin ever talk to you about his work?' Penny said.

'Sometimes.'

'Was it possible that the manuscript which is missing might have been going to bring up the whole Marius/Margaret thing?'

Peter spooned several thousand carbohydrates down his throat. 'Why do you imagine that?' he asked. Even with cream on his upper lip, he managed a judge-like severity.

'It seems such a nifty motive for murder. Old wounds being reopened. Margaret's name – thinly disguised, of course – being dragged through the mud again. Anyone might have felt that the thing must be stopped at all costs.'

'Anyone meaning Marius?'

'Possibly.'

Peter might be greedy. He wasn't stupid. 'Penelope,' he said, laying down his spoon to emphasise his seriousness, 'I have been a writer of fiction all my adult life. Had I been gifted with an imagination like yours, who knows to what unimaginable heights I might by now have climbed. Hosting the South Bank Show? Chairman of British Rail? A tax exile in Ireland? There would have been no stopping me.' He wiped his upper lip. 'Don't you think you are carrying your penchant for the macabre just a little too far this time? The doctor says Max died of a coronary. You can't seriously be suggesting that he's wrong. That my oldest friend murdered my only relative.'

'I'm merely suggesting that it's a possibility. Marius seemed rather agitated to me yesterday. When you kept needling him about Margaret.'

'Me? Needling?'

160

'You. Needling. Spearing, even. And that's another thing. What happened to the baby?'

'I don't know. Margaret simply disappeared. Dropped out of our lives. And the baby with her.'

'And Marius has had no contact with her for, what, eighteen years?'

'Not as far as I know.'

'Yet he still gets fighting mad at the very mention of her name. Seems to me his passion is by no means spent.'

'Perhaps he realises that by his own code, he didn't treat her all that honourably.' Peter pulled his nose back and forth. 'Thank God I've always been an utter cad. It makes life so much easier.'

'He had a terrific opportunity to nick the manuscript,' Penny said.

'Nick?'

'Steal, Peter,' said Penny. 'No one would suspect a thing if they saw Marius Knight coming from Maunciple's rooms with papers in his hand. And, as his friend, he presumably had free access.'

A curly-headed boy in granny glasses sculled past them, wearing a white vest banded in navy-blue. The navy-blue had run into the white. His biceps looked as though they had been inflated with a foot-pump. On the opposite bank, another boy in a baseball cap appeared on a bicycle and started yelling through a megaphone.

'Stop messing about, Tim. This isn't the bloody *Wind In The Willows*. Put your back into it, can't you?'

The curly-headed boy held up two fingers. His rowing-shell veered sharply towards the bank. Both he and the boy with the bicycle disappeared round a bend in the river.

'Marius wouldn't hurt a fly,' Peter said.

'He might if the fly wrote a book which told in intimate detail how his marriage was destroyed.' Penny saw again the elegant italic hand and the list of titles. *Time's Eunuch*. It could certainly be said to fit Marius Knight.

'Nonsense.'

'If you don't like that theory, what about this.' Penny rested

161

her elbows on the table and her chin on her hand. 'Let's face it, your cousin wasn't exactly Mr Lovable, was he? Suppose this missing book actually showed that nothing at all had happened. That he'd never seduced Margaret. That the baby was Marius's. That the marriage need never have broken up. Wouldn't that be even more of a motive? Two lives – three, if you count the child's – disrupted out of sheer malice.'

'Yes,' Peter said quietly. He wiped his face with his hand. His eyes sagged. He looked older than he had done two minutes before. 'I think it might.' He made an effort and straightened his shoulders. 'But I don't believe it was.'

Penny remembered Marius Knight admitting he had slipped out during the madrigal concert. He hadn't mentioned that the convenience had been inconveniently closed. Nor, for that matter, had Dominic Austen. Nor Charles Yeoman. Commonly known as Chips. Why hadn't they? Natural delicacy of feeling? A common wish not to admit that, caught short, they had been forced, for the sake of their bladders, to defile holy ground? Or for some other more sinister reason?

And where did Margaret Curteis-Squire fit into all this, if at all?

'Sacred blue,' she said. Hercule Poirot wasn't the only gazebo with brains. Her own little grey cells were standing to attention. And saluting. Peter had just given them something to get excited about, all right. Whatever Yeoman said, she was more than ever convinced that the death of Max Maunciple and the theft of his manuscript were linked.

The field, as far as she was concerned, was still wide open.

162

She dropped Peter back at Ashmole and parked her Porsche next to a little crimson car in the forecourt. A heavy summer heat hung over the school chapel, flattening its gothic exuberances. Latter-day pilgrims sat about under the chestnuts, eating sandwiches or leafing wearily through guidebooks. Boys in boaters and ribboned coats sauntered by on their way to the river. Girls swirled about in dark skirts of Indian cotton. Americans took pictures of them. In a corner of the Great Court, by the souvenir kiosk, two Texans were haggling with a hard-faced kid for the purchase of his boater. They kept saying the folks back home in Dallas would be tickled pink. Penny thought it unlikely. The kid concluded negotiations for the slightly shop-soiled article for a price that, if properly invested, would keep him financially secure for the rest of his days.

On her way to the High Street, Penny passed a bookshop. An assistant kneeled in the window, removing a display of a bestselling paperback that had made it impossible for any normal person to look at a goldfish again without blushing. A pile of glossy large-format books lay waiting to be set up in its place. At the sight of the cover of the top one, Penny's heart jumped. She saw a well-remembered smile. A face made beautiful by the bones underneath. Botticelli tendrils of blonde hair. Marfa. Penny had taken the photograph herself. And all the others in the book. Washington, seen in relation to the women who lived and worked there. Women doing ordinary and extraordinary things. Women who didn't know they were being photographed. Women who were young. Women who were old. Women who weren't beautiful. Women who were.

Perhaps one day she would do the same book from the man's point of view. It would show a very different Washington. She hoped the profits from this one would be good. Once they had been maximised with the aid of Miss Ivory's infallible horse sense, they could be used to buy and distribute some of the thousands of tons of cereal needed in famine-stricken African countries.

In the High Street, she sauntered about. She looked aimless. She wasn't. She paused to examine the pictures in the window of an art gallery. Perhaps this was where David Marriner did his shopping. Across the road, a party of Italian tourists were gesticulating at a ducking-stool. They seemed to think it was an excellent idea. When she returned for the third time to the pedestrianised area, she saw what she was looking for. Margaret Curteis-Squire. In this particular week, it was inevitable that those parents who had travelled to Canterbury for the annual summer rites at the Abbott's School would be congregating here about now. It was four o'clock. Teatime. Penny reckoned the chances were that Margaret had arranged to meet her son. Penny knew she certainly would have done, if he were her son. Every chance she got.

She watched Margaret turn into a tearoom that had packets of fudge in the window. Also ginger cakes that looked home-made, and jars of humbugs. There were several of those seated at the tables inside. They were talking of modern youth and the decline in standards as though they themselves had never harboured a lusty thought in their lives. They wore white collars and suitably striped shirts. They looked like solicitors. Or estate agents. Funny how humbugs were invariably male.

Margaret had found a table at the back.

'Mind if I join you?' Penny said.

Margaret looked up. 'As a matter of fact – ' she began.

' – you do,' said Penny. 'But I won't be awfully long.'

Today Margaret wore a necklace that could have been made out of lizards' eyes. It went well with the black linen dress she wore. There were clusters of lizards' eyes in her ears, too. Black is the colour of mourning. And Max Maunciple had just been consigned to ashes. Knowing what she now did, Penny thought

164

the two facts were unconnected.

'I just wanted to ask you if you were the same Margaret who was once married to Marius Knight,' she said.

Like a badly-constructed robot, Margaret lifted a hand to her throat. Penny had seen her do it before. The intricately-wrought bracelet on her arm fell down towards her elbow. There were three heart-shaped medallions on it, each with a single word engraved in fine copperplate script. *Amor. Vincit. Omnia.* The scar tissue across the inside of her wrists was very white against her tan.

'Why do you want to know?' she said, as though it hurt. Her dark eyes were frightened.

Penny put a hand on her arm. Margaret's flesh was warm and soft, no longer young yet still desirable. And undoubtedly desired. 'Please,' she said. 'I'm not trying to cause you any more trouble. I just need to know some things. Max Maunciple's death wasn't a natural one.'

'That's what I thought,' Margaret said. 'It didn't look quite right.'

'You saw him dead?'

'Yes.'

'You had a motive for killing him,' Penny said.

'What motive?' Margaret's voice made Penny want to clear her throat.

'He was going to tell Marius just who Adam was. Not outright. Through his next book.'

Margaret made a sound that was something like a laugh but much more like a gasp. A woman came up to them in a black nylon dress and a tiny frilled apron. You could tell her feet were killing her. 'Tea and cakes,' she stated, busily writing it down on her pad.

'Not for me,' said Penny. 'I'll have scones.'

'So will I,' Margaret said.

The waitress crossed out what she had written and started again. She breathed. She was something of a breath artist. By the simple act of breathing, she conveyed a great deal, most of it denunciatory.

'And I'll have China tea, please,' said Penny.

The waitress scrubbed at her pad again.

'So will I,' said Margaret.

The waitress breathed some more and clomped away.

'Who *is* Adam?' Margaret said. She looked down at the table as she spoke. There was a high flush along her cheekbones. Her eyelids shone as though they had been oiled.

'Mr Knight's son,' Penny said, guessing. 'The likeness is obvious.'

'To anyone who knows,' said Margaret. She didn't deny it.

'And Mr Knight doesn't.'

'No.'

'But Max Maunciple did.'

'Yes. I don't know how. He'd found out everything.'

Neither woman spoke for a moment. Across the room, Penny could see their waitress picking cakes off a tray with stainless steel tongs, and breathing. Uh-oh.

'I should never have come here; I knew it was dangerous,' said Margaret. 'I've always got out of it in the past. Adam never understood why I never came. But this term, Donald – my husband – had to go to a conference in Singapore. I thought I'd risk it, since it was Adam's last term. I hoped I'd get away without seeing Marius. I suppose it was Peter Corax who told you. I thought I saw him in the town.'

'He only told me because I dragged it out of him.'

Their waitress creaked back with a trayful of green crockery. The steam from their teapot-spout was unmistakably Indian. There was a plate of cakes. Several of them had cream and red stuff issuing from their sides. Margaret didn't seem to notice. Penny did. She decided she'd had enough confrontation for the moment. And a woman who could breathe like that would take some confronting.

'I always understood Marius,' Margaret said suddenly. 'Even when he was telling me to go, I knew exactly why. He felt – besmirched. He could never really believe that I loved him, being so insecure about the difference in our ages. And Max didn't help.' She looked back across eighteen years. Whatever they were like now, they probably hadn't been too good to begin with. Penny poured tea. 'You probably don't know yet how easily a misplaced word, an insult shouted in anger or grief, can become a rock on which a marriage founders. Especially if the marriage contains a partner as introspective as Marius. Had I been older, I would never have gone. I'd have forced him to face the kind of man his so-called friend Max was. I'd have made him see the lies for what they were. But I was young then. The young are always so proud. So sure they can win. When I left, I swore I'd never speak to Marius again, that I'd show him I didn't need him to survive.'

'But you did.' Penny's eyes dropped to Margaret's wrists and then away. 'Survive, I mean.'

'Barely. Almost not. I was pregnant. Jobless. Practically penniless, since I'd refused any help from Marius.' Margaret stirred her tea, although she'd put no sugar in. 'Then I met Donald. He's a doctor. I was in a pretty bad way by then. He put me back together. We got married.'

'And you never got in touch with Mr Knight?'

'Only through solicitors, to arrange a divorce. At first I thought, why should I? Then there seemed no point. I felt that by believing Max rather than me, he'd forfeited any right to know about Adam. Donald adopted him when we married. He thought I was a widow. It was just one of those strange coincidences that Donald had been at Abbott's himself and wanted Adam to come too. By then, I felt less angry about Marius. When I found out he was one of the Housemasters, I asked for Adam to go into his House. It was all he was ever going to have of his son.'

Penny knew that even if Margaret had killed Max, which seemed less likely, the more she talked, she would do nothing about it. He'd done too much damage already to both her and Marius.

Margaret was still talking. 'When I got back into the atmosphere of a big school again, after all these years, the past came back to me so vividly,' she said. 'My first teaching job after Oxford. Those few months with Marius. And Max. I wanted to talk to Max. I thought – I don't know what I thought. Perhaps that I could make him see what he'd done to us all. The misery he'd caused. Especially to Marius. I've got Adam. And

Donald. Marius has nothing.' She smiled rather shyly at
Penny. 'There was a poem he always used to quote when we
were young, to explain how I had transformed his life. After all,
he was getting on for forty when we met.' She cleared her
throat. '*Birds build – but not I build; no, but strain, time's eunuch, and
not breed one work that wakes. Mine, O thou lord of life, send my roots
rain.*' There were tears in her eyes. 'I was his rain.'

What a bastard Maunciple had been, thought Penny. To
discover, perhaps by idly leafing through his friend's manuscript, that he *had* bred one work which waked, and that Max
had deprived him of it, was a factor likely to turn a far more
temperate man than Marius Knight into a murderer.

'What happened when you got to Mr Maunciple's rooms on
the night of the concert?' Penny said.

Margaret tilted her head to one side. The tears seemed to
have dried up. There was suddenly something rather steely
about her. Perhaps Max Maunciple had seen that steel.
Perhaps that was why he'd considered the title: *Beauty Is Skin
Deep*.

'I was at the concert,' Margaret said. 'You told me you saw
me there.'

'There was no wind at all that night,' said Penny. 'Not the
slightest breeze. Adam's music stayed right where it was
supposed to. The whole time.'

Margaret did something rather curious with her lips.
Probably what the books call pursing them. Penny had never
been quite sure what it meant. She'd certainly never had a
purse that looked like a mouth. Or vice versa. Margaret drank
some of her tea. She poked at a cake with a two-pronged fork.
She took a breath deep enough to lift her shoulders.

'All right,' she said. 'I did leave the cloisters that night. As
soon as I saw Max wasn't there, I realised it was my chance to –
to have it out with him. It seemed quite safe. I wouldn't tell him
my present surname. Nor my present circumstances. There
was no way he need connect me with Adam.'

'What happened?' Penny repeated.

'When I got to his rooms, I knocked. Nobody came. I pushed
open the door and went in. He was lying back in his chair with

168

his mouth open. Dead to the world.' Margaret gave a queer little laugh. 'I went over and shook him. Having screwed myself up to it, I was determined to have my say. He fell against the arm of the chair like a – in such a loose kind of way that I realised he must be dead.' She sipped her tea. 'I felt completely cool about it. Not shocked. Not frightened. Not even glad.'

'What did you do?'

'Nothing. Absolutely nothing.'

'Why not?'

'I couldn't afford to. If the police had come, they'd have asked me questions. I couldn't risk Marius finding out that I was Adam's mother.'

'Because of Adam?'

'Because of all of them. Marius. Adam. And particularly Donald. You can see what a betrayal it would be if he knew that Adam's own father was his Housemaster. Yet Marius had some rights, too.'

She twisted the ruby on her right hand, staring out of the teashop window. A party of Asiatic nuns wimpled past, almond eyes black beneath the white bands across their foreheads. Christianity and the mysterious East had always seemed to Penny as incongruous as a boxer in ballet shoes. Though proselytising was one of the tenets of the Church, she had never been able to comprehend the degree of arrogance that could declare all other religions wrong. Never would.

'Do you have a job?' she said.

Margaret looked puzzled. 'I work sometimes as a receptionist at Donald's surgery,' she said. 'Why?'

Penny didn't answer.

'Miss Wanawake,' Margaret said. 'I understand that the official verdict on Max's death was that it was caused by heart-failure, brought on by excessive consumption of alcohol. Yet, if I understand your implications correctly, you think not only that he was murdered, but that he was poisoned. Possibly by some undetectable compound. Possibly by me.'

'Uh –'

'Don't you think that your imagination is running away with you?'

169

Sometimes this occurred to Penny herself. She wasn't going to admit it. 'Someone had emptied gin down Mr Maunciple's kitchen sink,' she said. 'The obvious assumption is that it contained something lethal and the murderer wanted to hide any traces of it. You not only had a motive, Mrs Curteis-Squire, you also had the means.' And the strength of character, though Penny didn't point that out.

'How am I supposed to have given Max this poisoned gin? I spent most of the afternoon and early evening skulking about in my hotel-room, where I couldn't bump into Marius.'

'You could have seen Mr Maunciple leaving the Great Court round seven. Most of the hotel bedrooms look out over it. You could easily have sneaked out and into his rooms. They're only a few yards from the hotel.'

'I am not,' Margaret said, 'a person who sneaks.' She seized the teapot and poured herself another cup of tea. It was among the more aggressive acts Penny had ever witnessed.

'What made you think Maunciple was going to spill the beans about Adam?' she said.

Margaret looked agitated. Her earrings shook. 'I saw his manuscript on a table as I was leaving. I had a quick look through it.' She lifted her teacup and put it down again. 'It was horrible. He was a hateful man. Quite hateful. Even though he was dead I wanted to – to spit on him. Mutilate him in some way.'

'Nasty, huh?'

'Filthy. Loathsome. He'd used our story, all right. Marius's and mine. Anyone who knew would have no difficulty in identifying us. I can just imagine how Donald would have felt, reading it. And my poor Marius. But even worse was the way he'd interwoven it in the vilest way with the death of some girl in the States. Her family would have suffered horribly when the book came out.'

Penny looked at an unappetising chocolate éclair which lay like a leprous finger on a plate between them. 'Was there anything to do with health farms in it?' she asked.

'Health farms?' Margaret seemed to be having trouble concentrating.

170

'Those places where they charge a small fortune to starve you to death.'

'Obviously I didn't have time to read it from cover to cover, but nothing leaped from the page. Not to do with health farms.'

'Did you take the manuscript with you?'

'I certainly intended to. I heard someone downstairs, pulling at the front door. I'd had trouble opening it myself. I tried to grab the typescript but half of it fell onto the floor. I didn't dare waste time picking it up. The last thing I wanted was to be found there. Especially with a dead body lying there. Actually, I was terrified it might be Marius.'

'So you left it and slipped across the passage into the kitchen.'

'How do you know?'

'It was the obvious thing to do. Besides, I smelled your perfume. Hermès.'

Margaret bit her lip. 'Whoever it was went straight into Max's room. I got outside as fast as I could. I wish I'd taken that manuscript with me. I really do.'

'If it's any comfort, whoever did must have destroyed it by now,' Penny said. 'There couldn't be any other reason for taking it.' Or could there? One of the other possible Maunciple titles had been *Told By An Idiot*.

'Maybe not.' Margaret was twisting her ring some more. And her mouth.

'Was anyone around outside when you left?'

'Quite a few people. There were other things going on that night, apart from the madrigal concert. One of the school bands was playing jazz somewhere. I could hear it. And there was a House play. If you mean did I see someone loitering suspiciously, carrying a blue bottle marked with a skull and crossbones, I'm afraid the answer's no. Anyway, I had rather a bad reaction when I got outside. Death isn't something I'd seen before. I really wasn't taking much in.'

Adam appeared beside their table. So did the waitress. She seemed to have forgotten about her feet. Which was understandable. Adam was very beautiful.

'Tea and cakes,' she said. She wrote it down.

'Not for me,' Penny said. 'I just ordered China tea and

171

scones.'

'So did I,' said Margaret.

Penny stood up. She leaned down and touched Margaret on the shoulder. 'I'll see you again, I expect,' she said. 'And please don't worry.'

'I will,' said Margaret.

Adam brushed at his cheeks with his eyelashes. He seemed more boyish than when she last saw him. 'Perhaps my mother would bring you up to my study for a cup of coffee, or something,' he said.

'I don't think I can manage that, darling,' Margaret said quickly.

'Great idea,' said Penny. She certainly wouldn't have wanted her own mother around for the type of something his eyes promised. But perhaps she was misreading the signals.

'I'll look forward to it,' said Adam. However much you shied away from clichés, a young god was what he looked like. He took her hand. Penny sucked in her stomach so hard it thudded against her backbone. She figured she only had about seventy years to go before she stopped being susceptible to the charm of young males. Today, it seemed like an awful long time.

She walked towards the till. The waitress shuffled after her. Penny paid her bill. She didn't tip the waitress. In the street, she saw two tall young men standing together with their heads bent. One was Yeoman. The other was Dominic Austen. Only Lot's wife after she'd looked back could not have wondered what they were talking about. Especially after the antipathy they'd displayed towards each other. Perhaps Austen was sounding Yeoman out about the possibility of a job as Poet-in-residence to the boys of the Detroit Police Department, in case the North Carolina position fell through. Perhaps he was telling Yeoman where he could buy a pair of maroon dungarees. Perhaps Yeoman was advising him to invest in a shredding machine.

Before she could drift over and find out, they both nodded several times and parted in different directions. Austen went towards the High Street. Yeoman went towards the cathedral. By the time she got there herself, he had disappeared.

FOURTEEN

In her room, Penny hung up the Kenzo-designed white dress and cape she had worn for Maunciple's obsequies. She took off her white shoes. She rubbed at the grass-stains on their high heels. White gives off the purest vibrations. Like peace. Like harmony. Grass-stains didn't help.

She wondered where Yeoman had gone. And when he would go. Had she deflected him from his first avowed intent to be a pilgrim? By now he ought to be communing with Julian of Norwich and the Cloud of Unknowing. Or standing at Glastonbury, soaking up history through the soles of his beaded moccasins. Instead, he was still here.

She took a shower. She wrapped herself in a bathtowel and rubbed steam off the bathroom mirror. She asked herself if Yeoman really needed so many damned vitamins as she replaced the ones that had fallen into the handbasin. Tonight, one of the featured entertainments laid on by the school was a reading of his poems by Dominic Austen. Yeoman had said there was no way he was going to miss seeing Austen make a klutz of himself reading that bullshit through a megaphone. Penny had agreed to go too. Not for the same reason. The alternative was a Chris Barber Jazz Band concert.

She picked up the phone. She dialled the number of her home in Chelsea. It rang and rang. From the first ring she knew the house was empty. As always, she felt the tremor between the shoulder-blades that was all she would allow herself of anxiety. Of *course* Barnaby was trustworthy, she told herself, replacing the receiver. She lay back on the bed and watched the early evening shadows outline the decorated stonework of the chapel.

It was so close it was almost in the room. The slanting sun struck brilliance from the bottles on the windowseat and the silver back of her hairbrush on the dressing-table. Of *course* he was. Yet to a thief – even a gentleman-thief like Barnaby – there must come a time when he made the definitive haul. When the temptation to keep it for himself became too much. Was this the time? She tried to remember what it had said in the paper about the break-in at Pensbury Lodge, nr. Andover. Several hundred thousand pounds' worth of jewellery taken. And detectives still checking the inventory of Mr Almouni's extensive collection of Oriental art. Penny had a feeling they would find some of that missing, too. Not much. Just one, maybe two, of the choicest pieces. And no one but Barnaby would see them again for a very long time.

She re-dialled her Chelsea number. You never knew: she might have dialled a wrong number the first time. Again she heard the empty hollow ring. She could imagine the sound beating in the white-painted hall, rippling against the shiny black-painted doors and on up the finely-curving staircase with its thick white carpet. No Barnaby. And no Miss Ivory, either. She was doubtless swapping fetlocks and form with like-minded members of the RGA, not giving a damn about the landscape outside the windows of their chartered coach with integral self-flushing toilet. Not unless it was a landscape with horses.

She dialled once more. Dammit. Did Barnaby know what a pain in the ass he was, not answering like that? Yeoman's hold-all was on the bed and she pulled it nearer with one hand while with the other she held the receiver close to her ear, willing Barnaby to answer. He didn't. She put the receiver down. OK, Barnaby Midas. That's your lot. See if I ever ring you again.

The hold-all was empty except for a plastic tub of vitamin pills. It must have got lost in the crush. Leyland Pharmaceuticals again. Either he had shares in the company, or the company had cornered the Michigan market in vitamins. Super Vitamin E, it said on the outside. 100 iu. Active Ingredients: d-Alpha Tocopheryl Acetate 100 iu. How many vitamins a day could a person ingest, for heaven's sake?

174

Admittedly Yeoman looked good. But he'd have looked good in a diving-suit. She peeked inside. Glistening red capsules. Each and every one stuffed full of d-Alpha Tocopheryl Acetate. Yum, yum.

Bells jangled. Five o'clock. And all's well. Or nearly all. She sat on the edge of the bed and considered. With the new motorway, she could reach Dover in twenty minutes or less. Plenty of time to check out the *Mary M*. Having established a connection between Marriner and Daguerre, she wanted to find out just what the connection was. There'd been nothing suspicious at all in Marriner's flat except the flat itself. The boat might be more rewarding. She wasn't worried that Marriner would be on board. Tomorrow was the last day of term, and this evening he would have to be on duty here at the school doing things more important than smuggling drugs. Like clipping boys round the ear. Writing reports. Getting chalk dust from under his nails. Pedagogical things. She wrote a note for Yeoman and put it on the pillow. Although all of Maunciple's titles might fit the Margaret/Marius story she'd heard an hour ago, she couldn't say the same about the Marriner/Daguerre thing. Except perhaps *Far Above Rubies*. Besides, if Margaret was to be believed, the manuscript had contained no reference to drugs. Yet there was unfinished business here. She was determined to finish it.

It actually took her fourteen minutes to get to Dover. The town sparkled as though someone had dusted it with glitter. France shimmered on the horizon, as indistinct as pearlised nail-varnish. She found a parking-place near the Wellington Docks. The harbour-master wasn't in his little office but she walked towards the pontoons at a pace that conveyed a general air of knowing exactly where she was going while at the same time being slow enough for her to suss out the whereabouts of the *Mary M*. Just in case he was watching her from a crow's-nest or something. She looked for a Westerley Centaur. With red spray dodgers. Almost at the end of the quay, she found it, lying five boats out. She climbed over the decks of the intervening four, smiling pleasantly at the retired naval gentleman enjoying an early gin-and-tonic over *The Times*.

175

From a nearby Moody, someone skeined a length of rope between thumb and elbow, watching her suspiciously. Man or woman? It was impossible to tell.

The hatch-cover of the *Mary M* was padlocked with a hefty bit of salt-stained galvanised iron. There'd be no fooling about with a credit card on this one. She took the cuticle-pusher from her manicure set and pulled off the tortoise-shell handle. Even using the very latest design in lock-picks, it took her considerably longer to open it than it would have done with a key. The creature on the Moody put down its rope in a neat coil and glared through its blue-rimmed glasses at her. Perhaps it was male, after all, despite its large bosom. If you could have a beer-belly, why not beer-boobs?

Penny waved charmingly at it as the padlock yielded. She dropped down through the hatch into the main cabin. It was the standard cruiser design. Neat little galley. Gimbelled stove with two rings. Comfortable saloon lined with cushioned bunks. Two more bunks in the forepeak. The head.

It didn't take her long to shake it down. As well as the more obvious places, she checked the cockpit lockers, the sailbags, the Ajax container beneath the little sink. She flashed a torch into the engine compartment. She searched the head, feeling behind the mirror, looking inside the sea-toilet. She hated the way it sloshed about. In the other cabin, none of the woodwork seemed movable. She lifted the cushions from the bunks, undid the zipped covers and looked inside. She checked the lockers underneath. Nothing.

What exactly was she hoping to find? What did X millions of pounds worth of drugs look like? Was she after a gallon-drum of white powder? A gross of empty Aspirin bottles? A twenty-year supply of condoms ready to be filled with heroin and swallowed? She honestly didn't know. Ignorance might be bliss but it wasn't a lot of help.

She crawled head-first to the end of the righthand quarter-berth, fighting the urge to scream. Claustrophobia. Put a sack over Penny's head and she'd defend to the death her right to get out of it as fast as possible. That was why she couldn't dive. Jump, yes. But ask her to get into a swimming-pool head-first,

176

and her toes refused to uncurl from the edge.

She patted the wooden walls of the berth. There was a bump. She froze. The boat rocked infinitesmally. Someone had come aboard. Someone who didn't want to broadcast the fact. What should she do? Stay there with her butt sticking out, hoping they wouldn't notice her? Or wriggle out as quickly as she could and take it on the chin? Whatever 'it' might be. Which she'd lay even money was David Marriner. She remembered his thyroid eyes and decided to wriggle. What the hell was he doing here? He ought to be at school.

There was another bump. A second person had climbed carefully aboard. Anybody want to bet it wasn't Daguerre? Nobody did.

'. . . cking black bitch,' she heard someone whisper. Penny tutted. How'd you like a guy who's not only a pusher but a racist as well? And some of his best customers were probably black. Some people had no business sense. She leaned against the chart-table and felt behind her for the heavy torch that had been lying there.

A pair of legs came backwards down the teak steps into the cabin. With it came the rest of David Marriner. She recognised him immediately. He had the fine clear eyes of a successful con-man. Or language teacher. He could have been carved out of solid adamant. Penny lifted the torch. It was heavy, yes. But unlikely to do much damage. David Marriner didn't look like the sort who could be felled by a rubber torch. Might as well try chopping logs with a glass hatchet.

Marriner stopped in front of her, brutal as the Barbican.

'My right arm has been registered as a lethal weapon,' she said. She had as much hope of stopping him with that one as CND had of banning cruise missiles.

'Let's see your licence,' he said. He was openly sneering. He clearly didn't believe her.

Another pair of legs appeared on the steps. She'd have recognised those tight jeans anywhere. The cabin was getting an overcrowded feel and Marriner moved further in to make more room for Daguerre. When the false Frenchman turned round, Penny saw that he was now cleanshaven. She shook her

177

head.

'*C'est magnifique mais ce n'est pas Daguerre,*' she said. 'What was it, one of those clip-on jobs?'

'Shut the hell up,' said Daguerre, 'before I blow your brains right out through your black asshole.'

He seemed considerably less insouciant than usual. If insouciant had ever been the right word. He ran a hand over his short dark hair as though wiping the surface clean. He used his left hand. His right hand held a gun. A squat Saturday Night Special. Penny knew very little about guns, except that they were dangerous. She didn't hold with them. Not as offensive weapons. Fine for wowing schoolkids in museums. Or as demonstrations of the gunsmith's art. Pretty nasty any other way. Anyone who'd seen what a gun could do to the human frame would feel the same way. Correction. Any sensitive person. From where Penny was standing, Daguerre looked damned short on sensitivity.

'Know what's wrong with this business?' he said to Marriner. The look he gave Penny was a long way from warm.

'The canteen lunches,' suggested Penny. She tried her Shirley Temple grin. It must have been ready for its ten-thousand mile service. She just couldn't get it to start.

'The goddam busybodies,' Daguerre said. 'That's what's wrong with it.'

'If it's not the Customs, it's the amateur bloody know-alls,' agreed Marriner.

'I can break your wrist with one lightning kick of my leg,' said Penny. You had to keep trying, didn't you?

'Shit, man,' said Daguerre. 'I'm so scared, think I'm gonna have to take a tranquiliser.' He must have thought she was lying.

'There are men with broken wrists all over England at this very moment. Ask them if you don't believe me,' Penny said.

She pressed back against the chart-table. She wished it would yield and give her more room. She wished Daguerre wouldn't aim his gun directly at her stomach. Boy, did she hate guns. They were so final. There was no arguing with a gun. Especially in a place this small. Maybe that was why poison

178

was supposed to be a woman's weapon. It gave the victim just that little edge on certainty. She wished, too, that Marriner wasn't coming towards her with a bit of rope in his hand. There was nowhere she could go. Sometimes she longed to be little and cute. A pocket-sized Venus. Now was one of the times. She might then just conceivably have been able to scuttle up the ladder past Daguerre, hop over the five boats between here and the pontoon, race towards the gates, jump into her car and head back to Canterbury before he could gun her down. On the other hand, she might just conceivably have not.

Marriner grabbed her. There was no point resisting him. The gun saw to that. He tied her wrists together behind her back with the skill of a man who knows that if he gets his knots wrong he could end up drifting into the Gulf Stream. Neither he nor Daguerre seemed worried that she might scream for help. She was grateful for that. The last thing she wanted at this moment was some foul rag stuffed down her throat. The first thing was a bourbon on the rocks.

'How about a drink, fellas,' she said. 'Then we could talk this thing over in a civilised fashion.' She was quite prepared to pass up the rocks if they were out of ice.

'Any talking you do's gonna be to the fishes,' Daguerre said quietly. He wiped his hair again. With his left hand. The gun remained steady, its primary target Penny's bladder. Which reminded her. Damn. Don't start thinking about that.

'Hey, bet you lifted that line out of *Moby Dick*,' she said. He stared at her coldly.

'What're we gonna do with her?' he said.

'Put me in the scuppers with the hosepipe on me,' Penny said helpfully. If she kept talking, maybe they wouldn't notice the way her teeth were trembling.

'There's not much we can do, now,' Marriner said. 'I've got to get back to school. I shouldn't be here at all. If I hadn't seen her greasing down the motorway at a thousand miles an hour, I wouldn't be.' He knelt and began to tie Penny's legs together. Which cut them out as defence mechanisms. Shucks.

'Lucky for us you did,' said Daguerre. 'Christ knows what she might have found if we hadn't got here.'

179

She must have missed something. If she ever got the chance to find out what, and where, she'd pass the information on to Mr Greenhill.

'Very lucky,' Marriner said. 'But like I say, I've got to get back to Canterbury. The Head Man's having his usual cocktail party for the staff, and I have to show up. If I want to keep my job. And make no mistake, I do.' He looked up at Penny from where he crouched at her feet, being efficient with the rope, and smiled. 'After all, it's such bloody good cover.'

She wondered whether falling on top of him would crush him to death. That would leave only Daguerre and his gun to deal with. Tied up as she was, it shouldn't present too much of a problem. For Daguerre.

'Hope you don't plan on *my* staying around to guard her,' Daguerre said. 'I got an important contact to meet in London.' He glanced at the thick black hairs of his wrist. Somewhere among them nestled a razor-thin watch. It went very nicely with his lips. 'Christ. I'm gonna miss my train if I don't move.'

He glared at Penny. He looked unfriendly. Penny decided the word she really wanted was louche, not insouciant at all. There was nothing like a thorough grounding in modern languages when you were looking for the *mot juste*.

'Are you taking a sample with you?' Marriner said.

'Natch.'

Daguerre went over to the other side of the cabin. A white opaque semi-sphere of plastic hung from the bulkhead. Any casual observer would have taken it for a lamp. Damn. If she'd been able to turn on the engine, she could have tested the lights. Then she'd have seen this was only a dummy. Daguerre unscrewed it carefully and carried it like a bowl to the galley-sink. Inside, Penny saw the proof she'd been looking for. A number of see-through bags plumply full of white powder. The way you read about in the papers. Daguerre got another plastic bag from a drawer and poured some of the powder into it. He screwed it up and twisted a wire tie round the top to secure it. He put it into his pocket.

'Just like that?' Marriner said. He had a greedy look on his face. 'That's practically pure smack.'

180

'You don't know squat,' Daguerre said. 'Cut this any more and it'll only be fit for flea-powder. You trying to tell me my business, or what? Just you stick to sailing the goddam boat, OK, and let me attend to the tricky stuff.' He sounded offensive. He looked it, too.

David Marriner was offended. You could tell from the way he went red. And the way he shoved Penny onto one of the cushioned bunks which ran along either length of the cabin. She was helpless to stop herself falling hard against the bulkhead. She half-lay, half-sat, her cheek stinging. She hadn't been this incapable since she left the womb. She felt fairly hopeless, as well. If they were aiming to leave her there tied up overnight, they'd certainly gag her as well. There were lots of things she liked in her mouth. Gags weren't any of them. And she was fresh out of that cute James Bond shit. No watches that turned into self-manipulating rope-cutters. No jet-propelled socks that would shoot her out through the hatch and on to dry land. Not even a simple earring that sent out a distress rocket when touched by a sweating finger. Which was what all eight of hers were doing.

Marriner started rummaging through a drawer in the galley. He came towards her with a tea-towel in his hand. It was made of Irish linen. It had a map of Cornwall printed on it, showing the places of historical interest.

'I've got sinus trouble,' Penny said quickly. 'Gag me, and I could drown in post-nasal drip.'

'Terrific,' said Marriner. 'That'll save us a lot of trouble.' He tried to stuff the towel in Penny's mouth but there was too much of it. He pulled out what he'd got in. He looked at it. He might be a whizz with knots but he obviously didn't know a thing about gags.

'Fa Chrissakes,' snapped Daguerre. He took the towel and folded it diagonally. He pulled it across Penny's mouth and tied both ends tightly at the back of her head. Her lips were stretched against her gums. Her teeth hung down over the edge of the towel and stuck up underneath. She felt like one of Shergar's foals having its teeth inspected prior to auction. Would anyone pay hundreds of thousands of pounds for her?

181

She doubted it. Not the way she took fences, anyway.

Marriner pulled her up from the bunk and took her in his arms. Given a Palm Court orchestra, they could have danced. Except he didn't have dancing in mind. He picked her up. He didn't even stagger. He carried her over to the oilskin locker and plonked her down inside. She fell, banging her head hard against the curve of the boat. She sagged as though stunned. The door clicked shut behind her. The locker was like a vertical coffin with a porthole in it. She braced herself upright and peered out. Nobody was likely to see her face against the thick glass. Especially with the sun going down behind the roofs of Dover. It was one of the few occasions when she could see the advantage of being white. Someone might have noticed her then. The boat tied alongside the *Mary M* was called *The Busted Flush*. Very original. Somehow she didn't think Travis MacGee was on board. Not with the hatch padlocked and canvas covers lashed over the tiller. Perhaps it wasn't entirely bad. She didn't think she could have coped with old Trav's sexist brand of therapy right then.

In the main cabin, she could hear the two men talking. 'I think she's safe in there,' Marriner was saying.

'She better be,' Daguerre replied. 'At least until we can put out to sea later on, and dump her.'

Penny was appalled at the lack of emotion in his voice as he said this. There was no denying she was frightened. Not Panic City. Not yet. But definitely Panic Hamlet. She struggled with the knots which tied her wrists. There wasn't the slightest give.

'Look,' Marriner said uneasily. 'I'm not really into violence.'

'You're into money, right? Then you're into violence,' said Daguerre. 'And if you're not into violence, what was that crap you were giving me about your Army service. Thought you said you'd killed dozens in your time.'

'That was different. That was on active service. I couldn't kill someone in cold blood.'

'You better get used to believing you could. That you have to,' Daguerre said. 'Look. I can catch the last train back tonight. Should be here just after midnight. Can you get away from your school then?'

182

'I think so.'

'And better check the tide-tables or whatever the hell they're called. I want to offload that soul sister just as soon's I can. I don't like leaving her here.'

Penny didn't like being left. She'd tell them so, straight out, if they'd let her.

'Even if she got out of the locker, which she won't, she's still got to get those knots undone,' Marriner said. 'I can guarantee she won't.'

'My feeling is, we should put a bullet in her right now,' said Daguerre.

Penny's feeling was that they shouldn't. She didn't think they were likely to consult her. Behind the tea-towel, she groaned faintly.

'If you think you're firing guns about in my boat, you can damn well think again,' Marriner said. 'A bullet would go right through the hull. That really would make us seaworthy.'

'There's not much else we can do, except leave her,' said Daguerre slowly. 'We can't take her with us. Not without attracting attention. She doesn't exactly blend in with the scenery, does she? And it would be far too dangerous to kill her now and leave a body.'

'Quite,' said Marriner. 'If anything happened to delay us, we'd have a hell of a lot of explaining to do. If she was found, I mean.'

Daguerre laughed nastily. 'But it would be easy to explain why she's trussed up like a Sumo wrestler's nuts, huh?'

'We could always say it was a game or something.'

'What the hell kind of game involves tying dames up and shoving them in a closet?' snarled Daguerre. 'Jesus. You English really are sick. Who'd you think would buy that piece of crap, if anyone *did* get on board?'

'Relax,' said Marriner. 'After all, she was trespassing. She'd picked the lock. We could always say she'd gone berserk and we'd had to restrain her. Or that we went to fetch the police but got held up. Anyway, who's likely to come aboard. Everything will be padlocked. No visible signs of life. And it'll be dark soon.'

'Still don't like it,' muttered Daguerre.

'Got a better suggestion?' Marriner sounded sulky.

Penny had several. She didn't think she'd be given the chance to put them forward. She didn't think she'd ben given the chance to do anything. She wriggled her wrists about as much as she could, which was not at all. She wished she'd told Yeoman where she was going. All she'd said was that she'd be back in time for Austen's poetry reading. She wished she wasn't here.

'Can you beat it?' she heard Daguerre say. 'First that old gimp in Canterbury, butting his nose in, telling me I shouldn't be allowed into the goddam country and he'd tell the authorities if he saw me again. Now this black cutie.'

'Old gimp,' Marriner said. 'You don't mean Max Maunciple, do you?'

'Maunciple? Some damned name like that. Walks around in funny shoes. That the guy?'

'Yes.'

'Yeah, well, I asked some kid in fancy dress who was hanging around. I'm pretty sure he said Maunciple.'

'He's dead,' Marriner said.

'Hey, that's great,' said Daguerre. You could tell he had the right impulses. 'You mean someone already did the job for us?'

'It was a heart-attack,' Marriner said.

There was silence for a while. Penny could hear the two of them moving about. Then Daguerre spoke again. 'Come on, come on. I gotta get going. If I miss this guy, we could be out a helluva lotta dough.'

'We can't have that, can we?' Marriner said.

'What about that skylight gizmo up front,' Daguerre said. 'Just in case Miss Ebony breaks out.'

'The forward hatch? We'll lash the liferaft on top,' Marriner said. 'Won't take more than a couple of minutes.'

'Jesus,' said Daguerre. 'If I miss my train.'

'I wish you'd stop moaning,' Marriner said. 'I haven't got much time, either. But it's better to be safe. Look. Want me to give her another crack on the head?'

'Thought you said you weren't into violence. OK, then.

184

Give her a tap. But watch it, for Godsake.'

Penny slumped to the floor of the locker. She snored a little, breathing shallowly through parted lips. She let her head loll like an abandoned ventriloquist's dummy. The locker door opened. 'She's still out for the count,' Marriner said. 'Must really have knocked herself out.'

Suddenly, his foot connected with Penny's ribs. If it hadn't been for the tea-towel, she would have gasped aloud. She couldn't help giving a violent jerk. He seemed to think it was the normal reaction. He closed the door again. She shuddered with pain. She felt nauseous. She used yoga techniques to force herself to relax, to think of nothing. Especially not about being nauseous. Gagged like this, if she threw up now, she was dead.

'What about the window?' Daguerre said. 'If she got free, could she . . . ?'

'The ports?' Marriner laughed. 'You try breaking one.' Daguerre obviously didn't bother. 'You take the tool-chest,' Marriner went on. 'I'll bring the cutlery. We can stow them in the cockpit until we get back. And there's a penknife in the chart-drawer. Get that as well. If she does free herself, she won't be able to get out of here, believe me.'

Penny heard the hatch slide shut and the sound of the padlock snapping to. She heard activity overhead as the two men lashed the liferaft valise across the forward hatch. There was the tread of feet on decking. A sudden lurch as first one, then the other, climbed on to the next boat. For a few seconds, the *Mary M* rocked. Then it was still. There was the faint sound of water moving against the hull. Voices raised in friendly greeting. Two good ole boys, sailing buddies, pals, saying goodnight to the other sailing folk. It was so touching, it brought tears to the eyes. And bile to the stomach. She felt all choked up. If she didn't get this map of Cornwall off her face, that was exactly what she'd be. Terminally. She made herself lie still. Any movement on a craft this small would be noticed if they looked back. She wanted them to think she was still unconscious. She waited.

FIFTEEN

Penny counted slowly to nine hundred. Not only did it keep her mind off her various discomforts, it also meant approximately fifteen minutes had passed. She eased herself upwards against the side of the boat and peered through the porthole. Her side felt stiff. There was no sign of Daguerre or Marriner. By squinting sideways, she had a fine view of the androgynous creature in the blue-rimmed specs waddling away along the quayside. A woman's bum, she decided. But definitely a man's walk. Ah well. What was gender anyway, but an arbitrary label devised for the convenience of civil servants?

When she judged it safe, she stood up on tiptoe and got the edge of the thick steel screw of the porthole in under the bottom edge of the tea-towel. She yanked her head sideways. There was much more give in Irish linen than there was in rope. She felt the knot behind her head tighten as the gag loosened. The skin round her mouth was tender. Her teeth were cold. She yanked some more. She stood tall and lifted the gag free of the porthole screw. After a bit of work with tongue and chin, the tea-towel slipped down around her neck. *Quel* utter relief. For a moment, she closed her eyes. Last time she'd been gagged had been in Zaire. For thirty-six hours, she'd been held by guerillas in the back of a stolen army jeep. She could still remember the pain of her constricted tongue. The feel of coarse cloth against the inside of her mouth. The exact texture of a combat boot only inches away from her nose. Being gagged was really the pits.

Her next task was to get out of the locker. With her hands tied behind her, she couldn't do much about the catch on the locker-door. She hoped that the door of the head, opposite, would also be shut. Otherwise she was liable to drown to death in the Lavac bowl. She threw herself against the door. It sprang open. She fell against the door of the head, which had been shut, thank God.

She hopped into the main cabin and sat down on one of the bunks. The ports were the obvious way out. If she could break one, she could saw away at the ropes around her wrists and ankles, using the broken edge. But she knew as well as Marriner that since they'd been built to withstand the onslaught of tempestuous seas in a Force Ten gale, they were unlikely to yield to the onslaught of Penny Wanawake's Adidas trainers. Even if they were the ones with green flashes. Besides, there was no way she could get enough purchase to swing her legs against them.

Although she knew it was useless, she hopped awkwardly about, looking for something she could conceivably cut the ropes on. She edged up to the drawers in the galley and pulled them open. Hop. Hop. Poetry in motion. There was nothing. Except matches. A potato masher. A burst teabag. Three pieces of string. An Irish linen tea-towel showing the historic places of Devon. She slammed the drawer shut with her knees.

She backed up to the chart-drawer and pulled that open. Pencils. Parallel rulers. Dividers. Three cocktail stirrers made of translucent red plastic. A splay-bristled toothbrush. There must be a way to cut the ropes which were biting into her ankles and wrists. She just had to work out what it was. For all his unusual sexual tendencies, Barnaby had never been into discipline and bondage. She might have enjoyed the present situation better if he had. She forced herself to concentrate. She did something she had sworn she would never do. Not ever. She thought back to the time she had agreed to crew for a friend in the Fastnet Race. Jesus. The mere memory made her shudder. Three days in a forty-footer, with a bunch of men who never seemed to stop farting. It had been hell out there.

She looked at the bunk along one side of the cabin. Underneath were the bilges. Storage space for things that didn't mind getting wet. She hopped over and pulled off the long cushion which served as both mattress and seating.

187

Underneath was a stretch of plasticised ply. It had two eighteen-inch square covers set into it, each with a finger-hole. Backing up, and bending her knees to get down that far, she felt around for the hole of one with her bound hands, then lifted it out. The space it left revealed the inside of the hull. And lots of canned food. The usual yachtsman's fare. Baked beans. Tinned stew. Diced vegetables. Tomatoes. Open them up, shove them into a pan, stir them round with a wooden spoon, and you had the sort of gourmet cooking that would make a maggot gag but kept round-the-world sailors circumnavigating.

The hull of a Westerley Centaur is made of fibreglass. GRP, officially. Glass Reinforced Plastic. GRP is lethal stuff. In a fibreglass boat, the wind isn't the only thing like a whetted knife. Where GRP is likely to come into contact with human flesh, the makers smooth it down and give it a gel coat. Where it isn't, they don't. Inside the bilges is one of the places they reckon the human body is unlikely to spend much time.

With considerable difficulty, Penny lay down on her back on the uncovered bunk. She drew her knees up to her chest. Her bound arms hung down into the bilge through the eighteen-inch-square hole. It was the kind of operation your average bed-of-nails man would have demanded danger money for. Gingerly, she felt around with her fingertips for a sharp edge. When she found it, she carefully began to work the ropes back and forth across it. She kept her hands as far apart as she could, knowing that fibres of glass in the fingertips ranks up there with having toenails pulled out by redhot pincers. She felt the first strands of rope begin to give. She sawed some more. She flexed her wrists and the rope pulled apart. It felt fantastic. Reprieve-wise, Daniel in the lion's den had nothing on Penny.

Sitting up, she rubbed her wrists for a bit. Then she began to work on the ropes around her ankles. Marriner might be a master of the round turn and two half-hitches, but Penny wouldn't lightly forget her experiences as a Guide. It didn't take long to untie herself.

The next thing was to get out of the boat itself. With the

188

liferaft lashed over it, the forward hatch was immovable. The other ports were too small for anyone larger than Tom Thumb to climb out of, even if she could have smashed them. Once again she recalled the Fastnet Race. In times of danger, one wasn't always true to oneself. Provided that Marriner was a little less than meticulous, there *was* a way out. And judging by the toothbrush in the chart-drawer, she reckoned he probably was.

She straightened up the bunk. Just in case she ever found herself again in the same position, she didn't want them to know how she'd escaped. She unbolted the three teak steps that led up to the cockpit and pulled them away. Behind them was the engine compartment. She crawled inside, smelling grease and diesel and dirty seawater. A miner's lamp would have come in handy. She remembered her white shoulder bag and backed out again. She wasn't leaving that for Daguerre and Marriner to find. She crawled back into the dark hole. Directly above the engine would be the hatch into the cockpit. She pushed upwards with her shoulders. Nothing happened. She gritted her teeth. If Marriner kept his engine hatch bolted down, she hadn't a hope. She heaved again. The hatch cover flew upward and she was out in the cockpit, with evening darkening about her.

She took several deep breaths. That'd show the bastards. Guess they'd think twice before they messed with her again. She wouldn't let them know about the flutter in her stomach, the tremble in her knees. Penny Wanawake, well-known escapologist. Once more, she picked the padlock on the main hatch. She jumped down into the cabin and pushed the teak steps back in place. She bolted them fast. Keep the buggers mystified. She unscrewed the false lamp on the bulkhead. The bags of what she was sure was heroine were still inside. She screwed it back into place again.

She walked to the stone house where HM Customs hung out. Her rolling gait owed less to a life on the ocean wave than to the release of nervous tension. The Customs officers listened with instant belief to what she had to say. They stuck their jaws out grimly. They said they'd wondered about the *Mary*

M. They called the police. They offered Penny a cup of tea. They said she oughtn't to be driving, not in her state. Looking down at her soiled white tracksuit, Penny thought they were probably right. She ought not to be doing anything in her state except lying in a hot tub. But she had to get back to Canterbury. She wanted to talk to Yeoman.

Back in her hotel room, she poured a generous slug of Jack Daniel's into a glass. The hell with the ice. She knocked it back. The hell with sippin' sweet. She poured another, feeling a lot less like a tray of Kitty Litter. She rang the house in Chelsea. Still no answer. Shit. Barnaby was in possession of several hundred thousand pounds' worth of diamonds. As the son of a South African diamond-merchant, he knew a lot about gems. They were his main passion in life, though he always tried to kid Penny that she was. But she wouldn't want to put him on the line about which came top of his personal pops. I could not love thee, dear, so much, loved I not diamonds more.

She showered for a long time, scrubbing herself all over. Difficult to tell if you're covered in oil when you're oil-coloured to begin with. She put on a silky white dress with a tightly pleated skirt. Round her neck she fastened the pearls her grandfather had given her when she was twenty-one. Three perfectly-matched strands, looped by diamond clasps. Princess Di had copied it for her going-away outfit. They were a little dressy, but the furthest she could get at such short notice from bilges and engines and tea-towels. As far as she was concerned, if she never saw the sea again, she wouldn't complain. They could stuff the tall ship. *And* the star to steer her by.

The Great Court was jumping like Oxford Street on the Saturday before Christmas. Last-night-of-term spirits were much in evidence. And alcoholic ones, as well. From the various school Houses came sounds of minstrelsy and mirth. Grave men, carrying armfuls of paper, smiled benevolently at the young, thinking of the long summer vacation ahead. What could only be rural deans clustered here and there. The darkness was soft beneath the great golden bulk of the chapel.

Penny made her way to the hall where Dominic Austen was giving his poetry recital. Outside the door, a woman in a Jaeger dress and a Margaret Thatcher hairdo held a boy by the arm. She said she'd never heard so much disgusting rubbish in her life. She said she didn't intend to sit there a moment longer to be sworn at. The man with her said he'd heard worse on a building-site. The woman said what on earth was he talking about, he'd never been on a building site in his life. The boy said you had to admit Mr Austen had street cred. The man said was this what he was bankrupting himself for and what in heaven's name was street cred? The woman said if he wasn't such a cheapskate he'd have sent his son to a decent school like King's in the first place. The man asked what the hell she meant by that. Penny left them to it.

The hall was packed. On a small stage stood Dominic Austen. He wore a turquoise boiler-suit with a nifty silk scarf round the neck. Penny wanted to ask him when he'd have her private plane ready for take-off. There was a table with a carafe of water on it and a glass inverted over the top. There was also an unlabelled triangular bottle. Austen kept drinking from it with much movement of his Adam's apple. This went down well with the parental section of the audience, confirming as it did every prejudice they'd ever had about these arty layabouts calling themselves poets who lived orf the State and had never done a hand's turn in their lives. Penny suspected the bottle contained cold tea. He might be a bit of a pseud – a lot of a pseud, even – but Dominic Austen was pretty shrewd. Falling down dead drunk in front of parents wouldn't go down too well with the Reverend John Shepherd.

Yeoman was standing at the back of the hall. When she got through the crush to his side, he pulled her close and held her arm tightly. 'Thank God you've arrived,' he said. 'I was beginning to worry.'

Penny smiled. 'Having fun?'

'It beats a panful of cold vomit.'

'You can't say fairer than that.'

Some oldish blimp with a purple face who couldn't possibly have been enjoying himself turned round and shushed them.

'It could get a whole heap better now you're here,' Yeoman whispered. 'What the hell kept you?'

'About half a mile of best-quality nylon rope.' Penny felt herself beginning to shake. She took a grip on herself.

So did Yeoman. 'Hey,' he said. 'What do you mean? Are you OK?'

'I will be, soon as this show gets off the road.'

She looked around. She saw Gerald Sumnour sitting in the middle of the hall. Next to him sat a boy who was unmistakably his son. The boy's mouth hung open. He was staring into the near distance. Right into the eyes of a girl with a thick auburn plait down her back. She was staring right back. They both seemed oblivious to anything going on around them.

On stage, Austen was looking shy. 'To end with,' he said, 'I thought I would read you what I'm working on at the moment. It's a sonnet sequence.' He added something about a multiplicity of significances that made Yeoman groan loudly. He launched into some crap about Jonah and the Whale. Man's long journey into the heart of darkness in quest of himself came into it. So did primal therapy and the neonatal wail.

'I presume that's a pun,' Penny said.

'Jesus.'

'Bet you he mentions Mistah Kurtz.'

'Trouble is, the guy doesn't know whether he's T.S. friggin' Eliot or a used dish-rag.'

'Neither of which has much street cred.'

'I really must insist that you go outside if you wish to converse,' said the purple-faced man. A woman three rows in front turned round and shushed him.

'What about it?' Yeoman asked. 'Do we take Buster Bloodvessel's advice?'

'I say we stick it out.'

'That would be the perfect comment.'

Austen was on to Persephone and Baldur the Beautiful now. He mentioned Orpheus. He mentioned the resurrection. Penny personally thought he was skating on pretty thin ice. If he brought Alice in Wonderland into it, she thought she might puke.

Marius Knight suddenly hurried up the aisle towards them. He must have been sitting at the front of the room. From the way his hand hovered in the region of his crotch, Penny guessed he had been caught short again. Ah, the indignities of old age. Except that fifty-five or so was hardly old age. Did he really have a weak bladder, or had he left the madrigal concert for a more sinister purpose? She remembered sudden anger and a sword-stick. She remembered a title in a black italic hand. *There Came A Big Spider*. If Marius had read enough of Max's latest book to learn that he had frightened Margaret away for nothing, his reaction would be nothing less than murderous, she was sure. He'd have no problem, either, in getting hold of something lethal to spike Max's gin. And no difficulty in substituting the bottle. Was there any way she'd ever prove it? And what would be gained if she did?

'Anyone ever tell you you're the sexiest thing in seven counties?' Yeoman said. His blue eyes glowed.

The purple-faced man turned round. 'Really,' he said.

'I wasn't talking to you, fella,' said Yeoman.

Penny looked demure. 'They usually say twelve,' she said.

There was an uncertain burst of clapping. When Dominic Austen snapped his folder shut, the clapping swelled into thunderous applause. For this relief, much thanks. Penny and Yeoman hurried out ahead of the crowd.

SIXTEEN

'Do you know what I wish?' Yeoman said the next morning.

'What?'

'That we hadn't just done that.'

'Why?'

'Then we could do it all over again.' Half-raised on his elbow, Yeoman looked down at Penny lying next to him.

'There is that,' she said. She smiled up at him. She liked Yeoman. She liked all sorts of people. But she particularly liked Yeoman. It wasn't that she was promiscuous. There was no percentage in that. Not in these herpes-haunted days. But she didn't see the sense in not making use of what came to hand. If the ingredients were first-class, the resulting dish could be a gourmet's dream. Yeoman was first class. No doubt about that.

'Come to think of it, what's to stop us?' he said.

'Business before pleasure,' Penny said. 'We've got to sort this Maunciple thing out. It's the last day of the term. Everyone will be scattered by this evening. Have you come to any conclusions?'

'Sure have. If I see that Marriner fellow, I'm gonna shove his teeth right down his goddam throat.'

'Apart from that?'

'I bet you have. And you're gonna tell me all about them right this minute.'

'Right.' Penny nodded so hard her beaded braids banged against her forehead.

Yeoman climbed out of bed and went over to the table with the tray of early-morning-tea fixings. He filled the kettle from

194

the bathroom. As he went past, Penny reached out and touched his naked butt. Just a reflex action.

'Don't do that,' he said, 'unless you're aiming to reach more than one kind of conclusion.'

Penny sat up and pulled the sheet up to cover her breasts. 'If that list of titles means anything at all,' she said, 'I figure we have five main suspects. Marius Knight. Kenneth Sumnour. Marriner and/or Daguerre. Margaret Curteis-Squire. Dominic Austen. Plus, of course, Mr X. Or any number of them.'

'Who's that?'

'The not-impossible he. Or she. Though I think we can discount Margaret for a start.'

'Why?'

'Because she's a woman.'

Yeoman swept a look around the room with his mouth twitched to one side. 'Well, how do you like that?' he said. 'What about the Equal Rights Amendment, huh? Equality of rights under the law doesn't mean they can get away with murder just on account of being female, you know. Or are you gonna pull the old premenstrual tension defence?' He leaned, naked, against the table, and folded his arms.

'Knock it off, Yeoman,' Penny said. 'And if you don't move ass pretty quick you are going to wish you were Hitler. At least he had one.'

'What're you talki – shee-it!' Yeoman leaped away from the table. The kettle had suddenly directed a fierce jet of steam at his balls.

'There must be easier methods of birth-control,' Penny said.

'You're pitiless. You know that? Absolutely pitiless.' Yeoman poured boiling water into the zinc teapot provided by the hotel. A bit later, he added two teabags.

'The reason I think Margaret's out of it is that she's happily married. I told you what she told me yesterday. Revenge simply doesn't sit on the boil for twenty years. Not for a woman. Not when she's happy. It becomes pointless beside the greater things. Birth and love and universal stuff like that.'

'What was that film with Anthony Quinn where Ingrid Bergman came back after twenty years,' said Yeoman. 'Offered

195

a fortune to the poverty-stricken village if they'd kill the man who'd done her wrong.'

'That was fiction. Besides, Ingrid suffered for every one of those twenty years,' said Penny. 'I'm talking ordinary, straightforward decent fact. Margaret also told me that when she read the manuscript, she wanted to stab Maunciple. Or mutilate him. If she'd just murdered him, I would have thought her revenge would have been complete. She didn't need that extra bit.'

Yeoman was making like a man who'd just made eye contact with the Medusa and discovered he'd left his shield at home. After a second or two, he unfroze. 'Let me get this straight,' he said. He seemed to be having trouble with his vocal chords. 'Are you saying she's actually read this book of Maunciple's?'

'Not read. Not cover to cover. But she's had a good look through.'

'Did she – uh – did she say what it was about?'

'It was about her and Mr Knight, apparently. The break-up of their marriage. Which explains why she was so agitated when she heard that it was missing. That was part of it.'

'What was the other part?'

'Just a sec. On top of that, Margaret has an alibi. There was only a brief period of about twenty minutes during which she could have got into Maunciple's rooms without being seen. Somewhere between seven o'clock and seven twenty. I checked downstairs with reception and they told me there had been some problem about her booking. She'd booked for five days and the room was only available for two. Something like that. She spent about half an hour with the manager, sorting it out and ringing her friends to see if she could go there. According to Marius Knight, Maunciple's broken toe was giving him so much pain that once we'd brought him over from Deal, he stayed home the rest of the day. Until sevenish.'

'So Margaret's out as a murder suspect. What about as a thief?'

'She was quite willing to admit that she'd have taken the manuscript if she'd had time to. I think she would have told me if she had.'

'Any other suspects we can eliminate?'

'That Sumnour man. It's possible he was afraid Maunciple was going to rake up that business about Mr Leon Goldman. But it's not a very strong motive. And if he was going to do something violent to Maunciple because of his son's A-Level results, he'd at least wait and see how James did. But in any case, I don't think poison would be Sumnour's way. I'm sure he's capable of kicking Maunciple's head to a bloody pulp in the heat of the moment. Or even using a gun, if he had one. But not poisoning.'

'I never met the guy,' Yeoman said. 'I'll take your word for it.' He peered into the zinc teapot. 'Think this stuff's ready yet?'

'As ready as it ever will be.'

Yeoman poured out two cups. He brought them over and sat down on the bed beside Penny. 'Hey, what was the other part of Maunciple's book about? Did Mrs Curteis-Squire say?'

'Nothing about a healthfarm. Another reason to get rid of Sumnour.'

'So what was it about?'

'Remember Maunciple telling us that very first day about some girl who killed herself in the States? It was about her.'

Yeoman got up and leaned out of the window. He said something indistinct. It sounded fairly intemperate. When he turned round he looked very tired. 'There's still Marius Knight. Or the drug-runners. Or the trendy poet.' He sounded as detached as an amputated arm.

'No. I told you. It obviously came as a big surprise to Daguerre to hear that Maunciple was dead. And I can't see Marriner committing murder on his own. He acts tough but he's as soft as a brush underneath.'

'That leaves us two,' said Yeoman. The St Christopher medal on his chest twinkled as he spoke.

'Three. Don't forget Mr X.'

'The way you're eliminating everybody, we're gonna need him. Though personally, I don't buy Mr X at all,' Yeoman said. He took Penny's cup away from her. He got back into bed. He touched one dark breast and then the other. 'Where do you think Marriner and Daguerre are right this minute?'

'I hope they're being mercilessly interrogated down at the local police station after an extremely uncomfortable night in a rat-infested cell,' Penny said. 'Pity our policemen are so wonderful. No chance of them using rubber hoses or the bastinado to force a confession out of them.'

Yeoman pulled Penny close to him. She could feel him shaking. 'I'm glad you're here,' he said.

'What's with you, Yeoman?'

'Nothing. Just the thought of you tied up on that boat. If they'd hurt you.'

The telephone rang.

Yeoman didn't move. Penny stretched out a hand and picked up the receiver.

'I'm quite sure you're up to some perfectly disgraceful antics with that young man from Detroit,' came Peter's voice.

'And you just got elected President of the Clean-Up-Canterbury Campaign, right?'

'My dear. I'm the last person who can afford to be judgmental.'

'I know.'

'The thing is, I need your help. Quite desperately.'

'What have you done this time?'

'Penelope, your lack of faith is most hurtful,' Peter said. 'Actually, what I need is your womanly skill.'

'You know how I feel about sexism, Peter. How desperate is desperate?'

'Dreadfully.'

'You want me to clean out your cousin's rooms for you.'

There was a silence on the end of the line. Then Peter said, 'Good God. You almost tempt me to believe in the gift.'

'Which gift is that? The one you're going to give me to mark your appreciation of the fact that I'll have done your dirty work?'

'The gift of second sight, my dear. As you well know. As a matter of fact,' Peter said candidly, 'I only asked you because I thought you might find it interesting. Knowing, as I do, your zest for poking around in other people's affairs.'

'Generous Peter.'

'We might even turn up that missing manuscript. I may say I've had the publishers screaming about it on the phone non-stop for the past two days.'

'Next time, tell them the chances of it still existing are nil.'

'How utterly fascinating.' A note of anticipatory glee crept into Peter's voice. 'You must tell me why you think so.'

'Later.'

'I suppose now is a bit early,' Peter said hopefully.

'You suppose right. I'll meet you in Maunciple's rooms this afternoon. After the Prizegiving I don't want to miss the tea on the lawn.'

'Nor me. After tea, then.'

Penny put down the phone and concentrated on the business in hand. Though hand was not the right word. She wondered whether Yeoman was finding it hard to say goodbye. He clearly had something on his mind.

The phone rang again. 'Penny?' It was Dominic Austen.

'Hi.'

'Am I interrupting anything?' Austen said.

'What do you think?'

'Good.' There was a pause. She heard him swallow. 'Would you like to pop round for a cup of coffee later this morning?'

Penny said nothing.

'A drop of Glenfiddich?'

'Now you're talking. You can't tell me on the phone?'

'No.' Austen swallowed again. He sounded agitated. Dimly in the background a female voice said loudly that it personally always fancied a nice kidney for breakfast. 'Not really.'

'Don't worry,' Penny said. 'I think I can guess what you're going to say.'

'You can?'

A second female voice said there was nothing to beat kedgeree but you couldn't count on a good kedgeree these days, know what she meant?

'We seem to be on a crossed line,' Penny said.

'No, it's my landlady. Mrs – uh – '

'Thing.'

'That's the one.'

199

'We'll stop by later.'

'We?' said Austen.

The first female announced that they didn't make sausages like they used to, not what she'd call sausages.

'Both of us,' Penny said.

Later, she and Yeoman stood before the door of Number 23 Prebend Street, staring at the lion's head. Before either of them could use it, Austen had opened the door. He stared at Yeoman with something very close to dislike.

'I don't know who asked you to come horning in,' he said.

'I did,' said Penny. She knew she was forcing an issue. She would like to have been sure exactly what it was.

'Why?' said Austen. His nose looked grindstone-sharp.

'I was terrified you might start reading your sonnet sequence again,' Penny said.

'I'm her bodyguard,' said Yeoman.

'All right. Come on up.' Austen spoke in surly tones.

'This makes the fabled hospitality of the east look a bit sick, doesn't it?' Penny said. She followed Austen up the steep stairs. Yeoman came last. If she should fall, she'd be all right. Unless Austen fell too.

Today, the poet's room smelled in a disquieting way of sweat and sperm. Penny tried not to look at the crumpled Kleenex on the floor. She couldn't tell whether his palms were hairier than last time they'd met. He took up a position beneath the tin mobile. It seemed a reckless thing to do. One false move and he'd be short of an ear.

'That manuscript,' he said. 'Maunciple's.'

'Yes,' Penny said.

'I have it.'

'Doesn't it feel good to get it off your chest?'

'That's not where I've got it.' Austen opened a drawer and took out three small glasses. He poured whisky into them. He handed one to Penny. And one to Yeoman. He spared no pains in making it clear how much he disliked doing it.

'Under the sofa, right?' Penny said.

'How do you know?'

'I figured it out.' Penny looked at the Chesterfield. It still

200

rested on a pile of papers. *Baghavad-Gita* had been replaced by a book on vegetarian cooking. Penny tutted. 'Books are our friends,' she said.

'Why did you take it?' asked Yeoman. He looked incredibly powerful. Penny hadn't realised how broad his shoulders were. She wondered if he'd put on his jacket without removing the coat-hanger.

'Sounds so stupid,' muttered Austen. He stared at the floor. He was wearing a long-sleeved grey T-shirt with THE FORCE BE WITH YOU on it in rubberised rainbow lettering.

'Crime always does,' Yeoman said. He looked solemn. And good. As though he'd just ridden into town to right a few wrongs before heading for the hills again.

'Crime?' Austen sounded annoyed. 'Look here. I only took it to bargain with. I'd have given it back, of course.'

'Of course,' Yeoman said nastily. He gave a knowing nod.

'Bargain?' said Penny. 'You mean pressurise.'

'All right. Pressurise. I wanted him to give me a decent letter of recommendation to those people in North Carolina, that's all. God knows I never meant anything like this to happen.'

'Murder?' said Yeoman.

'Yes. Christ,' Austen said. He gave the impression that his eyeballs were breaking out into a sweat. 'I didn't have anything to do with his death, I swear. I only took the manuscript as a lark, really. Spur of the moment. Sort of a practical joke.' He gave a kind of laugh.

Yeoman walked across the floor to stand in front of him. He kicked at the pile of running magazines as he passed them. 'If we want to listen to crap, we can go to one of your poetry-readings,' he said. 'Practical joke. It was blackmail.'

'Blackmail's an ugly word,' said Austen. He lifted his glass to his mouth as though he weren't quite certain of hitting a bull's-eye.

Penny said nothing. He was right.

Yeoman was staring at the sofa. 'And that's it?' he said. 'Right there. Maunciple's manuscript.'

'Yes,' said Austen. 'You see, I nipped in during the concert, just to have a quick word. See if he'd change his mind about

201

that letter. He was sitting there, pissed to the earlobes, or so I thought. I couldn't get a word of sense out of the old. . . . I was about to leave when I saw all these papers lying on the floor. I bent down to pick them up, automatic sort of thing anyone might do, and then I saw what they were. It seemed a gift from heaven, frankly. So I took them. The whole damned lot.'

'You think the cops are gonna hack that?' Yeoman asked grimly.

'They'd better,' Austen said. 'It's the truth.' He sounded doubtful.

'Why did you come back after the concert?' asked Penny.

'I thought he might have recovered and be in a fit state to take in what I wanted to say.'

'Either you write me a nice letter, or I total your book,' said Yeoman.

' – uh – something like that,' Austen said uneasily.

'You're a real slob, you know that?' Yeoman lifted the opera hat from the Styrofoam head and put it on his own. He looked at himself in the square of mirror above the basin.

'And you're a Boy Scout, right?' sneered Austen. He turned to Penny. 'When I saw all those people in there, and Maunciple dead, I nearly had a fit. Christ.' His hand shook as he poured more whisky into his glass.

'Why are you telling us now?' Penny said. 'Why not just return the manuscript?'

'I can't, can I? Maunciple's rooms have been locked up ever since he died. Short of leaving it on the altar-steps in a handbag, I didn't know what else to do.'

'A *hand*bag?' said Penny.

'I could have destroyed it,' Austen said. 'It ought to be destroyed. But I couldn't be responsible for getting rid of another man's work, whatever my personal opinion of it. Think of Isabel Burton destroying her husband's notebooks. And with all the fuss your boyfriend over there's been kicking up, I couldn't quite see myself handing it in to the police. They'd want to know where I got hold of it, and I'm not very good at lying.'

'He's not my boyfriend,' said Penny.

'Well, whatever.' He stared accusingly at Yeoman. 'Yesterday, he asked me point-blank if I'd got it.'

'Did you?' Penny asked. Yeoman was pouring more whisky into his glass. He sipped it. He nodded.

'Yes, I did. And the creep denied it.'

'Thought you weren't very good at lying,' Penny said to Austen.

'I'm not. But the way he was glaring at me, I wouldn't have told him the time, let alone that I'd got the damned thing.' Austen had a small skull earring on today. He jiggled it between thumb and forefinger in a manner that suggested inner disturbance. He gazed at the photograph of his naked torso on the wall as though seeking inspiration. 'I didn't murder Maunciple, though.'

'I'm not a violent man,' said Yeoman. He gave a boa constrictor's smile. 'Why should you be afraid of me?'

'Not violent, maybe,' Austen said. 'But dangerous. You're not someone I'd want to get on the wrong side of.'

'Which side is that?' asked Penny.

'The inside.' Austen rubbed one of the letters of the slogan across his chest. It squeaked faintly. He riffled a hand through his hair in a Byronic way and groaned. 'Oh God. What shall I do with that manuscript? I don't want it.'

'Leave it lay,' Penny said. 'I'll tell his cousin where it is, and he can decide what to do with it. Maybe I can persuade him to destroy it. He must have a better nature I can appeal to.'

'I wouldn't bet on it,' Yeoman said.

'Are you coming to the Prize-giving this afternoon?' Penny said to Austen. 'You could tell him yourself.'

'I doubt it,' said Austen. 'I feel like drinking myself into an early grave.' He took a gloomy look at the level of whisky in the bottle standing on the elephant's foot. 'Some hopes.' Penny couldn't help noticing that two eyes and a smile had been added to the largest of the toenails with a felt-tip pen.

Some hours later, Penny found herself seated at an unsteady card-table on the grass of something called Swithun's Quad. Large trees grew here and there. Fenced flowers bloomed. In the interim since leaving Austen, Penny had sat in the cathedral. She had confirmed her own suspicions. She hadn't liked doing it. She knew who. She was guessing why. She wondered what she ought to do about it.

She had subsequently attended the school's Prize-giving. A real treat. For the most part the ceremony had consisted of the same boys going up again and again to collect books from a visiting notable. The Headmaster had delivered a speech about building funds and scholarships to major universities. He had talked tenderly of departing ground-staff and the retirement of an ancient mathematical master, citing anecdotes which raised a chuckle or two among the older members of staff. He managed to say nothing at all about the missing member of the Modern Languages Department, currently languishing in the House of Correction. He spoke glowingly of the sad loss of Max Maunciple. He spoke less glowingly of the English Department's courageous experiment in engaging a Poet-in-residence. He had then lowered his voice and clutched at the sides of his academic gown. He told the parents they should not encourage their offspring in misbehaviour during the holidays as it was then impossible to maintain discipline when they returned to school. Penny pricked up her ears. So did the younger members of the staff. The Headmaster spoke of sheep being encumbered in the mire. All he meant, as it turned out, was that the younger generation shouldn't be encouraged to drink gin-and-tonics and stay up late.

Now it was teatime. Under the trees, the band of the school's Corps played stirring tunes. Boys of all sizes moved about in a windslip of emotional goodbyes. It was interesting to see how much more emotion they used saying goodbyes to the girls. Many of them wore a red rose in their lapel. Some carried silver-topped canes. Clergymen of various ranks sipped decorously from teacups. Over all brooded the belfry tower and the spires of the chapel.

Penny could see Kenneth Sumnour sitting uneasily at a table as though afraid it was going to collapse into his lap. His skin was worse than ever. If he'd washed his hair recently, he must be using the wrong shampoo. He was looking at his son who was looking at an auburn-plaited girl. The son's expression was besotted. The son's mouth hung open. Penny could see why it annoyed his father so much.

The saintly man whom Penny had last seen breaking the speed-limit in his little crimson car stood laughing with a couple of boys, showing a lot of perfect teeth. Close to, he looked a great deal less saintly. He looked as if he might very well succumb if someone offered him all the kingdoms of the earth for his very own. He kept running a finger round the inside of his clerical collar. Nearby, a lady in a hat with a spotted net drawn close over her face was holding a cup of tea in one black-gloved hand. For the life of her, Penny couldn't see how she drank from it.

Adam Curteis-Squire walked past. He looked magnificent. The ornate silver top of the cane he carried glinted. Over his school clothes he wore a royal-blue gown. He seemed worried.

'Adam.' Penny touched his arm. 'It's all right.'

'What is?' he said. A frown appeared between his golden brows.

'That Daguerre creep's been picked up by the police,' said Penny. 'And Marriner. There won't be any more trouble from either of them.'

Adam's face lit up. 'Thank goodness,' he said. 'That's wonderful.'

'I expect you've been in a bit of a dilemma,' said Penny.

'One doesn't tell tales,' Adam said.

'Perhaps one doesn't fully realise the long-term effects of hard drugs,' said Penny. She'd forgotten how young eighteen really was.

'One did one's best to keep an eye on the younger boys,' said Adam.

'I'm sure one did,' said Penny. 'Tell me. What exactly did you have against Mr Maunciple? Apart from general loathing.'

'He kept trying to imply something about my Housemaster,' Adam said. He blushed. 'Mr Knight. Just because he's unmarried. That we had a – you know – a special relationship. And that was why I was Head of House.'

'Typical,' said Penny.

'Apart from my father,' Adam said, 'Mr Knight is the best

205

person I know.'

'I do hope you're right,' Penny said. She sighed. She looked over at Marius Knight, who sat with Peter Corax in front of a large pile of cakes. She put out her hand. 'Well, goodbye, Adam. I wish you the best of everything.'

Adam took it. He smiled. 'I'd like that,' he said. 'If you're ever up in Cambridge, do come and see me. Clare College.'

'I will,' Penny said.

She went over to join Peter, who was alone, Marius Knight being engaged by the lady in the spotted net. 'My dear,' he said, 'wasn't that the youth I saw with Marg –'

Penny seized him by the pure wool of his handwoven tie. 'Peter. You are not to say a word about that boy. Not now. Not ever. To anyone. Do you understand?'

'Goodness,' said Peter. He reached for a Bakewell tart. 'You'll be strutting about the place in black leather boots and chains before long. Too masterful for words.'

'I'm ready if you are,' Penny said severely. 'Shall we go and start cleaning up your cousin's place?'

SEVENTEEN

Peter opened the door into Maunciple's rooms. They had been locked up since the day after his death. There was dust on the polished surfaces and the piles of books. The room smelled as though galloping dry rot had infected the fixtures and fittings. A spider had put in a lot of hard work among the lustres of the chandeliers.

Peter went over to the satinwood cabinet. 'It's mine, you know,' he said. 'Belonged to my mother. I've been trying to make Max give it back to me for years. Don't ask me how he got it in the first place.'

Penny didn't. She started opening drawers. Most of them seemed to be crammed with papers. 'You'll have to deal with these,' she said. 'I might chuck out something priceless.'

'Oh Lord,' said Peter. 'How on earth do you tell?' He was looking sartorially dreadful, in a vast blue-and-white striped shirt and what he called his Tropical Kit, a sloppy white linen suit that could have provided all the sail for Marriner's Westerley Centaur and still left enough for table-napkins.

'That's showbiz.' Penny took a roll of heavy-duty refuse bags in snail-green plastic from her bag.

'My dear. Forward planning.' Peter looked smug. Penny knew he felt very contemporary, using a phrase coined in the last twenty years.

'Why did your cousin keep his shoes in here?' she said. She had pulled open the drawers of the walnut davenport and was looking at a collection of unattractive footwear. 'We can dump these for a start, can't we?'

Peter didn't answer. He was staring at the contents of the

satinwood cabinet. 'Hang about,' he said, in what he supposed to be the accents of the Common Man. In his terms, this embraced anyone who had not benefitted from an Oxbridge education. 'Some sod's been at the booze.'

'What do you mean?'

'When I arrived here the other day – the night Max died,' said Peter, 'he offered me a drink. I was so late that I refused. But I distinctly remember thinking he must be doing extraordinarily well out of those frightful books of his if he could afford to have nine bottles of gin standing about. As you know, Penelope, I am not averse to the odd noggin myself from time to time – '

'Quite.'

' – but I certainly can't run to buying the stuff by the caseload. Even if he drank the best part of a bottle the night he died, there's still one missing.'

'There were nine bottles here that night,' Penny said. 'I counted them myself. Seven in the cupboard. One beside Mr Maunciple's chair. And one in the trash.'

'Max can't possibly have got through nearly two bottles between the time Marius picked me up for that madrigal affair, and the time we got back and found him dead.'

'He didn't, Peter,' Penny said gently. 'I'm afraid I wasn't joking the other day, when I said he'd been murdered.'

'The doctor said Max died of a coronary,' said Peter. 'What evidence do you have for saying that?' He subsided into a chair. He put his hand on an Oxford Concise Dictionary as though it gave him comfort.

'That extra bottle, for starters. Otherwise, not much except a lot of supposition. It's unfortunate that the empty bottle has long since gone. I just wish I'd had the sense to sniff it. I bet it wouldn't have smelled of anything.'

'What would that have proved?'

'That someone had washed it out. Pretty thoroughly. And who would have done that except a murderer? What other choice did he have? It was a warm night. Nobody was wearing coats. He had no way of sneaking that bottle out, with so many people around. So he had to wash it out, to remove any trace of the poison, and take a chance on leaving it here.'

'Poison?'

'Not that we'll ever prove it,' Penny said. 'Not with your cousin reduced to a thimbleful of ashes.'

Peter stroked his striped belly. He stared up at the cobwebbed chandelier. '*Nil nisi bonum* and all that,' he said slowly. 'I can't say I'd go so far as to pin a medal on whoever did it, but I certainly wouldn't want to hunt him to the ends of the earth in the interests of justice.'

'Neither would I. Just so's I know.'

'What were you going to tell me about Max's manuscript? That it had been destroyed.'

'It hasn't, after all. Dominic Austen had taken it. He had some lunatic notion of forcing your cousin into recommending him for a job in the States.'

'Who's Dominic Austen?'

'The Poet-in-residence.'

'The man must be insane.'

'I wouldn't go that far,' said Penny. She looked away as the flies of Peter's Tropical Kit began very slowly to open.

'How far would you go?'

'Confused. No further than that.'

'And in his confusion, this poet chappie made off with Max's latest book? He should be locked up.'

'I think your cousin was being a little uncharitable.'

'He could be a bit of a bugger, could old Max,' Peter said. 'Well, back to the slaughterhouse, eh?' He got up. He went over to the davenport and began pulling Maunciple's shoes out of it with the air of one determined not to shrink from atrocity. 'What about the stuff in his bedroom? Clothes, and so forth.'

'They could go to Oxfam.'

Peter looked doubtful. 'He wasn't what you'd call a snappy dresser,' he said. He regarded his own trousers and quickly pulled up the zip.

'One of those traits that runs in families, perhaps,' Penny said. 'I'll go and see what I can do.'

The aftermath of death is not glamorous. One man's

comfort is another man's disgust. The shirt with the frayed collar kept for gardening, the knickers that are perfectly wearable but grey from overwashing, the old sweater worn in bed on freezing February nights, tend to stand for all your shirts, knickers and sweaters. Given advance notice, you could have gotten rid of them. But you never are. The Grim Reaper doesn't leave calling cards. So those who clear up after you wrinkle their noses and remember you ever afterwards as a tramp or a slut.

Penny did her best to be kind. She emptied the contents of Maunciple's chest-of-drawers and wardrobe. She sorted through them. Anything that might conceivably be of use to those in need, she put into one pile. The rest she stuffed into plastic bags. When she had finished, she reached down two suitcases from the top of a cupboard. One had a PAA label still attached to the handle. Presumably from Maunciple's sabbatical last year. The other was covered in circular stickers which suggested that a visit to Silver Springs, Florida, was not something the thinking man would want to pass up. She filled them with the usable clothes.

Back in Maunciple's sitting-room, she found Peter sitting at the table, chuckling. 'What a marvellous writer Juvenal was,' he said, without shame. 'Just listen to this.' He reeled off several lines. His Latin was of the hard-c, soft-v school.

Penny did exasperated things with her face. 'You can read Juvenal at home,' she said. She went over to the file drawer of Maunciple's desk. 'As I remember, he was the guy said something that really fits your cousin.'

'I'm sure he did,' said Peter. 'What, in particular, were you thinking of?'

'Something about no one ever becoming a bad-ass in one fell swoop.'

'A somewhat free translation,' Penny said. '*Nemo repente fuit turpissime*. Yes. I suppose it's one way of putting it.'

'We'll be here for a week if we don't make a start on these papers,' Penny said. On the floor by her foot lay a dried rosebud. She knew Peter would, if given the slightest encouragement, start reciting the *Aeneid* at break-neck speed.

210

He often did. Especially if there were work to be done. 'Why don't I bundle together all the files to do with his work? They'll have to go up to London to be properly sorted through. You can deal with the personal stuff.'

'Good idea,' Peter said unenthusiastically. He closed the Juvenal with reluctance.

Penny pulled open the file drawer of Maunciple's desk. She studied the plastic clips on the dark-green folders. *Tennis Balls, My Liege. Star-Scattered on the Grass. Taffy Was a Thief.* And so on, through what would have to be called Maunciple's literary oeuvre, for want of a worse word. There were the seven titles of his published penny-dreadfuls. And one file tagged simply No 8. The manuscript of which was probably still propping up Dominic Austen's sofa.

She took it out and opened it. There were letters to and from Maunciple's publishers concerning contracts and deadlines. There were pieces of yellow paper containing notes written in Maunciple's spiky black script. There was an old magazine from a school in Dorset, nearly twenty years old. It was folded open at a page marked VALETE. '*And this term we also say goodbye to Mr and Mrs Marius Knight. Marius has always been* . . .' No mention of the fact that Mr and Mrs were going their separate ways. There was a copy of a birth-certificate for Adam Anthony Knight, with a covering compliments slip from Somerset House. No father was mentioned in the space provided. There was a copy of an adoption-notice for the same child by Donald Curteis-Squire. How had Maunciple obtained that? What evil streak had sent him looking?

There were clippings from the campus newspaper of the University of Michigan. And from the *Ann Arbor News*. Both contained comprehensive reports on the death by suicide of Deborah Lucy Leyland, daughter of Mr and Mrs Wallace T. Leyland, at an address in Barton Hills. A carbon flimsy of a letter from Max Maunciple offered perfunctory condolences to the bereaved parents. It hoped they didn't blame him, in spite of the note their daughter left. There was a second newspaper clipping. 'The recent death of Mrs Wallace T. Leyland has brought double tragedy to the Vice President of Leyland

211

Pharmaceuticals . . .' There followed a list of mourners at Mrs Leyland's funeral. The list was long. The clipping had been folded over. Part of it was torn away. A second carbon flimsy offered belated sympathy from Maunciple. It added a remark or two about his next book which, although it didn't actually say in so many words that all was grist to a writer's mill, made his meaning perfectly clear. It was dated a couple of months back.

At the back of the file, slipped in among several letters, was a photograph. It looked like a graduation picture. The girl in it wore a gown and mortar-board, the tassel hanging down her cheek. She had grey eyes. Light brown hair. Fine teeth. The standard model of the all-American girl. But with a little something extra. A compassionate mouth. A jawline that showed determination. A level gaze that didn't look as if it missed much. Not a beauty, this girl, but one to give herself to a cause and, once having given, not to fail it.

Penny guessed that in Max Maunciple, Deborah Lucy Leyland had found a cause. And that she had not been able to cope when it failed her. She guessed those eyes that didn't look as if they missed much had missed the cruelty that was as integral a part of Maunciple as mercury is to a thermometer.

She turned over a few more pages in the file. She nodded to herself. Maunciple was better dead. She found a torn piece of newsprint. It was the missing piece of the cutting concerning the Leyland funeral. She looked at it briefly. She stood.

'Where are you – ' began Peter.

'I'll be back,' she said.

'But what shall I – '

'Keep at it.'

She ran down the stairs into the Great Court. Late afternoon shadows slanted across the grass. There was a distant sound of martial music. Nearer at hand, a lawnmower whirred. She ran between roses towards the main road and dodged across between heavy traffic. Dicing with death. But Penny Wanawake was not one to put her own personal safety first when others were threatened. No, sir. She didn't want to think about the degree of threat. The door of 23 Prebend

212

Street was shut. She didn't bother using the lion. She put a shoulder to it. As she had suspected, the door and its jamb were soon parted. She raced up the stairs to Dominic Austen's room and opened the door.

The poet lay on his big Chesterfield. He looked terrible. So did the sofa. It sagged forward, its missing leg supported now only by the vegetarian cookbook. The papers were gone. When Dominic Austen opened his eyes at Penny's insistent voice, they seemed almost the same colour as his face. Above his head, Che Guevara's beret hung like a burnt doughnut. The Styrofoam head lay on the floor, gazing blindly up at Marilyn's tits. The skull earring hung across Austen's cheek. *Memento mori*. Dead symbolic.

Penny went downstairs again and knocked at a door which led to the back regions of the house. A lady with a foam of incredible red hair on top of her head came out. She shut the door very carefully behind her. She gave the impression that she had just figured out how to turn guano into gold and didn't want Penny to sneak a look at her research notes.

'Mrs MacGonagall,' Penny said. 'You'd better ring for an ambulance. Mr Austen is ill.'

'Drunk, more like,' said Mrs MacGonagall. 'Or stoned. He's been up there all afternoon puffing away at those joints. I could smell it. Him and his American friend. It's all very well him wanting to legalise cannabis. I kept telling him. If you start on the soft stuff, sooner or later you'll end up mainlining heroin or sniffing coke. That's what I tell him. Course, he doesn't take a blind bit of notice, but no one could say I haven't tried.' She jerked her chin sharply upwards a couple of times.

'He may have been poisoned,' Penny said.

'Poisoned?' Mrs MacGonagall made a snuffling sound. 'Self-administered, more than like. I could tell you a thing or two about Mr Dominic Austen that would make your hair curl.'

'My hair's curly enough,' Penny said. 'Look. Do you want a man's death on your conscience?'

'Call him a man?' said Mrs MacGonagall. 'With budgie

213

feathers stuck through his ear? A bit of a poofter, if you ask me. All these girls keep coming to the house, but we all know what that means, don't we? He's trying to prove something, isn't he? Hiding from himself. Know what I mean?'

'Have you got a phone?' Penny said. She stepped closer, invading the landlady's private *pagus*. The landlady didn't move.

'Not what you'd call a phone,' she said.

'Whatever you call it, Mrs MacGonagall, have you got one?'

'It's a pay-phone,' Mrs MacGonagall said. 'Under the stairs.'

Penny found the phone. She didn't have 10p. She made for it. She dialled 999. She said a man needed urgent attention. She gave the address.

'When the ambulance men arrive, perhaps you'd be good enough to direct them upstairs,' she said to Mrs MacGonagall when she had put down the receiver. She used the voice her mother employed when asking the member of the general public who had just thrown a cigarette butt into the carp-pond at Hurley Court to remove it. She ran back upstairs.

She dragged Dominic Austen upright. She tried to walk him round the room. He was wearing some kind of perfume for which the only adequate description was unacceptable. He groaned a lot. His knees sagged.

'Walk,' Penny said. 'Just walk. They'll be here soon to take you to the hospital to pump out your stomach.'

'Shtummuck,' mumbled Austen. He threw up suddenly.

Gaahd. 'He took the manuscript with him, did he?' Penny asked. She looked away from Austen who was messily wiping his mouth on his sleeve.

Austen fell on to the sofa again. His eyes closed. He began to snore. Penny slapped him. It was much harder to do than it sounds. The average person does not gratuitously offer violence to other average persons. Not easily. The noise of her palm on his cheek sounded very loud. She could feel the shape of his teeth through his skin. She didn't do it again. He didn't open his eyes.

'Did he take the manuscript?' she said again.

214

This time Austen nodded. He moved his hand vaguely in the direction of the floor. 'Washte . . . goo . . . drink,' he muttered.

Penny picked up the Glenfiddich bottle which lay spilled on the bare boards. She sniffed it. It smelled of nothing but pure malt whisky. She thought it extremely likely that if the contents were analysed, they would be found to contain some kind of fast-acting barbiturate. She wondered sadly whether the dose the thief had given Austen was strong enough to kill him, or whether it had only been intended to send him into a deep sleep. For a moment she stood still, staring down at the label. Then she took it over to the basin and emptied the contents. She ran water and thoroughly rinsed it. She put it back on the floor on its side.

There was the noise of feet in the hall below. Two large men came in. They wore air-force blue shirts and dark ties. One of them had rimless glasses. They eyed the pool of vomit with the air of connoisseurs.

'Those stairs,' one of them said. He lifted Dominic's eyelids.

'Don't fancy getting him down that little lot,' said the other. He made noises with his tongue against the roof of his mouth.

Mrs MacGonagall appeared just inside the door. 'Just watch my carpets when you bring him down,' she said, 'that's all. Only put them down in April.' She saw the mess on the floor. 'Here. Who's going to clear that up, then?'

'Not me,' said Penny. 'Know what I mean?'

The two men gathered Dominic together. 'The force be bloody with you,' one of them said.

'That's rich,' said the other. They manoeuvred the dangling poet out of the room and down the stairs. They had the intent look of men scaling Mount Everest. Not because it was there but because it was the only way to get to the other side. In the grey street, people were gaping at the ambulance as though waiting for it to announce the start of World War III.

When it had driven off, Penny walked slowly back to the school. She saw Peter standing in the big hanging window of Max Maunciple's lodgings. He had a glass in one hand and a book in the other. She went in through the back entrance of the hotel, past the geraniums and lobelias and the beds of

215

tobacco plants. Wisteria clambered over the iron railings of the stone steps leading up to the first floor. She didn't want to go up to her room. She didn't want what she would probably find there.

When she opened the door, Yeoman turned from the window. 'I saw you coming,' he said. 'Here.' He handed her a drink. 'You look as if you could use it.'

'Is it safe?' she asked. She didn't keep the bitterness out of her voice. She lifted the phone and asked if some icecubes could be sent up to her room.

'Penny,' Yeoman said. 'I'm glad you came back before I left.'

Looking up at his face, she felt tears forming at the backs of her eyes. She shook her head slowly so that the white beads knocked against each other. It was a sad sort of noise. She could see his packed hold-all standing by the door.

Yeoman was wearing his pink suit. He held his arms wide. Penny stood in close to his chest. She sniffed.

'You're not going to cry,' he said, 'are you?'

'No,' said Penny. 'Not yet. It's just you smell like you've been burning leaves and they haven't started to turn yet, let alone fall.'

'Wrong kind of leaves.'

A strong smell of smoke was coming from the bathroom. Penny disengaged herself from Yeoman and went in. A red-headed man was kneeling on the floor, trying to sweep ash down the plughole of the bath with the aid of the detachable shower-head. His feet were bare. They were also black and wet. So were his cream trousers, which had been pulled up to his knees.

'Have you joined the Masons, or are you just growing old?' Penny said.

'Maybe I like the bottoms of my trousers rolled,' Barnaby said. He rose to his feet. 'God. This stuff is difficult to get rid of.'

The bath was covered with ash. The enamel was blackened with smoke. Here and there a word or two stood out on a scrap of charred paper. 'Hate.' 'the car.' 'she said.' An effort had

216

been made to stomp the ash into powder. It hadn't been entirely successful. The water had turned it into an inky mush in which dead matches floated like funeral barges.

'Maunciple's last manuscript, I presume,' Penny said.

'Right.'

'The only copy?'

'So they say.'

'They?' Penny was impressed with Barnaby's tie, which featured crossed golf-clubs cradling a ball. They were dark-blue on a red silk background.

'Your friend next door.' Barnaby jerked his head towards the bedroom. 'The cop.'

'May one ask what you're doing here?'

'One may.'

'What are you doing here?' Penny saw that all the vitamin pills had gone. And Yeoman's shaving gear. It made the place look empty.

'Giving in to the urge to see you again,' said Barnaby. 'And conspiring to pervert the course of justice.' He looked down at his dirty hands.

Penny felt the tears again. This time they were in her throat. Justice. What exactly was justice? Who had the right to judge? Was it Camus who said we needn't wait for the Day of Judgment since it took place every day? She knew her mouth had turned down.

Barnaby took her into his arms. 'Come to me, my melancholy baby,' he said softly. He kissed her hard. Over his shoulder she saw Yeoman watching them. She pulled away from Barnaby.

'This is my regular guy,' she said.

'We've met,' Yeoman said. He gave her his terrific smile. Had it always been sad round the edges? Or had she just not noticed before?

'Yeoman,' she said. 'Oh, Yeoman.'

'There's nothing I can say,' he said.

'There is. Just tell me how many of those red capsule things you put into that bottle of whisky.'

He didn't answer.

217

'It matters to me, Yeoman. A lot.'

'To me, too, baby. You think I was trying to put him away?'

'That's what's bothering me.'

'Relax, honey. There was only enough to put him to sleep while I got the manuscript out from under that sofa. That's what this whole thing's been about.'

'Why did you leave the bottle there? He might have drunk more.'

'I knocked it over before I left so he wouldn't.'

'Was Deborah Leyland your fiancée?'

Yeoman closed his eyes. 'My half-sister.'

'What did Maunciple do to her?'

Barnaby began splashing water into the bath again. Penny looked at him. He jerked his head towards the bedroom. Penny took Yeoman's arm and led him out.

'Tell me,' she said.

'My mother married Wallace Leyland when I was eight,' Yeoman said. 'Deb was their only child. Perhaps they – all of us – overprotected her. When she met Maunciple, she didn't know what had hit her. Never mind that he was old and fat and a drunk. He flattered her. Arranged dinners *à deux* in his apartment on campus. He called her his Little Miss Muffet. Asked her opinion of his work. She fell for the whole goddammed line. When he told her he couldn't live without her, she believed him. I think she saw herself as the helpmeet, the woman who smoothed the thorny path of Genius.'

'Genius,' said Penny. 'Oh, boy.'

'Anyway, she went to – she slept with him. That's all he was after. When the time came, he told her he was back off to England. Without her. Goodbye, kiddo, it's been great knowing you. Just like that. She was completely stunned.'

Yeoman shrugged. It was the gesture of one who wasn't bothered. Except you could see he was. That he'd be bothered for the rest of his life. He stretched his lips over his teeth then covered them with his hand. 'I loved her,' he said.

Penny hunched herself up in the corner of the window-seat. Outside, late-model cars drove slowly round the quadrangle of the Great Court towards the gatehouse. They were full of hi-fi equipment and tennis-racquets and boys. A small crimson car suddenly queue-jumped by driving across the grass. No one, so far, had thought to put up a notice saying DO NOT DRIVE ON THE GRASS. 'He was a bastard,' she said. 'A real bastard.'

'She drove out to our parents' place by the lake and took an overdose. The same stuff I gave Maunciple. They didn't find her for nearly a week. She left a note saying she was pregnant by that – that filthy shithead.' Yeoman began to weep. 'It destroyed my mother,' he said.

You too, Penny thought.

'She died six months later in a car accident. My mother. Wallace managed to hush up the fact that she was stuffed to the eyeballs with tranquilizers at the time. Pills were the only way she could get through the days.' Yeoman shrugged again. 'Maybe Deb was naive and foolish. Maybe she should have seen through all that bullshit he was handing her. But she'd been loved so much all her life. She didn't know about people like Maunciple. She was a born victim. I guess that's why Maunciple picked on her.' He turned away. His head drooped. 'She wasn't anything special to look at,' he said. There were darker streaks on the lapels of his jacket, where tears had fallen.

Barnaby came out of the bathroom. He went over and stood beside Penny. Neither of them spoke. Yeoman wrenched his mouth about as though keeping it still was too painful.

'Maunciple actually wrote to Wallace when he heard about Mom.' He semi-laughed. 'Unbelievable.'

'Why?' Penny said.

'So sorry to hear about your wife, old boy, and hope you don't mind if my next book tells the whole goddam story. More or less. That's when Wallace and I decided to do something about it.'

Penny held up her hand. 'Don't tell me what you decided to do,' she said. 'It'll make it so much easier.'

'That's why I was in Deal when I met you,' Yeoman said. 'I'd arrived in Canterbury the day before and discovered Maunciple had gone over there. I was trying to find him. I

219

had to get that manuscript. I knew there was only one, that that was how he worked. I knew everything about him. Every little detail. Deborah was obsessed with him. She could talk about him for hours. I listened because I loved her.' He stared at Penny. 'I mean, really loved her.'

Penny sighed. This was why there was no Mrs Charles Yeoman. 'No wonder you were so agitated when the book went missing,' she said.

Yeoman's eyes seemed fuller of black flecks than previously. Beneath the tan, his face was pale. 'I had to find that manuscript. For Wallace's sake. And my mother's. I thought that with you and me both looking, we'd be sure to find it.'

'And with me busy searching for the wrong murderer, I was out of your hair.'

'Right.'

'From the very beginning, you were the logical person,' Penny said. 'You had the best opportunity. You even bought a bottle of gin quite openly for him. I suppose you poured away an inch or two to make sure he would start that bottle. And if the manuscript hadn't been stolen, you'd have left that very night.'

'Maybe. Maybe not.'

'You don't have to kid me, Yeoman. I guess I just didn't want to believe it was you. Even after I'd found those red capsules which couldn't possibly have been vitamins. It wasn't until I was going through Maunciple's files that I realised the motive.'

Yeoman stared at them both without smiling. Then he held his hands out, the wrists together. 'It's a fair cop,' he said. 'I'll come quietly.'

Penny stood up. 'I'm going outside now,' she said. 'I may be gone some time.' She went out of the room and closed the door behind her.

She sat in the hotel lounge until Barnaby came to get her. She gazed at nothing in particular. Dead lilac petals lay scattered on the polished surface of the table. Some of the brass had tarnished and needed cleaning. Bells rang from the clocktower. Never send to know for whom the bell tolls. She felt elegiac. Even tearful.

'He's gone,' Barnaby said.

'Where to.'

'Gatwick.'

'Goodbye, Mr Chips.'

'He didn't seem too happy about it,' said Barnaby. He held her hand tightly.

'I don't think he'll let himself get away with it, even though we have. I hope we've done the right thing.'

'The name's Wanawake, not God.'

Penny scrunched her eyes up. 'Gatwick, huh? You can't get there from here.'

'I know. Except by car. That's why I gave him your keys.'

'What?'

'We can pick them up from there tomorrow.'

'That just about takes the –'

'He seemed like a nice guy.'

'He is.'

'Fond of you, too.'

Penny winked. 'He certainly knew how to make a person feel six feet tall.'

They went upstairs together. The room seemed empty. Exit one passionate man whose pilgrimage was over.

'He got that suit in Regent Street,' Barnaby said. 'I asked him.'

'It was a bargain. Two-thirds off in the sale.'

'He was robbed.'

Penny put her arms round him. 'It's wonderful to see you.'

'Bet you thought I'd scarpered with the loot, didn't you?'

'The thought never crossed my mind.'

'I'm delighted to hear it.' Barnaby pushed Penny backwards on to the bed. 'I hope you haven't developed a thing about policemen.'

'No. But I'll tell you what.' Penny tugged at Barnaby's tie.

'What?'

'I think I may have developed one about golf-club secretaries.'

'What a fantastic coincidence. You're looking right at one.'

221

Barnaby began to undo the buttons of Penny's silk blouse. His hair was as soft as suede across her nipples. 'Subscription is £6,000 per annum but includes a limited number of green fees and entitles you to the services of our golf pro.'

'The services of the secretary will do me just fine.'

Barnaby pulled her skirt off. 'Do I remember you expressing a desire to be loaded down with expensive jewels,' he said.

'Gee, you never forget a thing, do you?'

'Memory like an elephant,' Barnaby said.

'That isn't the only thing.'

Barnaby opened his black leather attaché case. It held a number of suede leather bags. He emptied several of them onto Penny's naked body. They were cold. They were shiny. They felt very expensive.

'Wow,' said Penny. 'We could build a hospital with that lot. When does Miss Ivory get back?'

'No need to wait until then. Apparently there's a dead cert called Holy Moses running at Market Rasen next Saturday. Antonia sent me a cable. Said not to miss it and would I put a pound on for her.'

'A pound. That's reckless. I thought she never ventured more than 10p.'

'It's being on holiday.'

'Holy Moses,' said Penny. 'By Bulrush Baby out of Grandma.'

'How do you know?'

'The owner happens to be my father.'

'How amazing,' said Barnaby. 'Enjoy these while you can. I'm taking them up to London tomorrow to convert them.' He knelt at the side of the bed. 'And take a shifty at these.'

He unrolled two pieces of parchment. Miniatures. One showed Rustum in a tiger-skin, facing Isfandiyar across a log-pile of broken lances. Above their heads was an exquisitely-blooming pomegranate tree. Clouds like dragon's breath curled in the gilded sky. The other showed the marriage of Khusraw and Shirin, the two star-crossed lovers finally united beneath a decorated duvet of scarlet and gold. Khusraw was bending tenderly over his bride, his handsome face close to her.

222

'Kind of gets you thinking, doesn't it?' Penny said. She shifted so that the diamonds slithered across her belly. A necklace of yellow diamonds slid slowly down her hip like a fabulous worm.

'It certainly does,' Barnaby said. 'And my brain just went into overdrive.'

He rolled up the two glowing miniatures. They would be added to his own private art collection beneath his Mayfair antique-shop. He put them carefully into a plastic cover and placed it in his attaché case. He took off his tie. And his shirt. And everything else. Beneath his clothes his skin was very white. Standard redhead's skin. He kissed Penny. Well below the bikini line.

Penny picked up some of the gems which covered her and let them slowly drop through her fingers. Barnaby kissed her again. In the same place.

There was a loud rapping at the door. 'Yer arsecubes,' came an Antipodean voice from outside in the passage.

'Thank you,' called Penny. 'Just leave them there. We'll get them in a minute.'

'Jesus,' said Barnaby. 'Arsecubes. Hope you weren't planning to put one in my drink.'

'I was,' said Penny. 'But I won't. Got any suggestions for what I can do instead?'

'Lots and lots,' Barnaby said. He nuzzled at her.

'A kiss on the crotch may be quite Continental, but diamonds are a girl's best friend,' said Penny.

'Bet I could change your mind on that one.'

'Try.'

Barnaby did. And succeeded.

The pool of water in the bowl outside the door had almost reached blood-temperature by the time Penny got around to collecting it.